The
EURASIANS

The
EURASIANS

Don Peter

Chapter 1

Gunfire burst rapidly in the dark, and confusion was everywhere. Suddenly, there was a loud explosion, followed by another, a few seconds later. Aaron ran as fast as he could toward the thick undergrowth. He stopped for a short while, took a deep breath, and crawled swiftly near a dead meranti tree. He gained his composure and worked to control his rapid breathing. Slowly, he lifted his head and peeked at a clearing in the distance. He waited in total darkness.

A few minutes later, he noticed shadows approaching him. Aaron quickly pulled back his head and shrank himself farther into the shadows. The footsteps drew closer and suddenly stopped. He heard voices and was startled to realize that the people were speaking in Javanese. *The enemy!* he thought.

While the voices mumbled nearby, Aaron thought about the unfortunate ones who'd died, and he feared that his turn might be next. Fifteen Malaysian soldiers and a British officer had been killed. Aaron waited for hours as the enemy sat tight, not moving.

Move away, you bastard! Aaron cursed at them in his mind. He moved his head up slowly to steal another peek at the enemy. *Dammit! I can't see a thing,* he thought.

***

Three and a half hours had passed, and no one had moved from his spot. Aaron endured the tropical humidity in the middle of a night infested with mosquitoes. The jungle heat was unbearable, and Aaron's clothes were soaking wet. Besides the sound of the enemy talking, Aaron couldn't help but notice the songs of insects that were oblivious to what was going on.

Aaron thought, *it is now or never! If I wait, chances are they will find me. If I strike now, at least I'll take a few of them with me to hell!*

Aaron slowly took out his grenade and released the pin. His machine gun was ready to be fired. He stood and tossed the grenade. A moment later, there was a loud explosion. Aaron could hear the men screaming in pain. Quickly, he rushed the enemy and fired on them with his machine gun. The enemy returned fire with equal enthusiasm.

Aaron collapsed; he could feel blood on his left arm and right leg. His eyes stared at the jungle canopy as he listened. He heard murmuring and shrieking all around him. *Any moment now,* he thought, *the survivors will cut me to pieces. At least I brought some of them with me, though.* The thought brought a smile to his bloody face.

The noises around him began to fade. He tried hard to remember his past—his mother, Siamese girlfriend, friends, schools, college, and career in the army—but his thoughts got dimmer and dimmer.

Aaron slowly opened his eyes. His vision was blurry, and he could not see what was around him. He closed his eyes again and then reopened them slowly. Everything was still unclear, but at least this time, he could keep his eyes open. The brightness caused his tears to flow, and he blinked rapidly. Slowly, his vision began to clear.

"Good morning, sir!"

The voice startled Aaron.

"How is he, Doctor?" the same voice said.

"He will be all right," the doctor replied. "In a few more days, he will be as good as new."

"My name, sir, is Lieutenant Abdul Aziz bin Salleh," the other voice said.

Aaron now saw a young man in a green uniform with the doctor. Once again, Aaron struggled to clear his eyes of the tears, and his vision returned partially.

"Am I in heaven or hell?" Aaron asked.

The young lieutenant smiled and said, "No, sir, not yet in heaven. You are now in the Duchess of Kent Hospital in Sandakan. May I sit down next to you, sir?"

Aaron tried to talk, but excruciating pain in his arm and leg rendered him suddenly speechless.

"I guess I can," Aziz said. He permitted himself to sit next to Aaron's bed. Aziz looked at the doctor, who nodded and left the room. A nurse was about to approach Aaron's bed to administer his medication, but the doctor prevented her from entering. Perplexed, she stayed in the hall.

"We found you unconscious, sir," Aziz explained. "We found you seriously injured in the jungle of Kalabakan. You were hit pretty badly, so you were rushed to the military hospital in Tawau. Nobody thought you would survive; you lost a lot of blood. However, the doctors and nurses worked around the clock to save you, and by the will of Allah, you were saved. You were semiconscious most of the time in Tawau, and that is why you were transferred here to a civilian hospital in Sandakan. The military hospital and the Tawau hospital were inadequate to look after you properly."

Aaron was pleased that his vision had cleared. He could also now withstand the brightness around him. He began to speak slowly. "What about the battle?" he asked in a low voice.

Aziz looked at him and smiled wider. "You all stopped the entire battalion of Indonesian troops," he told Aaron. "But you didn't fight the whole battalion. What I mean is that when you managed to stop the part finders, the whole Sukarno battalion for the Kalabakan operation got cold feet. We counted the dead enemy, and well, there were ninety-six, to be exact. Your British officers are happy with that achievement, sir. It would be quite a big mess if not for all of you."

"What about the rest?" Aaron asked.

Aziz pulled back his smile and kept quiet for a few seconds. "They are all dead."

Aaron sighed. He thought about his Malay friends and the British officer. Days before they'd been assigned to Kalabakan, they'd been having a good time in Penang. Aaron Johnson and Stephen McCoy were pilots of the British Royal Air Force, but MI5 had assigned them both to monitor the Indonesian strength at the Borneo border. They worked closely together with the Australian, New Zealand, and Malaysian armies.

His deep thoughts continued, and he remembered the time Mohammad Abdullah, one of the Malay soldiers, had invited Steve and him to his house. Mohammad's house was on the Slim River, a kampong not far from the capital of Malaya, Kuala Lumpur. Aaron's mind flew back to happier memories.

"This is my lovely wife, Aminah," Mohammad had said. Pointing to the baby on their bed, he'd added, "And this is our son, who was just born. If my religion and culture allowed, I would like to name him Aaron or Stephen," Mohammad had said jokingly. All of them had laughed.

Now, Aaron thought soberly, *both Stephen and Mohammad are dead, as are fourteen other Malay boys. Aminah has become a widow at the age of nineteen, and her son is now without a father.*

Aziz suddenly interrupted his train of thought. "Sir? Are you okay?" he asked.

The question pulled Aaron back to the present. He looked at Aziz and asked for his assistance. "Would you help me to sit down, please?"

"Oh, sure," Aziz replied. As he helped Aaron to sit upright, he noticed that Aaron was still feeling some pain. The movement affected his arms and legs. Aziz lifted the top part of the bed so that Aaron could rest while sitting. Once Aziz was sure that Aaron was resting comfortably, he sat down.

"Who are you?" Aaron said, confused. "I mean, why are you with me?"

"I am assigned to look after you, sir, to see that everything is okay. There are three of us who will take turns monitoring you until you recover completely. I will be with you until fifteen hundred hours, and then you will be looked after by Lieutenant Ismail bin Hussein."

Aaron smiled, gave a slow nod, and looked around. He noticed he was in the first-class ward, and the room was only for him. The staff had put beautiful flowers on the table close by. Looking outside, he could see the clear blue sky.

"What's the date?" Aaron asked.

"It is October, sir. The twenty-third of October 1964," Aziz answered.

"I'm so sorry, but I'd like to keep to myself for a while, if you don't mind," Aaron told Aziz.

"No, not at all," Aziz said. "I would like to go outside to smoke, sir—with your permission."

"Go ahead," Aaron replied with comfort. He watched the young lieutenant walk out. After his sentry was gone, Aaron took a deep breath, closed his eyes, and searched his memories. *How in the world did I end up in North Borneo?*

Slowly, his memory of the circumstances returned to him. *I'm here in response to the threat by Sukarno, the president of Indonesia.*

Based on the Malaysian Agreement, which was signed last year in London, North Borneo and Sarawak, a British colony in Borneo, had opted to join Malaya and Singapore to form a new country called Malaysia. The people of these two Bornean states had exercised their choice for such a union. As a result, on September 16, 1963, Malaysia was born. *The anti-Western nationalist Sukarno threatened to declare war if the idea of Malaysia was implemented, and he made good on his threat*, Aaron thought. *Now here I am, thousands of miles from England, to protect her former colonial empire and her new allies.*

Chapter 2

MEI LING STARED OUT the window at the tall coconut palms scattered not far away. She studied them in earnest, noting the leaves, fruit, and trunks and how tall the trees were. As she looked at the fruit, she wished she could drink its lovely juice. She felt thirsty. A moment later, she noticed the many people walking freely.

Why are those people so lucky, Mei Ling thought, *when I have to endure boredom?* She saw children and teenagers playing outside; she saw adults hawking to potential customers as they passed by. *Boring! Boring!* she thought.

Then, slowly, her mind shifted to the beautiful beach. She had seen this beach in one of the magazines available at the community library. The picture showed beautiful white sand and a blue sky reflected by the crystal sea. However, the beach was far away, and no such beach existed in her hometown, Sandakan. "The beach here is brown and dirty. The sand is rocky," she said, visualizing the terrain.

"Ho, Mei Ling!" A sudden scream awakened her. "You are not working!"

Mei Ling was now alert, and she looked up at her employer, Mrs. Yap. She sensed trouble, as always. Mrs. Yap's eyes glowed, and her arms were crossed. Mrs. Yap stepped slowly but surely toward Mei Ling and then stopped. Mei Ling noticed that all of her workmates were now looking at her; some were giggling and smiling, and others were without expression.

"Do you want to work or not?"

Mei Ling put her head down.

6

"If not because of your parents, I would never consider employing you!"

"Forgive me, Mrs. Yap. I will not do it again."

"That is what you said yesterday and the day before yesterday! You have been saying that since you started work!"

Mei Ling tightened her lips. She knew it was futile to apologize or make excuses. In truth, she didn't like working there. In fact, she didn't want to work in any factories at all. Her parents had persuaded her to work at this noodle factory, which was hot and stuffy, with a hot-tempered boss.

"I am giving you one last chance! If you don't work properly, you are fired!"

Mei Ling was used to Mrs. Yap's scolding and threats. They didn't bother her much. Besides, the pay was so miserable that it did not make any difference if she continued working or not.

"Start working!" Mrs. Yap shouted at her in Cantonese.

Mrs. Yap looked around, and suddenly, all the other workers turned away from the scene and continued their chores. This time, Mrs. Yap shouted at them in Mandarin. Slowly, she walked into her small office. The factory Mei Ling worked at was three miles from the heart of Sandakan.

Everyone waited impatiently for the clock to strike six. At five past six in the evening, the workers all jumped up at the same time, packed up their things, and left the factory. All of them were eager to go home. Another dreaded workday was over. Mei Ling was the one who felt most relieved. She faced no more boringness for the day. Soon Mei Ling was the only employee left.

"Why are you still here?" Mrs. Yap asked her as she began shutting off the lights.

"I am still looking for my things. Just a minute."

"Hurry up! I don't have time to wait for you!"

Mei Ling kept quiet. She refused to respond to Mrs. Yap. To her, Mrs. Yap was disgusting. She did not bring anything useful to Mei Ling's life and did nothing to contribute to her future. Suddenly, Mei

Ling felt an urge to leave this miserable place as quickly as possible. However, she knew more suffering would come tomorrow, the next workday.

As she walked out, Mei Ling felt happy but agitated. While leaving the factory compound, she dwelled on another nightmarish condition: her home. She walked rapidly. Then she slowed down.

Maybe I'll go to town for a little while, she said to herself. *I'll tell my parents that I'm late because I was involved in overtime. Yes! My parents won't know.*

There were many new blocks of shops and houses in Sandakan. Prosperity was returning because Sandakan was rich in tropical timber. There had been an increasing demand for the wood, especially from Japan, which had sought to develop its economy rapidly after the Second World War ravaged the country. Another boom had followed because of the Korean War, and soon another impending conflict, the escalation of the Vietnam War, would bolster Japan's economy. Japan prospered, and so did Sandakan.

In Sandakan, there were many Malay soldiers and local police forces, and there were also some British military advisers and army officers. Mei Ling observed the soldiers patrolling around town. The British were spending their time at the Sandakan Turf Club, which used to be exclusively for European administrators, businessmen, and planters before North Borneo helped to form Malaysia.

She walked along the shops and occasionally stopped to glance at the multitudes of jewelry and nice clothes from overseas that waited for rich customers in Sandakan to buy them. Many individuals had become prosperous overnight because of the sudden demand for tropical timber.

However, Mei Ling couldn't afford these luxuries, no matter how much she wanted them. She came from a poor family. Her father was a vegetable farmer. Her mother was a housewife who also helped at the farm. She had an older brother who had gone to Hong Kong, sponsored by a Singaporean trader doing business in Sandakan. He never bothered to write or send money home. Being stuck in poverty was a nightmare she dreaded.

And my miserable pay—only five dollars a month! she thought to herself.

She wandered aimlessly around town, praying for a miracle, wishing that somebody could buy her the goods she desired. She looked at the dirty brown sea, which upstream logging polluted. She prayed for time to stop, but it continued. It was almost time to go home.

As she was heading back, she passed the Sandakan Turf Club. It was not exclusively European anymore; it was open to everyone who could afford to drink, dance, and gamble. Mei Ling watched from a distance. *If only I could meet one of them!* she thought.

The luxurious lifestyle of those at the clubhouse played in Mei Ling's mind. She was almost twenty years old, and her skin was tan compared to that of most Chinese girls. She'd probably inherited the skin from her mother's mother, who/ was a Sino-Filipino from the Visayan stock.

She'd also inherited her grandmother's round eyes. Her body was well developed, with nice curves in the right places. She was exceptionally attractive.

As she arrived home, what she anticipated occurred.

"Why are you late?" The yelling came from the vegetable farm not far from her father's old wooden house. "You know you are supposed to help me out on the farm."

Her father, a skinny middle-aged man whose father came from Kwantung, China, decades ago, looked at her and shook his head. Mei Ling's parents had told her that her grandfather had been a wealthy man by the time he was thirty-five. However, by the age of forty-two, his life had returned to poverty because of his addiction to opium. Her father had inherited the suffering. He had never been lucky enough to get out of this cycle of poverty, unlike some of his close friends, who had made themselves rich or at least comfortable.

Mei Ling did not answer her father. She went straight to her mother, who was more understanding. Her mother was in the kitchen, cooking and preparing for their dinner. Mei Ling looked at the food. It was the same dry rice, soya bean curd, vegetables from the farm, and salted fish that they had every day.

"Mama, I had overtime, and that is why I'm late," she lied.

"That's okay with me, Mei Ling. But you know, we have nobody to depend on to help us on the farm," her mother said. Mei Ling looked at her mother and smiled. Then she looked at the cooking, frowned, and turned away.

"Mama, why do we have the same food all the time?" she asked, though she knew the answer. "It is always the same food. I am very bored with the same food."

Her mother looked at her and spoke softly. "In China, where your grandfather came from, he had nothing to eat at all. Consider yourself lucky, Mei Ling."

"We are not lucky, Mama! We are poor. I don't like being poor," Mei Ling replied with frustration.

Her mother shook her head and continued her cooking. Mei Ling saw her father slogging at the vegetable farm. She wondered to herself why her parents were unsuccessful. Why did her family have to endure such humiliation? She became angry while thinking about her grandfather.

"Why did he squander all his money? Why?" She looked around her house and saw nothing but misery.

The toilet was several yards away from the house. At night, she had to run there to answer the call of nature. Then she had to run back to the house after she was through, because she was scared of the darkness. It was worse when it rained. The toilet was made of thin zinc, which had rusted and filled with small holes. The waste was deposited in a used diesel drum buried underneath.

There was no electricity or running water in the house. They obtained water from the well nearby, and during heavy rain, it became muddy. There were many holes in their house's roof, which her father had not yet fixed. She was certain he never would fix them.

Despite their poverty-stricken home, her father managed to house an idol in a small red box on an altar placed on the floor near their dining room. The idol was the god of prosperity, and their offerings were apples and oranges.

Mei Ling approached the idol, looked at it carefully, and whispered, "If you are indeed the god of prosperity, make us rich. Make us rich!" She looked at the fruit and saw that it had rotted. "No wonder we are not rich! Father only offered him apples and oranges! Maybe Father should offer him roasted pig or duck," Mei Ling said.

However, she knew that her parents could hardly afford even apples and oranges. That was the best they could offer to their god. Mei Ling was tempted to take the fruit from the god, but she feared retribution from him.

When it was late evening, her father came home, feeling tired. The workload doubled by the day because Mei Ling was not there to help. Her father took off his straw hat, placed it on the table, and then grabbed some joss sticks, burned them, knelt down, and prayed.

Mei Ling watched her father. After he prayed, he rose and sat on a wooden chair near the dining room door. He grabbed his hat and used it as a fan because it was hot inside the house.

"There is no news from Ah Kow!" Mei Ling's father's voice broke the silence in the house. "No news at all! He didn't send any letter. We cannot expect any money from him." He stared at Mei Ling. "I hope you won't be like your brother, Mei Ling," he said sternly.

"Come! Let us eat." A cheerful voice came from the kitchen. Her mother had finished her cooking. When there was no special occasion, all of them ate in the kitchen. Only on grand days, such as the Chinese Lunar New Year, did they eat at the dining table.

Mei Ling looked at her food. Then she looked outside the house. Her mother held her hand and nodded, as if pleading for her to eat.

At night, Mei Ling went to the vegetable farm alone. It was dark, and creepy noises frightened her. She never liked to walk outside her house at night. The insects and snakes were her secondary concern, but what frightened her most were the ghosts of the dead, for there was a Chinese cemetery nearby.

The darkness grew intense. She had waited for an hour. She was becoming paranoid, as she saw an image moving in the darkness. She moved closer to some bamboo trees nearby and waited. The image was getting closer. She shook her head and looked again, and the image was gone. She continued waiting.

Suddenly, she heard an eerie voice behind her. She became stiff. She couldn't move. She closed her eyes tightly, and then she screamed, but a hand covered her mouth so that she couldn't scream anymore. She turned to the right.

"Ha-ha!" Ah Seng said, laughing. "I scared you, didn't I?"

Mei Ling was too scared and angry to respond. She hit him on the chest. Ah Seng screamed, still laughing.

"Not too loud, stupid! My parents can hear you!" Mei Ling said.

They both kept quiet for a while. Ah Seng took out a cigarette, lit it, and smoked. Mei Ling kept quiet. "Want some?" Ah Seng offered the cigarette to Mei Ling. Mei Ling shook her head.

"You are late. Why are you late?" she said.

"I've got a job to do! It's lucky that I can escape and come see you. Otherwise, I'd still be at my workplace, and you would be waiting here by yourself."

Ah Seng took out another cigarette as he finished the first one. As he puffed out smoke, he looked at Mei Ling. He quickly looked at her face, body, and legs. *She is so sweet and young!* his scheming thoughts cried.

Despite the darkness, he could see and admire Mei Ling's beauty. He was one of the neighbors' kids, and he was seven years older than Mei Ling. His continued, persistent catcalls had at last paid off, at least for the moment.

Chapter 3

"GOOD-BYE, MR. JOHNSON!" THE nurses said. They were saying farewell to Aaron.

"Hope you have another gunshot wound so that we can treat you again," one of the nurses said, giggling.

"How cruel of you! You want me to be shot again?" Aaron jokingly replied.

"Yes!" they all said at the same time.

Packing his belongings, Aaron looked at them and smiled. The hospital staff had been good to him, especially the nurses. They were all sad to see him leave, and he had liked it there. In fact, he wouldn't have minded staying a bit longer to be pampered.

Blond and blue-eyed Aaron was well built and six foot tall. He was now ready to leave the hospital. He was well dressed for any occasion. This time, he wore his Royal British Air Force uniform—not because he expected to continue his work immediately but because he wanted to celebrate the fact that he had survived and was okay.

As he walked toward the hospital entrance, the nurses followed him, as if trying to persuade him not to leave. At the entrance, Aaron looked at them one more time and smiled. "Thank you! Thanks, all of you," he said with deep appreciation.

"Take care, soldier!" one of the nurses exclaimed.

"Write to us!" another cried.

A Malaysian military Land Rover approached Aaron. Aziz bin Salleh got out of the vehicle. "Good to see you again, sir!" he said to Aaron. Aziz invited Aaron to step into the vehicle.

While putting one of his legs in, Aaron looked at the nurses one more time and waved at them. "Good-bye, girls!"

They all shouted, "Good-bye, Mr. Johnson!" one last time.

While on their way to their destination, which was unknown to Aaron, Aaron took the opportunity to observe the surrounding areas. He saw tall jungle trees, including mangroves, and eagles flying above.

"Sir, you will be staying at the government rest house," Aziz said eventually, revealing their destination. "We will bring your bag to your room at the rest house, but before that, there is someone who would like to see you. He will be waiting for you at the police headquarters."

At the Sandakan police headquarters, Aziz and Aaron climbed the stairs and entered a room. Aziz performed the introductions. "Sir, this is Colonel Nigel O'Brian. Colonel, this is Captain Johnson."

"A very good morning, Mr. Johnson. We have been waiting for you to recover, and indeed you have."

Aaron looked at the colonel. He was about fifty years old, was slightly balding, and wore a plain white shirt with baggy brown trousers. "Good morning, sir," Aaron said.

"I hope we have not kept you waiting, sir," Aziz said.

"Goodness! No, not at all," the colonel replied.

"I have to help Mr. Johnson with his room, Colonel. Will you excuse me?"

"Go ahead, sonny! Mr. Johnson and I have a lot of things to talk about. Don't we, Mr. Johnson?"

As Aziz left the room, the colonel invited Aaron to sit down. "Would you like coffee or tea, Mr. Johnson?" he said.

"I think I will have tea, sir," Aaron replied.

Aaron looked at the colonel as he poured tea for both of them. The colonel sat on his chair and smiled at Aaron.

"Mr. Johnson, the Royal British Air Force was very relieved to hear you were okay but was very grieved by the death of Captain McCoy. It is indeed—"

Suddenly, Aaron interjected. "And the other Malaysian soldiers, sir. Don't forget that, sir."

The colonel stopped for a few seconds, smiled widely, and then continued. "Ah, yes. And the other fourteen Malaysian soldiers. As I was saying, it was indeed a tragic incident. However, those who died did not die in vain, Mr. Johnson. As you know, based on our intelligence sources, most of the Indonesian troops have withdrawn from the Malaysian border."

As the colonel sipped his tea, he looked at Aaron and continued. "Mr. Johnson, let me tell you that just like you, I was selected by the British MI5 to help out the Malaysian army and police in monitoring the border between the Malaysian and Indonesian Borneo. You, Mr. Johnson, are assigned to help me out. Bear in mind that this is highly classified."

The colonel put a briefcase on his desk, unlocked it, and took out a file marked, "Top Secret." The colonel put his glasses on. He browsed the document, took off his glasses, and looked at Aaron.

"It's just a continuation of existing operations, Mr. Johnson. But this one is more clandestine." The colonel smiled. "Her Majesty's government, in collaboration with the Malaysians, Australians, and New Zealanders, is going to conduct Operation Charet. This includes the Royal British Air Force."

"What, if I may ask, is my duty, sir?"

"The purpose of Operation Charet is to obtain information on Indonesian troops along the border and weed out Indonesian infiltrators by ambushing them wherever possible." The colonel closed his briefcase, locked it, and stood up. "Any more tea, Mr. Johnson?"

"No, sir, I haven't finished this one." Aaron pointed to his cup.

"However, you, Mr. Johnson, are only required to patrol along the border, gathering intelligence, not to pursue the Indonesians. You are to coordinate with the Malaysian rangers and border scouts. All of these men are indigenous people of Borneo, the Iban and Murut. They can smell the enemy coming from any direction miles away. They say these people can even smell the boundaries of the border."

"Who says, sir? May I ask?"

The colonel stopped and looked at Aaron. He smiled again but did not answer his question. "Remember, every month, you are required to write reports on the development of your activities. Each report is to be stamped 'Secret,' and only I am authorized to see them."

"When can I go home, sir?" Aaron asked.

The colonel, who was facing the window, turned toward Aaron. "Oh, just a minute." He sat down, took out another file, and looked at it. He put his fingers on his forehead and looked at the papers inside more earnestly. "Well, Mr. Johnson, it will be a year or two before you can go back."

"One or two years, sir? Don't you think that is rather long for me? I have already served six months in this wilderness. Don't they consider that?"

"Her Majesty's government needs your service, son. They need you to help out."

Aaron stood up and slowly walked toward the window. He looked out at the sea and thought for a while. At the hospital, Aaron had thought he might be sent back to Penang immediately. He looked at the colonel, who looked away from him and pondered the file.

Aaron slowly turned from the window and said, "Very well, sir. After serving another two years, I want to go back. No more extensions."

"Very good to hear that, Mr. Johnson," the colonel responded. "I am very relieved you said that. Indeed I am."

Chapter 4

FOR MORE THAN THREE weeks, Mei Ling had not entered her workplace. She pretended to go to fool her parents, and she felt lucky that her employer did not inform them that she had skipped work. Ever since she'd met Ah Seng, she had been following him to the beach, to an isolated location not frequented by many people.

Ah Seng looked at Mei Ling. He took out a pack of cigarettes and offered one to her. "Better learn to smoke," he said. "A grown-up girl must know how to smoke."

Mei Ling shook her head and looked at the beach around them. It was full of rocks and dead coral, and the sea was muddy because of the numerous mangrove swarms around. It was not an idealistic beach like the one she had seen in the magazine. However, this was the best spot in Sandakan, according to Ah Seng, so she had to be contented with it.

Ah Seng moved closer to Mei Ling. "What are you doing?" she asked nervously.

"I just want to be close to you," he said. Ah Seng kept getting closer. Then he put his hand on Mei Ling's hand, and suddenly, Mei Ling could feel her body hair stand on end.

Slowly, Ah Seng put his right arm around Mei Ling. Mei Ling at first objected, but after a while, she felt the pleasure of a man's touch. However, she continued to feel nervous. Ah Seng pushed his face close to Mei Ling's. After a while, he managed to kiss her.

They had been at the beach for more than an hour, and both of them were now naked. Mei Ling felt shy and embarrassed.

"You will feel uncomfortable at first, but after a while, you will enjoy it," Ah Seng assured Mei Ling.

"What are you going to do?" she asked, knowing his intention.

Minutes later, Mei Ling cried out. Her cry later changed into a groan. Nobody witnessed the event, except for the surrounding beach, the sea, the swarm, and an eagle. However, the eagle was not interested in them. It was looking at its prey, a small squirrel a mile away. This squirrel would feed the eagle's chicks.

Mei Ling groaned, quieting down. This time, Ah Seng was the one making all the noise. Mei Ling covered his mouth with her small hand.

"Somebody might hear," she said while closing her eyes.

Both of them panted heavily. They looked at the sky.

"Mei Ling, you are now a woman. You are no longer a girl," Ah Seng told Mei Ling as he rubbed his hand against her hair.

It was a painful experience for Mei Ling, and the pain would continue for another week. Ah Seng smiled, took out another cigarette, and puffed on it. He thought about how lucky he was. *Three virgins this year!*

After the visit to the beach, Mei Ling continued to follow Ah Seng. She began to smoke, gamble, and drink. A few months later, Ah Seng encouraged his other male companions to have a go with Mei Ling. They took turns sleeping with her.

When her parents learned that she wasn't going to work, her father scolded her. To avoid hearing her parents complain, she left and stayed with some friends who had similar interests and lifestyles. She supported her habits by becoming a part-time nightclub hostess.

For months, she never saw her parents. Her parents sent friends looking for her, but she told them to leave her alone. She threatened to run to Celebes if her parents persisted.

After a while, she felt she should see them, but she didn't miss them. In fact, she felt relieved that they didn't bother her. When she returned home, she saw a lot of people in her house. There were police everywhere. She saw one of the neighbors weeping. Then a senior police officer approached her and spoke to her in Malay. She could understand only a little.

"Are you Mei Ling?"

She kept quiet.

"Are these your parents?"

Still, she kept quiet. One of the neighbors indicated to the police that she was Mei Ling.

The officer said, "I am sorry to say this, but your parents have been murdered. The motive was robbery."

The neighbor translated to Mei Ling what the policeman had said. Mei Ling immediately dropped down and sat on the ground. She did not know whether to be sad or happy. She felt sad because only now did she realize she missed her parents, especially her mother, but at the same time, she also felt sort of relieved that they would not be able to control her anymore. Mei Ling continued sitting on the ground alone. Everybody thought she was grieving and should be left alone for a while.

The police also left Mei Ling on her own and combed the area for evidence. For the first time, Mei Ling sobbed.

***

Seven days later, at the funeral, Mei Ling looked at her parents one last time. She insisted on dressing them in red cloth, and she put mirrors on each body.

"Rise up as ghosts, Mama and Papa, and hunt down those who killed you!" She spoke to them softly, hoping they could hear and understand her. As she and her parents were poor, not many people came to the funeral. Not even Ah Seng turned up. After all, Ah Seng had gotten what he wanted, and he had been avoiding her. As the coffins were lowered into the respective graves, Mei Ling whispered one more time to her parents. "Go after Ah Seng too! And ask our ancestors to make me rich. Do you hear me?"

A few weeks later, Mei Ling managed to sell off her parents' land. She sold it for eight hundred and fifty Malaysian dollars, which was a lot of money to her. She made attempts to inform her brother of the deaths of their parents, but there was no news of his whereabouts.

With the money, she could spend her time at the clubhouse, drinking, dancing, and enjoying the place she used to pass by and admire. She felt this was the only place that could bring her happiness.

Chapter 5

S ANDAKAN, ONCE THE CAPITAL of colonial North Borneo, was located at the far eastern corner of East Malaysia. It had a population of sixty-three thousand. Because of the vigorous trading activities, migrants from Kwantung, China, were attracted to this town. That was why the British administrators referred to Sandakan as Little Hong Kong. Sandakan was the only town in North Borneo where most of the Chinese spoke Cantonese. Many settled at Farm River Village, including Mei Ling's grandfather. In the olden days, Sandakan was also an important fortress, essential in protecting the east coast of North Borneo from marauding Suluk pirates from the southern Philippines.

Aaron took his time walking around Sandakan. At the market, he observed the petty traders exchanging manufactured goods from Britain and China, brought by the Chinese traders, in return for Filipino bird nests, copra, fish products, and turtle eggs. There were thousands of turtle eggs openly sold on the streets' walkways. Aaron had learned during his free time at the clubhouse that the former British authority had tried to ban the sale of turtle eggs but had failed—because they too loved it.

Aaron climbed up a hill nearby that overlooked all of Sandakan, which was built along the bank next to the sea. The air was fresh, and it was windy up there. As he reached the top, he panted and then smiled. *What a wonderful view,* he thought to himself. *Wonderful!*

He saw many European-style bungalows dotting the hill. One of them was an abandoned, deteriorating shack. Someone at the club had

21

told him it used to be the home of Agnes Keith, author of the book *Land below the Wind*; words mentioned meant for North Borneo, a place protected from the destructive typhoons which didn't spared her northern neighbor, the Philippines.

The sky was blue, and eagles were flying all over the town. Eagles were beautiful creatures. One landed on a tree close to Aaron. It was a big brown one.

"Hey there, old fellow! I wish I could fly like you do, to see the view from up there," Aaron said to the bird. "Can't do that right now. My plane is back at Penang, you know."

The eagle looked at Aaron as if it understood him. Then, swiftly, it glided away. It had to take the opportunity to catch the thermal heat from the ground to help it float higher. That way, it didn't have to flap all the time. The heat helped eagles to glide upward.

Aaron counted the eagles. There were twenty-six of them, maybe slightly fewer, because he might have counted some twice. Aaron looked around and noticed a Chinese cemetery nearby. There was a sudden quietness, and Aaron felt slightly eerie watching the graves with pictures of the deceased. He took a deep breath and approached one of the tombs. He looked at it carefully. He looked at the people in the pictures, but the Chinese characters meant nothing to him. A sudden, strong breeze came from the sea, as if the dead were aware of his presence.

That night, Aaron drank beer alone at the clubhouse. He enjoyed the swing music, though it was nearly drowned out by the murmuring of patrons who had come to enjoy the same thing as Aaron. Aaron looked around and noticed that the patrons were mostly Europeans and some Chinese businessmen. What he enjoyed most was eating a spicy biscuit called a *maruku*. It increased the pleasure of drinking beer.

"Hi there, pal!" Someone loudly greeted him from behind. "All by yourself, I see."

Aaron turned around. It was Sam Stawski, whom he'd gotten acquainted with at the clubhouse. Aaron smiled, took Sam's right hand, and shook it. "It's wonderful to see you, Sam. Come join me here. I am alone, you know."

"I can see that, Al," Sam replied.

"Why do you always call me Al?" Aaron asked, feeling a bit irritated.

Sam smiled. "It's easy to remember. Besides, it would sound funny if I called you Ar."

"Whatever," Aaron said softly.

As Sam sat down, a waitress approached them. "The usual, Mr. Stawski?" she asked.

"Yes, the usual," he replied.

"How about you, Mr. Johnson? Would you like another jug?" she asked.

"Well, all right. Another jug will be fine. Thank you," Aaron replied. When the waitress left, he said, "So, Sam, how was your day today?"

"Lousy! I lost a couple hundred bucks at a Chinese mah-jongg game in town. There are illegal gambling dens disguised as Chinese clan associations in shop houses all over town, and I played in one of them. How about you, Al? How was your day?"

"Well, I enjoyed a stroll—sightseeing, I suppose."

"In Sandakan? This is not Singapore, you know. Nothing to see here!"

"Well, at least I did not lose two hundred bucks, Sam," Aaron jokingly replied.

The waitress approached Sam and gave him a bottle of Johnny Walker. Aaron knew from his first encounter with Sam that he was an American businessman dealing with petroleum tools and die equipment that he supplied to his Indonesian customers through Tawau, the major town in Sabah, bordering Indonesia.

There were oil explorations going on in Indonesian Borneo, and Sam had been doing well until the Indonesian confrontation with Malaysia erupted in 1963. Now Sam was praying for the war to end so that he could start his business again. Aaron remembered that Sam had told him he came from Allentown, Pennsylvania.

They conversed through the night, joking, laughing, and enjoying the music while drinking. Suddenly, there was nothing to talk about, and both of them became quiet. Each was overwhelmed by his own thoughts. A moment later, Sam had an idea to break the silence.

"Al, look at those chicks over there! What fine ladies."

Aaron turned around and looked. They were indeed pretty ladies, and all of them were Chinese. Aaron turned back, looked at Sam, and smiled. He continued drinking, pretending to be oblivious. "They are pretty, Sam."

Sam was watching them with seriousness. He closed his eyes and sipped the whiskey in his hand. Then he opened his eyes and smiled at them. Two smiled back. Sam put his head close to Aaron. "I would like a taste of one of them, Al. I am sinking in, Al. Sinking in real deep!"

"Good for you, Sam. Cheers to you!"

"That one in blue, the one in red, the one in yellow—they are all pretty, Al!"

Aaron turned around one more time and watched the girls carefully. Then one of the girls looked at him and smiled. Aaron looked back to make sure, and the girl kept looking at him and again smiled. Aaron faced Sam and took a deep breath. "Sam, I'd rather have that one in pink."

Sam looked at her. He turned to Aaron and shook his head. "Are you kidding, Al?"

Aaron felt a rush of blood to his face. Everything around him seemed blurred. He stood up. "I think I would like to go now. It's rather ridiculous. I can see that." Aaron felt embarrassed and irritated by Sam.

Sam quickly stood up and held both of Aaron's shoulders. "Okay, okay! Don't get jumpy. Come on, Al. All right, I'm sorry. Sit down," Sam said. "Wow, you're quite sensitive, pal!"

They continued drinking, Aaron with his beer and Sam with his whiskey. Sam gulped his last glass and stood up. "I'm going to approach the red one. Boy, isn't she hot?" He walked toward the girls.

For half an hour, Aaron sat alone. He watched as Sam and the girls laughed and giggled. There were some British patrons observing Sam, and based on their facial expressions, they didn't seem happy with him. They looked at Aaron. Aaron smiled sheepishly and gave them a nod. They did not smile back. Then they continued drinking, choosing to ignore the commotion created by Sam.

While Aaron was drinking, a young girl slowly approached him. "Can I sit with you?" the girl asked Aaron in broken English. Aaron felt uncomfortable when he noticed that a number of the people around were observing him. Slowly, the people turned away from Aaron and continued their business.

"I am sorry. I will go now." The girl, feeling disappointed, began moving away.

Aaron quickly stood up. "No, please. Don't go away. Please sit. I am sorry I acted that way," Aaron said. Slowly, the girl sat down. She was the one in pink whom Aaron had indicated to Sam. Aaron looked at Sam. Sam gave him a thumbs-up. Then Aaron looked at the girl again.

"My name is Elaine," she said, giving her hand to Aaron.

Aaron took her hand and shook it. "My name is Aaron—Aaron Johnson. Can I offer you a drink?"

Elaine said no to Aaron's offer. She still had a glass of stout in her hand.

They spent time together until everybody had left. Sam too had left an hour earlier with the girl he'd had his eye on. She'd agreed to follow Sam back to his hotel room. Aaron smiled at Elaine.

"Closing time!" the bartender told them.

"How much?" Aaron asked.

The bartender looked at him and smiled. "Sam paid for all of you."

Aaron sat back and smiled. "Thank you, Sam!" he said softly. "Shall I walk you to your house?" Aaron asked Elaine.

Elaine smiled and nodded. They both stood up and walked toward the empty street. They walked slowly, as if trying to enjoy as much time as possible with each other's companionship. They talked and talked, and for Aaron, the time passed quickly. Before he realized it, they had reached the house of Elaine. It was in town, on top of a shop house with many small rooms. She shared one of the rooms with the girl who'd gone out with Sam, Dora. Elaine felt uncomfortable. She stopped, wrapped her arms around herself, and sighed. "What's the matter, Elaine?" Aaron politely asked her.

"Dora, my friend, is not in our room. I am afraid to be alone. I'm always with Dora."

Aaron thought for a while. "Why not follow me back to my room at the rest house?"

"No!" she said in a loud voice.

Aaron was surprised and embarrassed. "I'm sorry, Elaine. I was just trying to help."

Elaine thought for a while. Then she looked at Aaron and smiled. "Okay, I'll follow you. I am scared to be alone here."

Aaron was happy and relieved that she would continue her journey with him. Inside Aaron's room, Elaine looked around as if she had never been in a rest house room. Aaron kept looking at her as she explored the surroundings like a small country girl brought to a big city.

"Coffee?" Aaron said. Aaron had made two cups, assuming Elaine would take one.

"Okay," she replied.

I was right! She accepted, Aaron thought.

For the whole night, they talked to each other, until it was almost dawn. They looked at each other. Both were sitting on Aaron's bed. Aaron slowly approached her, sat close to her, and held her tightly. Aaron, who was twenty-five years old, was holding a woman five years his junior. Slowly, Aaron put his face close to Elaine's. He moved closer and closer and then kissed her. Aaron pulled her down onto the bed. His left hand searched for the light switch. He found it and turned off the light.

Chapter 6

ELAINE TOLD AARON ALL about herself. She told him that she came from a rich family, but both of her parents and her brother had been kidnapped and murdered. Elaine claimed that her parents' properties had been divided among her aunts and uncles, and she had been left with nothing. She loved school but had been forced to give it up because she couldn't afford to pay the fees. She'd found herself a job at the factory, but her employer mistreated her. That was why she has no choice but to work at the club as a part-time hostess.

Elaine also told Aaron that Dora had taken her in as a roommate not because she pitied her but because she wanted to make her a slave. She had to wash Dora's clothes, clean her room, and cook. Elaine said that she would have left Dora a long time ago, but since Dora had been her connection to the clubhouse, she had to tolerate Dora's attitude.

Aaron believed her. He suddenly felt a sense of responsibility to look after her. He could not leave her to face the world alone. Aaron decided he would rent a modest house not far from town and ask Elaine to stay with him. The government could compensate him for his dwelling. He was entitled to a lodging allowance, which he had not utilized.

For weeks, Aaron and Elaine spent time together. When Aaron was on duty, she would stay with Dora and spend her day at the clubhouse. Aaron drove her around in his Mini Cooper provided by the government. It was a small but hardy vehicle. Elaine enjoyed the rides because she had never been inside a car.

"Where are you taking me, honey?" she asked one day.

"It is a surprise, Elaine! I hope you will bear with me for a while."

She had improved her English since spending time with Aaron for three months. Aaron had tied his handkerchief around her eyes. Slowly, he guided Elaine along the way. He kept quiet for a while. Then he stopped, and Elaine stopped too.

"For a moment, Elaine, I want you to stand right here. There you are."

Aaron slowly removed the handkerchief from her eyes. When she opened them, she saw a house in front of her. She was overwhelmed. Slowly, she moved inside to explore the interior. The home was partly furnished, and it even had a new refrigerator. Two of the four bedrooms had an attached bathroom. Elaine put her hand on her mouth. She was speechless.

Aaron observed her carefully as she moved from one room to another. *Why does she look so surprised with this house if she comes from a rich family?* Aaron thought to himself. *Oh well. I don't care to answer that question.* Aaron continued looking at her. *Isn't she lovely? I am in love with her!*

The veranda was adjacent to a well-maintained garden with multitudes of tropical flowers. Elaine sat down on a rattan chair and watched the surrounding area. She was surprised to find that the chair could rock. The gentle movements made her want to slumber.

"I hope you like it, Elaine."

Elaine looked at Aaron and then turned back to the garden. "I used to stay in a bigger house than this," she bragged.

"Oh. Sure you did," he responded.

"But, honey, I like it, and I want to stay with you here."

"Elaine, there is another thing I would like to say to you." Aaron paused for a while and took a deep breath. "I love you, and I want to marry you."

"You do?" Elaine replied with surprise. "Why?" She couldn't believe her ears. To her, this was a fantasy coming true. Many Chinese girls dreamed of being married to a white man. How could she be so lucky? Was she dreaming? Was she hearing him right?

"I love you, and I want to marry you," Aaron repeated one more time.

Elaine looked at Aaron and gave him a smile, as she usually did. She took his hands and held them tightly. She nodded. Aaron was happy that she'd accepted his offer. He had been traveling around the world and felt it was high time to settle down.

What a place to settle down. However, love could overcome all difficulties and challenges. One month later, they were married at the courthouse, and they were registered. Only seven people witnessed their wedding. Among those who attended were Sam and Aziz. Aaron was delighted to see Aziz. Despite his busy schedule, he had come. Aaron hugged Aziz tightly.

Mama, Papa, thank you. You both answered my prayer, Elaine thought to herself. However, on her birth certificate, Elaine was not Elaine. Dora had given her that name so that she could blend in well at the clubhouse. The registrar required them to present their birth certificates. The record gave Elaine's name as Ho Mei Ling.

Aaron couldn't be bothered to see why her name was different on her birth certificate, nor was he bothered to thoroughly check Elaine's background. He had found the perfect girl. That was the important part.

Elaine pleaded with Aaron to have a Buddhist priest bless their marriage. Aaron hesitated at first but later accepted. After all, it was a unique experience.

After their brief honeymoon, it was back to business again. Every month, for three weeks, Aaron was to fulfill his duty at the border, but he left a lot of his money with Elaine. Because of his love for her, he never questioned how she used the money. He never questioned why there was never enough food every time he came back from the border, since he gave almost all of his pay for their household expenditures. The money was never enough. Little did he know that she was using the money to satisfy her craving for gambling. She was a compulsive gambler.

His blindness was all because of love.

Whenever Aaron was back from the border, Aaron and Elaine had to stay home. Unlike before, Aaron could not afford to take her out. He couldn't afford to take her to a decent restaurant. Instead, once a while, Aaron would take her out to nearby hawker stalls. There, all the foods were cheap. Aaron wanted to ask Elaine about the money, but since he had given her the responsibility of managing it, he figured, *Why should I ask?*

Again, his foolishness all boiled down to love.

Chapter 7

"AH, THERE YOU ARE! A very good afternoon to you, Mr. Johnson. A very good afternoon indeed," Colonel O'Brian said, greeting Aaron as he entered his office.

"Good afternoon, sir," Aaron responded.

"Please, Mr. Johnson, do have a seat. Coffee or tea?"

Aaron paused for a while. "Coffee this time, sir."

"I heard you were married, Captain," the colonel said while pouring the coffee.

"Yes, sir. I invited you, sir, to my wedding."

"Oh yes! Very sorry that I was unable to attend your wedding. What a pity that was. I was on official duty in Kuala Lumpur. Congratulations, Captain Johnson. Here you are. Your coffee, Captain."

"Thank you, sir."

As the colonel sat down, he opened a file on his desk. As he flipped through, as he always did, he read the reports to himself. Then he closed the file and looked at Aaron. He smiled widely. "You have done a splendid job, Mr. Johnson. Indeed a job well done. Your monthly reports were very helpful to both the British and Malaysian governments in making a fairly good assessment of the Indonesian infiltrators' movements and activities along the border in Borneo. All the required and necessary precautions have been taken into consideration, as you recommended, Captain."

The colonel smiled. "Operation Charet is a complete success! We managed to stop the Indonesians from using guerrilla tactics. By the way, the presence of our Avro Vulcan bombers in Butterworth, Penang, was also considered an effective deterrence against the Indonesians, who might otherwise have embarked on a large-scale offensive. I'm sure you are aware of that, Mr. Johnson?"

"Yes, sir, I am very much aware of that," Aaron responded while sipping his coffee. Aaron was happy to hear that his superiors appreciated his work. Aaron crossed his legs and waited for the colonel, who was still reading some papers, to continue.

"I have got one more piece of good news for you, son." The colonel leaned back in his chair and laced his fingers together. "I told Her Majesty's government that you would like to go back to Penang to your old job, the RAF. You have already served almost a year for this assignment, and the government has decided that you have served very well. The Malaysian government, however, was reluctant to let you go, but they too decided to respect your wish."

Aaron put down his cup and looked at the colonel. The colonel was surprised that Aaron seemed unhappy about the news. Aaron kept quiet. O'Brian waited for him to speak.

"Sir, a few months ago, I would have been very happy to hear this."

"Well, what changed?" The colonel waited.

"I would like to continue my service in North Borneo, sir. Please help me to stay on."

The colonel leaned backward and then stood up and walked to the window, as he usually did. He thought. He gave a nod. "I don't see any problem with that, Mr. Johnson. After all, it was your choice to go back or stay on."

"And another thing, sir. I would like to be a Malaysian."

The colonel was shocked at Aaron's request. "Do you consider yourself to be loyal, Mr. Johnson? After all the country has done for you?"

Aaron kept quiet. He cleared his throat and stood up. "Frankly, sir, I love jolly good old England, and I appreciate what she has done for all of us, but I love my wife very much, sir. She doesn't want to leave her friends, and besides, I have grown to love the wilderness here." Aaron paused. Slowly, he sat down again.

"I see. Well, that's your choice, Captain Johnson. I see no problem with you continuing your mission at the border. However, becoming a Malaysian won't be easy."

The colonel walked to his seat, sat down, and grabbed his cup of coffee. Both of them kept quiet. Suddenly, the colonel looked at Aaron. This time, he didn't smile. "I will be required to have an audience with the Malaysian home minister. He may be able to help out," the colonel told Aaron. "It will not be easy, though, to fulfill your request of changing citizenship. Well, Mr. Johnson, you can go on with your mission and your marriage, of course. You are dismissed for now, Captain."

Aaron stood up straight and saluted the colonel. "Thank you, sir." As Aaron walked out of the office, O'Brian's voice called out from behind him.

"Send my regards to your wife. And keep up the good work."

"I will, sir," Aaron answered without looking back.

Aaron continued his job at the border. Elaine kept gambling away all his pay. In 1966, the Indonesian confrontation with Malaysia was over when the new Indonesian president, Suharto, took over leadership from Sukarno. A few months later, Devin, Aaron's illegitimate son with a Siamese peasant girl who'd stayed with him in Penang, came to join his father in Sandakan. Aaron hadn't loved her, but he'd felt guilty when she'd become pregnant. He'd felt responsible for her and had decided to marry her after she gave birth. However, she'd died while delivering Devin.

Devin's maternal grandparents had been looking after him. Aaron had paid for Devin's education, but Devin had stopped schooling at the age of eight. His grandparents had tried to persuade him to continue studying, but Devin refused.

They couldn't handle him, so Aaron, who had partially settled down, asked them to send Devin to stay with him. Devin was now ten years old. Elaine was too busy gambling to think about the presence of Devin in her life. She employed a maid to look after him.

Five years later, Aaron was accepted as a Malaysian citizen. He was transferred to the capital of North Borneo, Jesselton. Aaron also managed to get Devin citizenship.

In their new home, Aaron took Elaine to the beach nearby. It had been difficult at first for Aaron to convince Elaine to leave her friends in Sandakan. However, Aaron had persuaded her and enticed her with stories of beautiful tropical beaches on the west coast of North Borneo.

"You always said the beach here was beautiful," she said softly to Aaron. Elaine was happy to see such a beautiful beach. No beach in Sandakan was comparable to this. She held Aaron tightly and asked him to kiss her. He did.

"I love you, Elaine."

"I love you too, honey."

Chapter 8

B LUE SKY AND THE deeper blue sea dominated the landscape of the beach. Tropical pines called aru had witnessed these surroundings for the past hundred years or more. The species was native to Australia, and now it was found there. There were thousands of them. Their scientific genus was *Casuarinas*. When the sea breeze blew into the plants' needle-like leaves, the sound of the wind made a beautiful rhythm. These trees kept growing taller and taller. There was no better feeling than resting under the casuarinas while enjoying the cool air coming from the sea. That was why people called the place Tanjung Aru, or, in Malay, Bay of the Casuarinas.

William was witnessing a boy and two girls playing along the sandy estuary. Another girl was staring at the South China Sea. William cleared his throat and approached them. Coming out from the shade, he could no longer feel the comfort of the mild wind. The heat of the midday sun was scorching his skin. *But if the other kids can stand the heat, why can't I?* he thought.

"Good afternoon!" he said in greeting to the boy playing in the sand. The boy looked up at William without responding. William noticed that the girls also looked at him, except for the one staring at the sea. William felt slightly embarrassed.

"Good afternoon," he said once more. Still, everybody was quiet.

The one still staring at the sea looked different. William was sure the other three were like him—Eurasian. He was hoping they'd notice him because of the distinctiveness they shared. William built up his courage, trying to start a conversation.

"I am a second-generation Eurasian."

The boy looked at him, stood up, and approached close to his face. He looked fiercely into William's eyes and said, "I don't care! I don't care if you are a first-generation European or Japanese or Indian."

William took a deep breath. He was embarrassed. He could feel the blood rushing to his ears. His greenish eyes turned watery. He perspired, but his sweat did not cool his thin body. The girls kept looking at him, which made him feel shy. *Why did I introduce myself ridiculously?* he thought.

The girls slowly turned away from him and continued playing in the sand. The boy still looked furious. His angry face suddenly turned into a broad smile.

"Hi! A very good afternoon to you," he said to William. "My name is Raymond—Raymond Johnson." He offered his hand to William.

Slowly, William took his hand, and they shook. William was still puzzled. "My name is William Stewart."

"Hello, William. Let me introduce you to my two sisters." Raymond took William by the hand and pulled the reluctant boy closer to the girls. "This is Theresa." Theresa didn't look up. "Don't be upset. She is always like this, even to us," Raymond explained.

"How are you, William? My name is Linda," the other sister said, introducing herself before Raymond did. She shook William's hand and then continued playing in the sand. "You have to understand Raymond. He likes to confuse people," Linda explained to William.

William looked at Theresa. She was not looking back.

"Come on, Will!" Raymond pulled William away from the girls to play in a different spot. "I'm sorry I behaved that way," he said.

"What did you do to me?" William pretended as if Raymond's weird reaction had not offended him. Both of them smiled and continued playing. William could not help noticing the girl whom Raymond had not introduced. She was still looking at the sea. William kept watching. At last, he couldn't tolerate his curiosity. "Is she your sister too?"

"Who? Which one? Oh! That one. She is not my sister. That's our maid's daughter. Dad took her mom in as a maid, and ever since, she is like our own sister. They came from the interior of Borneo—Keningau, to be exact."

"Why is she just staring?" William asked, looking puzzled.

"She is wondering why this river is so wide that she cannot see the other side of the riverbank. And this river is so salty that she is wondering who would release so much salt into the river!"

William became more puzzled.

"Okay, her name is Titty, and she has never seen a sea before. She comes from a place where there are only rivers. Not even lakes can be found there."

William slowly smiled. Finally, he understood. He turned his attention to playing in the sand with Raymond. Slowly, he lifted his head and stole a peek at Theresa. Theresa was beautiful; she was a fair girl with brunette hair and green eyes like his. The heat was getting unbearable.

"Okay, I think we have had enough fun. Let's get back to the shade." Theresa, the oldest, gave the command. All of them quickly rushed to the nearest tree. Fifteen minutes later, their father came.

"All right, children, time to go back home," he said.

It was Aaron Johnson. He had put on weight, and he had a short beard. Despite his age, he was still handsome. His clothing was sloppy. However, Aaron's smile and cheerfulness were soothing to William.

"Dad, this is William," Raymond said, introducing them.

"How do you do?" Aaron said.

"I am fine, sir," William answered with respect.

Aaron smiled at William. He looked at his watch. "It's time to go back for lunch. I hope your mother will be around."

"She's never around," Linda said.

"Would you like a lift, son?" Aaron said, offering a ride to William.

William thought for a while. "I don't think so, sir. In a moment, my mother will be fetching me here. She will be worried if I'm not here waiting for her."

Aaron paused. "All right then." He paused again and then walked toward his old Ford Cortina, and all of the other kids followed him.

As Raymond walked toward the car, he stopped and turned around. "I hope to see you again, William."

William smiled. "Where do you stay, Raymond?"

"House number eight. Near the hospital mortuary. It's the only government housing estate near the hospital." Raymond turned and ran toward his father's car.

As the car moved away, William was all alone. He walked out of the shade of the tree, kicked twigs around, and squeezed his feet into the sand. He sat down. He stood up again and walked around some more. Suddenly, he visualized Theresa. He did not do so on purpose; the vision just came. He thought for a moment about how beautiful Theresa was. He sat down again. *How I wish I could meet her again.* William was infatuated with Theresa.

"William!" A shout in the distance awoke William from his daydream. He looked toward the strong voice. It was his father. William slowly stood up.

"Hurry up! I haven't got all day to wait for you!" his father said.

William immediately grabbed his shoes and rushed toward his father's car barefoot. Inside the car, he continued to think about Theresa, even though Theresa was two years older than he was. His infatuation grew stronger.

"You have got a lot of work to do, Son," his father said while driving. "First, you have to help your mother finish the housework. Then you have to focus on your homework."

"Yes, Father."

But William was not thinking about those tasks. He was focusing on images of Theresa. He really wanted to see her again, but there was no way to find her now. He couldn't remember the address Raymond had given him.

How am I going to find them again? He sighed with disappointment as he thought of the remote possibility of bumping into them.

Chapter 9

WILLIAM STEWART CAME FROM a small town called Tenom, a remote place in Malaysian Borneo. They'd moved to Jesselton, the capital of British North Borneo. His father, David Stewart, was a successful real estate broker. William's grandfather was an American planter from California. His grandmother was Malay. His grandfather had left his father and grandmother when his father was only five years old.

William's mother, Kamariah, was an influential woman who had strong family ties with the local political elites. She had a successful restaurant business in town, with a good location, and she consistently socialized with other women of her status, doing charity works.

William had three brothers: Murphy, James, and David Stewart Jr. William were the eldest. William's father was a disciplined person, and his children had to live regimented lives. William and his brothers woke up early in the morning, went to school, came home and did their homework, and then had to help with the house chores. William's father deliberately did not employ servants, even though he could afford to do so.

William's mother was understanding. When they were young, she used to sing by their bedsides, and despite her busy schedule, she still found time to be with them. Sometimes William and his brothers despised their father's strict behavior. Their father was conscious of his status as the leader of the household, and he did not openly show love and affection to his children. But as for their mother, they loved her dearly. She was not only understanding but also loving and caring.

William was playing in the school yard with several of his classmates. He attended one of the most reputable junior high schools in the capital. William built a sandcastle with a limited amount of sand within the compound. He somehow had forgotten that he would be in trouble with the teacher for being dirty after the recess. He'd also forgotten to brush his teeth that morning and even had forgotten about Theresa.

"William, look! New intake," one of his classmates said to him. William ignored him and continued building the castle. "William! For heaven's sake! We are all already thirteen, and only you seem to be playing with sand."

William ignored his comments. He kept playing with his fragile castle. He slowly turned his face toward the new students in the distance. He turned away and then suddenly turned back and looked at the new arrivals.

He stood up immediately. His friends were startled. He couldn't believe his eyes. He walked nearer to them, leaving his friends behind. The new arrivals were Raymond and his sisters. Quickly, he rushed to them. As he approached them, a teacher suddenly said, "Stop, you dirty clown!" All the students looked at him. So did Raymond and his sisters. Theresa seemed disgusted with William.

"You go to the washroom right now, and clean yourself up!" commanded the teacher. The teacher slowly turned away from William and smiled at Raymond. "Come! I will show you to your class. It is a good thing your father chose this school for the three of you."

Raymond followed the teacher, turned back, and signaled to William. "Meet you later," he said in a low voice.

William smiled. He walked backward gently and then turned and ran.

Chapter 10

AARON JOHNSON CAME HOME from work. He was tired and haggard, and he was an unhappy man today. They now lived in an affluent neighborhood only three miles from the city. His house was a big detached bungalow surrounded by a well-maintained garden.

Despite the big house and beautiful garden, the home had only a few pieces of old furniture, a small refrigerator, a black-and-white television set, two broken-down air conditioners, and a bed with a smelly mattress.

The kitchen cupboard was almost empty. The garage where Aaron parked his old car was littered with rubbish and old newspapers. Aaron and the Johnson children only changed their clothes once a year, during Christmas. As for Elaine, she got new clothes every month. She was always outside the house, and she dined on good food with her friends. Aaron and his kids were left to fend for themselves. They had to figure out what to eat at home, if there was any food, or outside if Aaron had the cash. This made Aaron sad.

Aaron walked slowly to the couch in the living room. He loosened his tie, put his bag down near the stairs, and dropped himself onto the soft, wrinkled seat. He closed his eyes and murmured.

Elaine, watching him from the kitchen, opened the refrigerator; took out a beer, which was the only drink in the fridge; closed it; and walked toward Aaron. She opened the beer and passed it to Aaron. Aaron looked at her, forced himself to smile a bit, and took the beer. Aaron kept looking at Elaine. She had grown prettier than ever, prettier than when he'd met her.

Elaine sat next to him. She rubbed her hand on the back of his neck.

Aaron again closed his eyes. "That's good, Elaine. I love it." Elaine rubbed harder. Aaron groaned with pleasure. Suddenly, he opened his eyes again, and his smile disappeared. He stared at the ceiling.

"What's the matter?" she asked. "Something's bothering you."

Aaron kept staring at the ceiling. He kept quiet. Elaine too kept quiet. A few seconds later, Aaron sat up straight, gulped some beer, and stared at her. He kept quiet. Then, slowly, he took a deep breath and mumbled something.

"I can't hear you," she said, feeling uneasy.

"Elaine!" At last his voice broke out. "You know how much I love you, and I give everything to you. I never interfere or ask questions about anything. We have been married for more than sixteen years now."

Aaron stood up and walked around the living room while holding the can of beer in his hand. Elaine looked at him lovingly. She smiled. However, Aaron did not smile back. He kept walking round and round, trying to say something he should have said a long time ago. Aaron took a deep breath and marshaled his courage to speak out this time.

"Elaine, I now have a job that offers a salary twice as high as most ministers in Malaysia. I give every single cent to you for you to manage the household." Aaron turned around and observed the surroundings. "But we have nothing! You just spend your time with all the Chinese ladies at the gambling club and finish off all the money."

"If you don't like me, why did you marry me?" Elaine exploded as she rose and walked toward the stairs. Aaron dropped the can of beer, rushed behind her, and pulled on her arm.

"Listen to me, Elaine!" Aaron roared. "You gamble, you smoke, and you always lie. You even lie about small issues!"

"Like what?" Elaine shouted.

"Many things!" Aaron spoke with a calmer tone. "Many things, Elaine. For example, you promise to spend some time with the kids once in a while. Do you ever do that? Never! You lie, Elaine. You always lie. And the children are beginning to behave like you." Aaron walked back to take his seat. Elaine slowly fell down and sat on the stairs. She wept.

Aaron shook his head. "Look around you, Elaine. What have we here now? Next to nothing!"

Aaron laid his head on the couch. His mind flowed to the not-so-distant past. While serving at the border, he'd received an offer letter from a security firm, Mega Shield, offering him a position as general manager of the company. The job would pay seven thousand Malaysian dollars per month and include other fringe benefits, such as a bungalow house. The firm was owned by a government agency, and he would always be attached to the city, without having to travel away from his family all the time. Aaron had been delighted and had accepted the offer without hesitation.

Aaron's mind wandered back to the present. Here he was, still as miserable as before. He looked at Elaine. She was still weeping.

Slowly, he stood up and walked toward her. He sat next to her and held her tightly. He shook her gently. "Think about it, Elaine. Are you hurt because I spoke something true, or are you hurt because I spoke something that isn't true?"

Elaine rubbed away her tears and looked at Aaron.

"I want you to change, Elaine."

Elaine looked at Aaron and smiled.

"There, there." Aaron spoke softly and held her more tightly.

Elaine said, "I want to go back to Sandakan alone, honey. Only for a short while."

Aaron relaxed his grip on Elaine. "What for?" he asked, puzzled.

She held a finger to his lips. She stroked Aaron's hair and smiled.

Aaron didn't respond to her gesture. He turned away from her. "What is it this time you are up to, Elaine? What?"

"Nothing. I just miss my friends back there. Besides, I want to pray at my parents' graves. I also want to give offering to my ancestors. Maybe more fortunes can come to us."

More misfortune to me! Aaron thought to himself.

"Please!" Elaine pleaded. "Tonight I will give you the best," she whispered into his ear. "You can do anything to me. For tonight, I give you permission to treat me not as a wife but as your slave. Only tonight. Okay?"

Aaron's grim face changed to smile when he heard Elaine's proposal. Seduction was Aaron's weakness and Elaine's strength. She was so seductive. Suddenly, Aaron forgot about his problem. Now he was looking forward to spending time with Elaine the whole night. He agreed to let Elaine go.

"But only for three days, okay?" he said.

Elaine nodded with a sinister smile.

Chapter 11

THE NEXT DAY, ELAINE flew to Sandakan. She took a cab into town, and she did not miss the chance to observe the surroundings. The areas she passed by were changing. Many new housing developments had sprung up.

As she approached a landmark, a bunch of overgrown bamboo trees, she asked the taxi driver to slow down and stop. It was a place she recognized, but the whole area had changed. There were no more wooden houses around and no more roads with potholes. If not for the bamboo trees, she would not have recognized the place. She saw the place where she used to stay and the land she had sold more than a decade ago.

"The land was sold a few weeks ago," the taxi driver said to her in Cantonese.

Elaine looked at him. "How much?"

The taxi driver paused. "If I am not mistaken, it was eight hundred thousand Malaysian dollars. If I am not mistaken!" He shifted the car into gear and slowly moved away. Elaine kept quiet the whole way to her destination. She did not want to observe the surroundings anymore.

Outside the entrance, Elaine stood still and read the signboard in Chinese: Far Sea Eastern Dragon LTD. She opened the glass door slowly and walked toward the reception. One of the employees stood up and smiled at her while she observed the surroundings.

"Can I help you, madam?" she said in Mandarin.

Elaine looked at her and smiled. "I am looking for Mr. Tan," she replied in Cantonese. "Tan Boon Seng."

"Do you have an appointment?" the receptionist asked politely.

Elaine walked closer to the counter. "Tell him Ho Mei Ling wants to see him."

The receptionist paused. "Wait a minute, and please do have a seat," she said to Elaine while pointing to a sofa nearby. Fifteen minutes later, the receptionist stood up and waved at Elaine. "You can come in now. Just go straight ahead to the biggest room."

Inside, multitudes of staff members were working around the clock. She moved toward the big room. She stopped and knocked. "Come in!" a voice instructed. She opened the wooden door and walked toward the man she wanted to see.

"Please sit down," he said. "It has been a long time. You want something to drink?"

Elaine smiled and said, "The wine that I am seeing in your cupboard."

He smiled and took a bottle. "How do you know about me, Mei Ling?" he said while pouring the wine into two glasses. He gave one to Mei Ling.

"I read about you in the Chinese newspaper. They say you have been a successful businessman dealing with shipping and forwarding."

He gulped the wine.

Elaine too drank hers and finished it off quickly, which surprised him. He smiled and poured some more into Elaine's glass.

"Ah Seng, you indeed have prospered. Your wife is lucky to have married you."

Ah Seng stopped and looked at the picture on top of the table. "She is a bitch!" he said, and he quickly drank the whole glass, as if to challenge Elaine. "She is a prostitute. I met her in Taiwan."

Elaine looked at the picture. "She is beautiful."

"Ah! She is barren," he said, continuing his criticism of his own wife. "So what can I do for you, Mei Ling?" Ah Seng looked at the attractive lady he'd deflowered years ago. He looked her up and down, from her hair to her legs. "It has been a long time, Mei Ling. Long, long time now." He continued looking.

"You know, Ah Seng, I cursed you when my parents died. You were not there to show your respect."

Ah Seng looked away from her. "I never had a chance to say I am sorry for what happened," he said, offering his belated condolences to Elaine. "Why did you curse me?" He suddenly realized what Elaine had said.

"You never gave me any money! It was me who fed you, remember?" Elaine shouted.

"Not so loud!" Ah Seng put his fingers on her lips.

"Why? Are you ashamed?"

Ah Seng raised his hand, indicating that was enough. He poured some more wine into their glasses and quickly drank. Elaine followed and finished hers in one go. By now, the whole bottle was finished.

"I have been saving this bottle for a grand occasion, you know," he told Elaine. "This is the occasion. So?"

Elaine stood up and came closer to Ah Seng. "I have a proposition for you." Elaine sat on his big table, removing the things on it. Ah Seng watched as some of the things fell over, but he did not protest. "I lift the curse, and you give me a big sum of money."

Ah Seng fell back into his big executive chair. He paused. He looked at Elaine and smiled.

"How about it?" Elaine pressed him for an answer.

"You know, my wife controls the financial aspect of this company. It is her capital. I only help to run the business. Most people rush to venture in harvesting timber in Sandakan. I deal with transporting and exporting their products. Not many of them have thought about it. I am smart, you know."

Ah Seng sat up straight. "However, I could find a way to manipulate those transactions without her knowing, but I can only do it once. Not anymore." He looked at Elaine while his hand caressed her smooth legs. He slowly put his hand inside her panties. Elaine politely pushed him away.

"However, there is a price for me to betray my wife," he said.

"And there is a price for me to betray my husband!" Elaine said.

Elaine smiled and turned away from his face. Ah Seng again pushed his hand deeper into Elaine's underwear. With his other hand, he slowly rubbed Elaine's breasts. Both Ah Seng and Elaine's breathing became faster.

"I want you, Mei Ling. For a good old time. I want to own you, and I want your husband to know it too. Sleep with me for one week."

Elaine smiled. "Three days," she said.

"Four days," he replied.

"Done! Hundred thousand Malaysian dollars."

Ah Seng spit out the wine in his mouth. He thought for a while. He looked at Elaine. She was far more beautiful than his old wife. He slowly smiled. "All right then. I can give you thirty thousand."

Elaine laughed. "Sixty. And no more negotiation!"

Chapter 12

Back at the capital, Elaine smiled at the airport while waiting for her husband to fetch her. She couldn't believe her luck. She'd stayed with Ah Seng for one week, though. Ah Seng had told her that this was the last time he could see her and strongly warned her not to come back. She didn't mind. She knew that Ah Seng's wife would be returning from her holiday in Taiwan, and there was no point for Elaine to continue meeting him. She had gotten the money wired into her account.

As she was waiting, Aaron and the kids slowly approached her.

"Mummy!" they called as they rushed to her. "Where have you been?"

She stood up and hugged them one by one. She then turned to Aaron, held him tightly, and gave him a kiss. "Honey! This time, my gambling paid off with the help of the fortune deity."

Aaron couldn't believe his ears. She had gone all the way to Sandakan to gamble? "My God, Elaine!" He spoke harshly but softly.

"I have won sixty thousand Malaysian dollars! Do you hear me, dear?"

Aaron had mixed feelings. He didn't know how to react. To him, this was both good and bad news. However, he smiled. "Okay, Elaine, if that's how you want it. Why don't we go home, and you can talk about your adventure in Sandakan?"

The whole family walked together, holding each other's hands, toward Aaron's old car. Elaine smiled at Aaron. He smiled back, oblivious to what had happened for the past several days.

Chapter 13

WILLIAM AND RAYMOND BECOME close. They were in the same class, they went out fishing and camping together, both of them joined the Boy Scouts, and they were both Eurasians. Raymond needed William as his closest companion. In class, Raymond always got second to last, and to cover his shortcoming, it was fortunate that he had William, who was always last in class.

Despite their closeness, there were apparent differences between them. While William talked about religion, Raymond talked about girls; while William was interested in language and history, Raymond was more concerned about biology, especially the subject of the human body. Indeed they were odd couple.

Every weekend, William would visit Raymond at his house, and then from there, they would travel by bus to town. On weekdays, Raymond would follow William to his house not far from the school. One day they found a thin fiberglass boat mold abandoned near a shipyard. They would paddle this flimsy object deep into the Mangrove River to catch black crabs.

On weekends, they would waste their time loitering at the shopping complex or cinemas, hoping to bump into their rich classmates, who would offer to buy them drinks or movie tickets. At night on the same day, they would gaze at the sea in front of the city, witnessing the sunset.

"What's interesting in life, Ray?" William asked.

Ray kept quiet. He took a deep breath and shook his head slowly. "You know," he said to William while watching the sea darken, "there

50

was one incident when my brother, Devin, and his friend Kloon were playing with rubber pieces that they called French caps." Raymond smiled and laughed.

"Caps made of rubber?" William asked innocently.

Raymond closed his eyes and shook his head again. William looked at Raymond. He understood that Raymond was feeling irritated with his question. Again, William tried to fit into Raymond's conversation. "So what happened?" William asked attentively.

"Well, my brother told me that it only fits the head of the bird below." He pointed between his thighs. "I tried to fit it, and Devin yelled at me, saying that I had to harden it first."

William was listening carefully.

"So I hardened it. I tried to fit the rubber on it, struggling and struggling. It managed to go halfway through. I forced it in again. Suddenly, it snapped and broke! Can you imagine? Both of the guys just stared at me." Raymond laughed. "Actually, I felt great. I felt like a hero!" he said, laughing harder.

William looked at him and joined him in laughing. "Excuse me. Ray?" William asked while laughing. "Is the French cap like the Muslim skullcap?" William continued laughing.

Raymond's face turned sour. He was not amused. He looked at William seriously. William slowed down his laughter. "Are you dumb?" Raymond shouted. He shook his head in disbelief. "You are dumb! You should drink more milk, you know. It will increase the fat inside your brain." Raymond stood up and walked away.

William was perplexed. He wondered for a while.

"What did I do wrong, Ray?" He stood up and shouted, "Wait for me, Ray!"

They walked to town. Raymond was walking with huge strides. William tried to follow his footsteps. Raymond couldn't tolerate any more conversations with William. He had to find other excitement to fill his time.

"Maybe there is a good movie today. We can find somebody to pay for us," Raymond said.

"Don't you think it is a bit late for movies?" William asked.

"Relax, Will! It'll be fine."

They both reached their respective homes at almost midnight. William was caned. Raymond received only nagging from his father. Each felt the punishment was unbearable. Both got grounded for two weeks and were unable to go out after school and during the weekend.

The next day, Raymond came to school with something for William to see. He took several items out of his bag and showed them to him. Several of their classmates also watched.

"Do you know what this is?" Raymond asked them.

All, including William, stared at each other. They shook their heads. Raymond gave a strong puff, and after a few minutes, the rubber item bulged and expanded. Raymond approached some of the girls sitting near the class windows.

"Do you want some balloons?" he said.

The girls looked at the so-called balloon with interest.

One said, "We are all fourteen, but we still like to play with balloons. Thank you, Raymond!"

"With pleasure," Raymond replied with a cunning smile.

"What's all this?" a voice suddenly screamed, exploding outside the classroom.

It was the principal, Mr. George Abraham. He moved into the class and looked at the boys with stern eyes. The boys quickly dispersed. He approached the girls slowly and looked at them seriously.

"Mr. George, Raymond was so kind to give us this balloon," one girl said.

The principal took a closer look at the rubbery thing. He suddenly straightened up and became more furious. All the other kids in the class quickly sat down and opened their books. Mr. George approached Raymond. He noticed Raymond was trying to suppress his giggling by biting his lips.

"Follow me to my office!" he commanded.

"Yes, sir," Raymond replied.

As the principal walked out, William approached Raymond. "Why does a balloon make Mr. George so angry?"

Raymond walked closer to William. "That, my friend, is the French cap."

William thought for a while. "Oh, I see." William continued thinking, looking more lost.

Raymond became a popular kid in his class, as well as in the school. He quickly built a network of friends among not only his juniors but also the seniors. He was an interesting person to mix with. Raymond was the first person to know and share his knowledge about how a child was born into the world.

"Your parents made love! That is why you were born," he said.

"I thought babies came from heaven and were put into my mother's stomach," said one classmate. Many of the boys rushed around Raymond to hear this new revelation. The girls watched and wondered.

"Yeah right," Raymond answered cynically.

"That's what my mother told me," another classmate confirmed.

Raymond brought a magazine to school and introduced *MAD Magazine* to the students. Soon both juniors and seniors were always hanging around him because of his humorous and hospitable personality. Girls began to send letters to him.

He had an athletic build, blue eyes, and slightly dark tan skin. His hair was blond, but he was slightly short. Teachers could see that Raymond had leadership qualities. He seemed to be the alpha male; however, he was inspiring his peers with negative facts.

William noticed that in his friendship with Raymond, he and Raymond were drifting further away from each other. It was not Raymond's fault, and William understood that, but he missed his companionship.

Chapter 14

DESPITE RAYMOND'S GROWING POPULARITY and despite the fact that he always spent more time with new friends, Raymond and William still spent their weekends together at the beach, pondering, watching, and admiring the sunset. They still had things to talk about. However, Raymond had less time to go fishing or boating with William.

They walked to a section crowded with people hurrying to take their baths in the sea before darkness took over the twilight. There were dozens of hawkers selling young coconuts, corn, tidbits, peanuts, and local fruit to locals and foreign tourists. William and Raymond chose this place because it had a good view of the setting sun.

They heard the sea crash against the shore as the last batches of gulls squeaked above the waves, heading for their resting places. The breeze moved the pine leaves of the aru trees, which wailed a beautiful melody in the midst of couples talking, giggling, and laughing. Raymond and William kept quiet for a while. They were sitting on a rock big enough for six people to sit on, watching as the sun went down.

"You know, Ray," William said, starting the conversation, "aren't you proud to be a Eurasian? I'm proud to be one." William smiled as he said these words. Raymond seemed not to notice what William had said. He kept watching the sea and the sunset.

"Not many of us here have the blood of a white man. What do you think, Ray?"

Raymond kept quiet. Then he sighed. "Why don't you grow up, William?" he said, breaking a twig in his hand. With it, he drew something in the sand. "Why don't you ever grow up?"

Raymond moved away from the rock and sat on the sand. People were now leaving the sea and moving into the hawkers' stalls not far away. Some got into their cars and drove away, but new people kept coming to enjoy the stalls.

"We are pariahs, William!"

William looked confused. "Why do you say that, Ray?"

"You think the whites will accept us? We are a half breed! The lowest of the low! Why do I say that? All right, first, all races have a place to go back to and call home. The Chinese can go back to China, the Indians can go to India, the Malays and Bumiputeras have their homeland here, and the Europeans have Europe. You got that?"

William thought about what Raymond had said. Then he smiled. "Maybe, Ray, when we grow up, we can carve out certain parts of Russia to create Eurasia. In that way, we too can have a country."

Raymond shook his head vigorously. "The problem with you, my friend, is that you always talk nonsense." Raymond stood up, cleaned the sticky sand from his clothes, and walked away from William toward one of the hawker stalls. He stopped, turned back toward William, and added, "And your nonsense is intolerable! Remember that!"

William watched him walk away, waited for a while, and then stood up and joined Raymond. "Wait for me, Ray!" he shouted. Raymond signaled for him to follow.

"Two coconuts, please," Raymond told the hawker.

He sat down. William joined Raymond and sat down too. The place was crowded with customers. William put his hand on his right cheek. Raymond sensed that something was wrong. "What is it now?" he asked.

William kept quiet.

"What?" Raymond said, insisting on an answer.

"Well, I don't drink or eat young coconut."

Raymond shook his head and slapped his forehead. He kept quiet for a moment. "Never mind! I'll take both!" he said angrily.

"Sorry," William said.

The crowd was getting bigger. Some of the people were waiting for seats. Fortunately, many of them had finished drinking and started to leave. However, a new group appeared, and the cycle went on. Raymond finished his fruit. He quickly took the other one meant for William. Raymond was thirsty, and he drank fast.

William looked at Raymond. "About Eurasia," he said. He stopped immediately as Raymond waved his hand, indicating he should stop.

"Why don't we talk about other things?" Raymond said to William.

William thought for a while. Suddenly, he put his arms on the table. "Do you have a girlfriend?" he asked Raymond.

Raymond released the straw from his mouth and smiled. "That is a good conversation. Yes! Her name is Winnie Kwan. I met her at my dad's friend's house. She happens to be his daughter."

"Is she pretty?"

"Indeed, very pretty. She goes to school at the Saint Francis Convent. She is the same age as both of us. What about you?"

"Will you marry her?" William asked, avoiding Raymond's question.

"I don't believe in marriage, Will. I'm an atheist, and I don't believe in any holy matrimony. You will see, William. I will be a bachelor for life. Mark my words!"

"I will get married and have children. I will build a big house for my future wife. And we will have many children and be happy forever. I will not have sex with her. I just want to love her." William was visualizing his dreams, and his eyes were facing away from Raymond.

"How will you have children if you do not have sex with your wife?" Raymond was getting irritated with William.

"Do you need sex to get children?" William asked, looking surprised.

"You are a hypocrite—do you know that? You are pretending to be holy," Raymond said with a raised voice.

"No! I am not pretending anything," William replied with embarrassment.

Both kept quiet. Raymond was playing with the straw. William was looking under the table. "So who is your girlfriend? Who is this unlucky girl you want to marry?" Raymond pressed for an answer.

Raymond could see that William was blushing and seemed nervous to answer. Raymond looked at the straw and kept playing with it. "It's okay. You don't have to tell me. What's the big deal anyway?" Raymond seemed to sulk.

William took a deep breath, trying to muster some courage. He released his breath slowly. "Actually, I don't have any girlfriend yet. I'm looking for one. But I think I found one."

"Go on," Raymond said, pressing William.

"It's your sister Theresa."

Raymond did not look at William. William too was looking away, at the crowd's movement.

"Hey there! How much for the coconuts?" Raymond asked with a loud voice.

The hawker approached. "Two dollars," he replied. Raymond paid the hawker and stood up. He indicated to William that he wanted to start moving away. William slowly stood up, and they walked toward the town.

"You know, Will, my sister is a championship trophy. All sorts of boys are attracted to her. You think you, whose brain is made of marshmallow, would stand a chance to win her? Dream on, baby! You are a dumb-ass—do you know that? She will not go for a dumb-ass!"

They kept walking along the pathway to town. William was slightly hurt at the remarks Raymond had made, but he was used to harsh criticism from his father, so what difference did it make with a friend? He bit his lip, trying to overcome the humiliation.

"Anyway, Will, you can try your luck." Raymond's words turned William's despair into some sort of hope. He immediately forgot what Raymond had said. Now he felt Raymond was a friend after all—an understanding one.

"Next week, on Friday, we are having a party at my house. I am inviting a lot of friends, and you can come if you want. There you can spend your entire time with Theresa." Raymond looked at William and patted his back.

William felt happy. It was eight o'clock now, and both of them had to be back at home soon or risk being grounded again.

"You want me to inform Theresa about your feelings?"

William looked panicked. He kept mum for a while. "No! Please don't. Please!" he pleaded to Raymond.

Raymond thought for a while and answered, "All right. I won't tell her. Trust me."

They went their separate ways. When William reached home, he obligingly helped out with the house chores, tidied his room, and went to bed early. His parents were surprised at his abnormal behavior. In bed, William couldn't sleep because he was thinking about the party at Raymond's house. He couldn't wait until Friday.

Chapter 15

A T LAST, IT WAS Friday night. For the past few days, William had been in his best form. He was cheerful, in high spirits, and always early to bed and early to rise for school.

He looked in the mirror. He put a cotton shirt over his T-shirt so that he would look a bit bigger and camouflage his skinny body. He used cologne, which he never did, and brushed his teeth three times that day instead of once, as he usually did.

He persuaded his mother to buy him new jeans, and he polished his shoes over and over again until they looked so shiny that they gave the impression he was wearing military parade boots.

William had to take two buses to travel from his house to Raymond's home. However, he traveled early, so he had plenty of time to wait for the other bus. While waiting, he walked around town to pass time.

He was anxious about the party. As the time approached, he climbed onto the second bus and sat close to the door. There were not many other people riding, so there was not much hassle.

The bus dropped him off outside the housing area where Raymond lived. He didn't mind because there was still plenty of time before the party, and besides, the distance from there to Raymond's house was not far. He walked slowly. Suddenly, he became nervous. He walked even slower. The reason was obvious. He was shy with Raymond's family, especially Theresa.

When he arrived, he noticed that everybody in the family was around. Raymond's mother was busy preparing food for the party.

Even Raymond's father was helping out. William saw Raymond and Devin preparing the music sets. As William walked toward Raymond's house, he saw Theresa preparing the tables. Raymond observed the surroundings. There were no other people aside from Raymond's family members and the maid and her daughter. However, it was still early. He approached Raymond.

"I'm too busy, Will!" Raymond was busy fixing the amplifier and the speakers. "Find somewhere to sit." Black discs were all over the floor nearby. William walked away from Raymond and tried to find a good sitting location. None of the other family members greeted him.

William saw Theresa looking at him. Quickly, he glanced somewhere else. He was too embarrassed to make eye contact with her. Even looking away, he noticed that Theresa was walking toward him. He started to sit down.

"Raymond told me everything," she said.

She was wiping plates for the party. William could feel blood rushing in his veins. He couldn't stand the embarrassment; he felt as if he was shrinking, and his feet were cold. He had trusted Raymond not to say anything to her, but Raymond had lied.

"Would you like to help me out?" she asked.

William felt the rushing blood suddenly stop. He felt his spirit brighten, and his body became warm again. He looked at Theresa and smiled broadly. "I would very much like to help you," he stammered.

She smiled. "Come!" she said.

Devin played a popular hit song over and over again. The title was "No One Came." Nobody was at the party except William and Raymond's family members. Much later, Raymond's father went out with some friends, and his mother went to the house next door to play mah-jongg. The maid and her daughter were already asleep. Linda persuaded Raymond's youngest sister, Susan, who was still a child, to get to bed.

The same song went on and on. Devin seemed to enjoy it.

William had the time of his life. He spent time talking to Theresa, and he had Theresa all to himself without any competition from others. Raymond ate the many foods his mother had prepared, but nobody could finish the food, no matter how much they ate.

Devin was fiddling with the discs but seemed content to continue the same song as a sign of sarcasm. William and Theresa continued to ignore the bad things happening and chose to continue conversing with each other.

"I'm going to convince the others to hold another party next Friday. Would you come?" Theresa said.

William could hardly believe Theresa's invitation to him. He looked up toward the sky and smiled.

"Well?" she demanded.

"It will be a great pleasure to come, Theresa. I will come."

Theresa looked at her watch. "It is getting late. You have a bus to catch, and I have a Bible to read. Thank you for coming, Will." Both of them slowly stood up. They shook hands. Theresa had a beautiful, soft hand.

"Good night, Theresa. See you in school."

"Good night, Will."

Chapter 16

WILLIAM LOOKED AT THE girl he was infatuated with. She was on her way to class, carrying her bag. Suddenly, a mild wind blew, and her curly brown hair danced to the rhythm of the morning breeze. Every time this happened, Theresa used her fingers to straighten out her hair.

William looked harder at her, concentrating. As Theresa was walking, she suddenly slowed down, and then she stopped. She held her bag to her chest, and with a sudden sense of intuition, she turned her heard toward William. William felt nervous with her eyes staring at him. He was about to turn away, but he cleared his throat and continued to look at her.

Theresa winked at him and slowly started walking again. Then, suddenly, she stopped. She turned her entire body and moved toward William. William straightened and couldn't figure out what to do. She approached him until she was close. William noticed that some of Theresa's classmates were watching them.

"Don't forget, Will. The Friday party is on again." She giggled a little and walked away from him.

William was still. Slowly, the crowd of schoolmates began to turn away and disperse. William stared at Theresa as she disappeared into her class. He slowly smiled. He was excited to visit Theresa's house again. He couldn't wait for Friday, which was still four days away. Someone patted William's shoulder from behind. He turned around. It was Raymond.

"What are you looking at, Will?"

William stood still and stared blankly at Raymond.

"Will? Hello!"

William jerked a little. "I am okay! Don't worry. I'm okay," he assured Raymond.

They looked at each other, and both suddenly had mental blocks; their minds were completely empty. Raymond again patted William's shoulder. "I want to tell you, Will, that the Friday party at my house is on again."

"Again?" William replied, pretending he didn't know.

"Yes, again!"

As they conversed, they walked toward their class. Moving together, they reached their class and sat down at their desk. Raymond and William shared a desk.

"Oh, one more thing, Will. You know, since the exam is getting closer, it won't be good if you are sitting with me."

"Why not?" William asked, feeling a bit hurt.

"You see, for the past five years, our school tests and examination results haven't looked promising for either you or me. Why? Because you are dumb, and you are dragging me down to your level."

William paused and pondered Raymond's words.

"I'll tell you what. I want to sit with Brian, and I suggest you sit with Chong. Both of them have brains, and I believe both of us will benefit if we sit separately," Raymond told William.

"Will Brian and Chong agree?" William said.

"Well, Brian is delighted to sit with me, but Chong is hesitating. But don't worry, Will. I will convince him. That's not a problem."

Raymond walked toward Chong. The teacher had not come in yet, and the class was noisy. Raymond sat on Chong's desk. He talked to him, and William could see that Chong was occasionally looking at him. Chong didn't look happy, but he kept nodding and listening to whatever Raymond was saying to him.

After a while, the teacher arrived. All of the students suddenly kept quiet and rushed to their own desks. Raymond was still talking to Chong. Seconds later, after the teacher entered, he moved away from Chong. Chong nodded one last time, and Raymond sat back in his chair.

While the teacher was standing in the front of the room, Raymond shifted himself closer to William. "Everything is okay," Raymond whispered. "Chong agreed to sit with you. Brian will move away from Chong, and he will be taking over your seat. You should thank me."

William pretended to smile, but he bit his lip tightly. He was upset Raymond had pushed him out. Slowly, his sadness disappeared, replaced by happiness about the upcoming Friday party and the opportunity to be with Theresa.

Chapter 17

I T WAS FRIDAY NIGHT again, the night William had waited for impatiently for the past few days. He again groomed himself while facing the mirror, trying to look his best. He had convinced his mother to buy him not only new clothes and trousers but also a new pair of shoes.

Again, he arrived early to the party, but this time, it was different. Everyone was busy again, but the scene was more hectic than the previous one. This time, there were a lot of people. He saw many girls and boys, mostly teenagers but also many older youths who had completed high school.

They must be the super seniors, William thought to himself.

William saw that Raymond was enjoying talking to the girls who were encircling him. Devin and his father were fixing the hi-fi equipment that they'd borrowed from their neighbor. The maid and Raymond's mother, as usual, were preparing the food.

Theresa and Linda were approaching one boy after another. Theresa also allocated some time for the seniors. They were laughing and enjoying themselves. One of the boys offered the two sisters whiskey, which they gladly accepted.

William felt out of place. He moved slowly toward the table filled with food and drinks. He helped himself to some sandwiches and a glass of punch. He kept eating the sandwiches.

Then he saw that Theresa was alone, helping herself to some food. He quickly approached her, confident that she now had the time to entertain him.

"Hi, Theresa!"

She looked toward him. "Hi, Will!"

As they were chatting, a well-built, well-dressed, handsome man approached Theresa. Theresa looked at him. "Hello, Mike! How are you these days?" She held on to him tightly and started to move away, forgetting about William. "Just a moment, Mike," she whispered.

She approached William. "Can you take a seat for a while? I will be back with you soon."

"Okay," William replied with a heavy heart.

Theresa walked toward Mike and moved away from William. He looked around at everyone. They all were too busy for him. He found himself a seat and sat down. Deep inside his heart, he was hoping Theresa would find time to be with him.

Raymond was talking and giggling with several girls. The hi-fi equipment was fixed, and Devin began to play music. The crowd continued to enjoy themselves and the different tunes. Theresa and Linda were engrossed with the boys who were courting them.

"Let's dance, boys and girls! The party is on!" Raymond cried.

While William was concentrating on the time, he felt a strong pull on his shirt. He turned around and saw Susan, the youngest sister of Raymond, who was only eight years old. William looked at her and smiled. He shook his head and then continued to look for Theresa.

"Uncle William, I want you to play with me," Susan told William. William just gave her a smile. She continued to pull his shirt. "Please, Uncle." William was getting irritated and annoyed.

"Please, Uncle! Please!" The persuasion continued.

"Look, little girl, it's past your bedtime, and I think you should be in bed right now. Please go!"

Susan refused to go away. William stood up and left Susan alone. Susan watched him move away. William watched with relief as Theresa approached him. This time, Theresa was going to allocate some of her precious moments for him. Theresa smiled at William. He smiled back. Theresa asked William to sit, and she sat next to him.

"I appreciate that you could come, Will."

William tilted his head a little bit, indicating that it was nothing. "You see, many people came to this party, so I'm kind of busy."

"That's okay," William replied.

"Can you do me a favor?" Theresa said.

"Sure. I'll do anything for you, Theresa," he said. Theresa kept quiet for a while, so he asked, "What is it, Theresa?"

Theresa pulled Susan onto her lap. "I want you to keep an eye on Susan. She wants you to play with her inside the house. Nobody seems to have the time for her. Just look at the crowd. You can help out, can't you, Will?"

William was shocked at the request. This was a terrible favor. But what could he do? He wanted to show Theresa that he felt love for her, not just infatuation, and this was a way to show his love to her. However, he also felt that Theresa was using him. These conflicting feelings were hurting him, and he could do nothing about it.

"Will you, William?" The persuasion continued.

William sighed. "All right," he agreed reluctantly and angrily.

"Yea!" Susan rejoiced.

"All right, Susan. Take Uncle inside the room and play with him. Thanks, Will!"

William walked slowly inside. There wasn't anybody there. Everyone was outside, enjoying the party. William observed the surroundings. Susan grabbed a lot of coloring books, crayons, and colored pencils. She placed them near William.

"Come, Uncle! Let's play!" she said.

William sat on the small chair nearby. He shook his head slowly. A small amount of tears came out of his eyes, as he was upset about what had happened to him. He reluctantly joined Susan in her games. Then he walked up to the window and watched the outside party that everyone except him was enjoying.

"Uncle, come. Let's continue!"

"Just a moment, Susan!"

Peeping through the window curtain, he noticed that Theresa was talking closely to Mike, and they were holding hands. He felt a sudden rush of blood and extreme jealousy. He could not understand why he was doing a favor for Theresa, while she was outside enjoying time with another man. He walked away from the window and came to Susan.

"Susan, I am not your babysitter, you know! And besides, it's high time for you to go to bed." Susan was indeed tired. This time, she didn't object to his suggestion, and she stood up, yawning.

"Thank you, son. I didn't get your name," Aaron said, coming into the room to put his daughter to bed.

"William, sir," William responded.

"Oh, William. I think I remember you. We met years ago at the beach, didn't we?"

"Yes, sir, we did."

"Are you all right, son?" Aaron noticed a disturbance in William.

"I am fine, sir. I am glad Susan accompanied me."

Aaron sensed that William was upset about something, but he was not going to pry. "All right then. It's time for me to take over from you here. I appreciate what you did for my daughter, and I thank you."

"Yes, sir. I know that, sir."

"Yes, of course you do. Thanks again, son."

Aaron carried Susan on his shoulder. Susan was half asleep. She looked at William and smiled. He didn't smile back at her. He was still irritated. Fortunately, Aaron didn't see his expression, because he was facing away from William.

"I like you, Uncle William!" Susan said while yawning.

"Good night, Susan!" William responded.

William watched the others having a good time. Raymond was enjoying with the girls, and Theresa and Linda were dancing with the boys. Devin was sitting alone in one corner by himself. His father watched him smoke but didn't care. William slipped away without telling anyone. After all, nobody cared to notice him.

Chapter 18

THE NATIONAL EXAMINATION WAS seven months away. The school was going to conduct a mock test in three weeks' time. Many of the students were busy preparing for the test, but many others couldn't be bothered.

The nerds, such as Brian and Chong, were the smartest and the most respected by the teachers. They were anticipating the day with enthusiasm. Raymond got involved with a group of classmates who participated in tutoring and extra classes to supplement their deficiencies, especially with mathematics and the Malay language, which were both compulsory subjects.

William was all alone to face the examination. He hadn't studied a bit, and he wasn't prepared for anything. His monthly class tests were always miserable. William was worried. Chong, who was supposed to help him with his studies, had left him to fend for himself. Raymond did not want to be involved with William until after the final national examination.

William walked around his neighborhood aimlessly. His mind was bogged down, and he couldn't think properly. There was a small coffee shop nearby that only had three tables and nine chairs. He stopped, looked at it, and moved toward it.

He sat down and requested a cup of tea. While waiting, William tried to figure out how he could catch up with his studies. He did not want to share his problem with his parents, because his father would be mad at him. So he kept quiet about it.

On the table was a small plate of hard-boiled eggs, ready for any customers who wanted to have a snack. William took an egg, cracked it open, and ate it. The tea arrived, and for William, the taste of the egg was much better with tea.

"Hello, William!" Ramlan Omar, one of his neighbors and a childhood friend, said. He was riding a bicycle. "Can I join you?"

"Sure. Why not?" William answered while putting the remaining egg inside his mouth.

"A cup of coffee, please." Ramlan looked carefully at William. He sensed that William was having some kind of problem. Suddenly, his bicycle fell down because he hadn't parked it properly. Ramlan quickly stood up and straightened it. He came back and joined William. "Can I help you, Will?"

"With what?" William replied. He had finished his egg and now was sipping his warm tea. Ramlan's coffee arrived, and he slowly sipped it. The sugar container did not have enough sugar, so he requested one more teaspoon.

"You have a problem, Will. I can see from your face." He continued to drink his coffee.

William sipped his tea slowly. "I am having problems with my studies."

Ramlan looked at William. "That should not be a problem."

"What do you mean? Is there any way I can catch up on my studies?"

Ramlan laughed. "There are seven Javanese traders staying at my house. They rented a big room in the basement. I was made to understand they are very well versed in the Holy Koran and also full of spiritual knowledge. I believe they can help you, William."

William found it hard to believe, but he was desperate. "You think they can help me?"

"Of course. I am positively sure about it. Why don't you come to my house tonight and see what they can do? Then you will believe me."

William thought for a while. Then he nodded. "All right. I'll come to your house tonight."

That night, William arrived early. Ramlan was waiting at the door of the rented room. "Come in," he told William.

The room was constructed of cheap wood and thin plywood. There was only one bulb to light the entire room. One of the tenants had stayed behind to help William. The others were out doing business at night. They were selling Indonesian emerald rings brought from Surabaya. Emeralds were popular there.

"This is Mas Nolla. I have explained your problem to him, and he said he understands. It's a universal problem, but in Indonesia, they know how to handle this situation. He has helped many students like you to do well in their studies."

Ramlan introduced Mas Nolla to William. They shook hands. There were no chairs or tables inside the room, so William just stood.

"Please sit down. You can sit there on the bed. I'll roll the mattress for you," Mas Nolla said, trying to make it comfortable for William. William slowly sat down. The bed wobbled, and there was a squeaking noise.

Almost immediately, Mas Nolla started to chant some Koran passages. The chanting lasted for fifteen minutes. Slowly, Mas Nolla took a black object from his bag. It was a necklace with hollow beads. He put it around William's neck.

"There! There! You will no longer have to worry about your studies. This amulet will help you to be confident, but you must maintain your faith in it all the time."

Mas Nolla took out his *kretek*—a famous Indonesian tobacco blended with cloves—and smoked. The room soon filled with a nice smell from the kretek smoke exhaled by Mas Nolla.

"The teachers overseeing you will be compelled to make you pass your test. Have strong faith," Mas Nolla said.

William held the necklace. "Does it mean I don't have to study?"

Mas Nolla smiled. He shook his head. "No! You don't have to study. You will pass!"

Ramlan was happy for William. William was in a much happier mood. At last, he'd solved his problem. He could now pass the exam with ease using a shortcut to studying.

"Thank you, Mas Nolla!" both of them told the Javanese.

"Hey! Wait a minute!" Mas Nolla cried, putting up his hand as he kept smoking. "Fifty dollars," he said slowly.

"Fifty dollars? I can't even afford ten bucks!" William faced Ramlan.

Ramlan quickly approached Mas Nolla and gave him the money. Mas Nolla nodded while puffing more smoke out. Ramlan moved back to William and asked William not to worry.

"Once you pass your test, then you can pay me back," Ramlan assured William.

William didn't like the idea of paying for black magic, but in Southeast Asia, it was common practice for the locals to rely on witch doctors called *bomoh*. William was determined to pay Ramlan once he could find the money. William didn't know Ramlan had used rental money paid by the tenants. Ramlan did this because he wanted to assure William that he had strong faith in Mas Nolla and also because he considered William his best friend.

William enjoyed himself and did not bother studying. All he had to do was have faith in his amulet. He spent the rest of the three weeks prior to the test fishing, playing football, and strolling in the city. William assured his parents that he would pass, but his parents were not convinced. William did not tell them about the magic that was going to take place. However, his parents trusted William, and they hoped he knew what he was doing.

The day of the exam arrived, and the students took their test.

One week later, everybody was anxious to receive his or her report card.

"William!" the teacher shouted. William approached the teacher. The teacher looked at him with a grim face. William was filled with confidence that his test score would be excellent. All he had to do was have faith.

He slowly opened his report card and peeped at his result. Suddenly, he felt overwhelmed. He'd gotten all red marks, except in English. He'd passed his English class with distinction. William sat slowly and pondered his future.

Raymond approached William. William kept quiet. He refused to discuss his results. Raymond watched William's sad face. Slowly, he left him alone.

While walking home, William angrily took off the necklace and opened the beads to see what was inside. To his horror, he found that the necklace was filled with burned papers and broken pieces of chicken bones. He rushed to meet Mas Nolla. Mas Nolla was at the house, and William confronted him.

"I failed every subject except one! It doesn't work!" he said angrily.

Mas Nolla kept calm and continued cleaning his rings. When he finished, he stood up and walked toward William. "You are the one who asked a favor from me. The problem is that you don't have faith."

"I want my money back!" William shouted, pulling on Mas Nolla's hand as Mas Nolla walked away.

Mas Nolla looked at him and pointed toward his pocket. He slowly put his hand inside and took out a small, curved dagger. Mas Nolla looked at it and turned it around. "You know, many have died because of this." Mas Nolla suddenly looked at William and smiled. "You still want your money back?"

William became frightened. He let go of Mas Nolla's hand and slowly left. Suddenly, he ran as fast as he could to his house. At home, William took a deep breath and decided that for the time being, he had to forget about Theresa and about fooling around; he had to focus on his studies. He had less than six months of school left, and he had to consult his parents about his problem. After all, they were the ones who could help him.

Chapter 19

Jesselton, the capital of North Borneo, had a population of approximately five hundred thousand people. It had some of the world's most beautiful beaches and islands. The most famous were Pulau Gaya and Pulau Tiga. Both of these islands were national park. Within two hours after enjoying the sunny beaches there, visitors could reach the highest mountain in Southeast Asia, Mount Kinabalu. They could spend the night there and enjoy the temperate coolness. Jesselton and its surrounding area developed rapidly. With the development, the nightlife flourished. The nights also grew longer, as people refused to sleep early.

The year was 1983. The examination was three weeks away. Raymond was walking with Alex Fernandez around the city. They walked without direction. The studies had taken a heavy toll on the students in the country.

"We have to get our minds off studying, Ray!" Alex said. He took out a pack of Salem cigarettes, helped himself to one stick, and offered the rest to Raymond. Raymond looked at the pack and took one.

They stopped by a coffee shop on one of the busy streets in town. They found themselves a place in the corner of the interior shop. The shop was packed with customers, mostly brokers. These people had small briefcases filled with Xerox copies of land titles that supposedly offered approved timber concessions. All they had to do was locate a willing buyer for the concessions, and the broker would arrange the transaction. If the deal was finalized, he would get his commission.

Raymond and Alex both ordered coffee and toasted bread. They watched the people talking, haggling, and negotiating. Alex puffed on his cigarette and faced Raymond. Raymond was still watching the people.

"Sometimes I asked myself, *why should I study so hard?*" Alex said. "You see those guys over there? They don't have any high school certificates. But they make tons of money." Alex was pointing at two young Chinese businessmen in the center of the shop.

"What do they do?" Raymond asked.

Alex sipped his coffee. "Well, they have strong connections to some high-ranking customs officers at the port. They bring in spare parts bit by bit from Hong Kong and Japan, which are subject to fifteen percent duty. Then they assemble the parts to make cars. A fully assembled car is subject to one hundred twenty percent duty. Then they can sell the car they assembled at half the market price!"

Raymond looked at the businessmen. He estimated that they were slightly older than he was, possibly in their early twenties. They looked simple, wearing jeans and round-necked T-shirts. However, their gold chains revealed that they were successful.

"But that is not the end of the story." Alex took another cigarette and lit it. "They also built strong connections with the transport department and the police so that they could use the chassis and frame numbers of stolen or condemned vehicles on new registration cards of the vehicles they assemble."

"Wow! That is a hell of a lot of complicated work," Raymond marveled.

"However, if the authorities take the trouble to check the chassis and frame numbers of the vehicles, then there will be trouble for these people," Alex said.

Raymond looked at Alex.

Alex grinned while puffing away the smoke. "So tell me: Is it worth studying?" Alex paused after the question and then said, "I think not, Ray! That man sitting over there has a bachelor's degree to his name but is earning much less than those two guys."

Raymond looked at the well-dressed man with long sleeves and a necktie. He was sitting alone and drinking Coca-Cola.

"He is a credit officer at a bank, working ten hours or more a day without any overtime pay."

"Alex, tell me one thing: How come you seem to know everybody here?"

"I am a man of the street. I spend most of my time hanging around these areas. Do you think I want to spend my time studying? No way!" Alex stood up. "Come, Ray! I want to show you something more interesting."

Alex took Raymond to an isolated location in the city. It was a run-down part of town, and the people there were unfamiliar with Raymond. They entered a door and took a staircase to a floor that had a lot of small rooms.

"Hi, Alex. Long time no see!" a girl who was barely twenty said to Alex.

"Hi, Susanti! This is my friend Raymond. Raymond, this is Susanti," Alex said, introducing them to each other. Raymond saw that females occupied all the rooms, and there were a lot of men moving around the rooms.

"Any new stock arriving?" Alex asked Susanti.

"Many of them. Mostly from the island of Sulawesi."

Raymond looked at Alex. "Alex, I think we should go home."

"Relax, man! The fun is just beginning," Alex told Raymond. He noticed that Raymond was getting nervous and concluded that he was new to this kind of experience.

"Okay, Ray. Let me explain. This is a brothel. You know what a brothel is?"

"I've heard about it. So?"

"So? These are the sorts of places for a man to seek pleasure. We only live once, Ray! What is the greatest pleasure for man? Making love to a girl, man!"

Susanti smiled at the two friends talking. She approached Raymond, who seemed jittery. She took him by his arm and dragged him to a nearby room. Raymond reluctantly followed her.

"I'll pay for the bill, Susanti. And, Ray, don't worry. I will be in the next room, enjoying!"

Susanti dragged Raymond inside. "This is Wati," she said, introducing a young woman to Raymond. Susanti quickly went outside and closed the door. Wati was sitting on the bed. Raymond was stunned. He couldn't move, and he kept standing straight. His eyes wildly looked around the room. He could hear clearly the action taking place in the next room, including giggling, groaning, and screaming, because the wall was so thin. He looked at the girl, who was equally nervous. He saw that she did not dare to make eye contact. Slowly, he gained some courage. He walked slowly toward her and sat down by her side.

They both kept quiet. Then he said, "Your name is Wati?" She nodded. "How long have you been here?" She still kept quiet. "How old are you?" Again, she kept quiet.

Finally, she broke her silence and asked, "What's your name?"

"Raymond. My name is Raymond."

Half an hour later, Raymond and Alex walked away from the slum. Alex offered a cigarette to Raymond. While walking, both of them smoked. Alex looked as if he'd had the greatest pleasure in his whole life. Raymond looked happy.

"She had a terrific body and a tight one too! She even gave me a chance to sodomize her! Can you imagine? I loved the way she screamed in pain. What about you?" Alex said.

Raymond kept quiet. He'd never expected that Alex could be so disgusting, even to Raymond, who had the reputation of being the most vulgar person in his school. Raymond inhaled his cigarette smoke deeply. He slowly noticed that Alex's life was full of fun. *Alex could be a good buddy to hang around with,* he thought to himself.

"Well? How was it with your girl? Was she hot?" Alex insisted on an answer.

"I didn't do anything to her."

Alex stopped walking. "You are a fool! I paid for you to enjoy! Goodness!"

"I love her, Alex."

Alex was shocked at Raymond's statement. He couldn't believe what he'd just heard. "Excuse me? Ray, could you repeat that?"

"I said I love her. Her name is Wati, and I did not do anything to her. I will be dating her, and I promised to pick her up tomorrow. I want to marry her."

"Do you know she is a prostitute? Are you out of your mind?" Alex spoke loudly.

"I don't care what you think, Alex. In the first place, you brought me there."

"I asked you to screw and forget. I did not ask you to fall in love!" Alex put his hand on his hip and shook his head. Then he raised his hand, indicating he didn't want to hear any more from Raymond. They continued walking.

Alex brought Raymond to a fancy restaurant. While having dinner, he tried to persuade Raymond to change his mind about the girl, but Raymond was adamant. He refused to accept any advice.

"Raymond, you can't get infatuated now. The examination is only a few weeks away. It will be a disaster to your studying."

"Alex, you yourself said that people who did not do well in their educations did well in business."

"Yes, I did say that, but you have to have a lot of experiences in this world. Not falling in love with a hooker!"

"Alex, one more condemnation from you, and you will not be my friend anymore."

"All right. It's your decision—on one condition. You help me tackle your sister Theresa."

Raymond smiled. "I can't help you with that. But I can tell you more about her—her likes and dislikes."

"That is what friends are for!"

Alex and Raymond continued their dinner.

Chapter 20

RAYMOND KEPT DATING WATI but fell short of making love to her. Finally, when the examination was a few days away and everybody was busy preparing for the final countdown, Raymond took her one evening to an abandoned building not far from Raymond's school.

Razor-sharp weeds and thorny shrubs surrounded the compound. After struggling, they finally got through the brush. There were no doors or windows to stop anybody from coming in, and they could easily move inside. It was dark and humid, and the place was littered with syringes and rusty needles.

It is an addict's den, Raymond thought to himself.

"I am scared, Raymond," Wati said.

"There is nothing to be scared about. I will protect you, Wati. I love you."

"I love you too, Raymond."

They walked into the deepest part of the house. It was silent, and then Raymond heard water dripping slowly. The sound of the water hitting the floor seemed loud in the quiet room. They began to hug and kiss each other. Raymond was excited. They fell to the ground, clinging tightly to each other, but it was uncomfortable.

"Just hold on, Wati." Raymond stood up and walked around the house. He was searching for some kind of bed, if there was any. Finally, he brought a big cardboard box, broke it up, and put it on the floor.

"There! Our makeshift bed for the night," he said to Wati.

"Raymond, please hold me again," she pleaded in a slow and loving voice. Raymond sat down and continued to kiss her. They took off their clothes. Raymond was breathing heavily, while Wati seemed relaxed and cool. Wati stopped and slightly pushed Raymond away.

"Are you sure you want to marry me, Ray?"

"Trust me, sweetheart. I love you, and I will marry you."

"I have heard those promises a hundred times. But it is all empty talk!"

"I am different, Wati. I will fulfill my pledge to you. Can we continue?"

She pushed Raymond away. She would have sex with anyone who paid, but to her, Raymond was different. She felt that this was the moment of truth, and she could not give in easily. She wanted to make sure Raymond was serious.

Raymond began to feel irritated and desperate. He pulled her to him strongly and gave her a deep kiss. This time, Wati became more receptive. She hugged him and tightened her grip on him. Slowly, they fell into their makeshift bed.

After an hour, Raymond took out a cigarette and smoked. He had begun to get addicted to nicotine. Wati was lying on his naked chest. Raymond looked down. He shook his head. *What a way to lose my virginity!* he thought.

"Anything wrong, dear?" Wati asked.

Raymond paused and then said, "There is nothing wrong, dear. Nothing at all."

Chapter 21

AARON JOHNSON RUSHED HOME from work. In his old Ford Cortina, he sped, ignoring the condition of his vehicle. It should have been overhauled months ago, but he couldn't afford it. While driving, he had a big smile on his face.

When he reached home, he was overjoyed to see all his family members there, including Elaine, his lovely wife. He got out of the car in a joyous mood and hugged and kissed Susan, who was the first to meet him at the door. Theresa was talking and gossiping with her mother on the veranda. Devin was fixing a bicycle for Raymond. Raymond was helping Devin out. Linda, as usual, was reading a romance novel in the living room.

"A very good evening to all of you, especially you, my lovely wife!" Aaron said.

Devin and Raymond couldn't tolerate their father's greeting, especially Devin, who was almost thirty. Theresa quickly stood up and hugged her father. Aaron quickened his pace toward Elaine and kissed her. Aaron stood up straight and expanded his chest.

"I have good news for all of us." Aaron paused. "We are going back to Sandakan." As he made this announcement, he noticed that all of their faces except for Elaine's and Susan turned somber. Aaron could see that Elaine was the happiest.

"When are we going, Daddy?" Susan asked her father. "Can we go today?"

Aaron smiled at Susan. He went into the living room, holding her, and sat on the sofa. He waved for all of them to come inside. Slowly, all of his kids except Devin walked into the living room and sat around him. Elaine stood up from the chair she was sitting in and sat next to Aaron on the couch.

"Why must we go back to Sandakan?" Linda asked with disappointment. "You know I don't like Sandakan."

Aaron was calm, and he kissed Linda on the cheek.

"Daddy, we will be leaving our friends here," Theresa protested.

Aaron still remained calm. "The first thing I have to tell you is that I have been offered a new job by a big plantation company. It offers twice what I am receiving now. I am now a plantation general manager for a palm oil and cocoa estate, and I get a free house and two four-wheel-drive vehicles. Don't you think I should be entitled to all these privileges?"

"Wow! You will be receiving a big salary? That means you can give me more money, right?" Elaine asked with eagerness. Aaron gave her a nod.

"You are going to have two new cars?" Raymond said.

Again, Aaron nodded. "They are Toyota Land Cruisers."

There was excitement in Raymond's face.

"Secondly, you all are big enough—but not you Susan—to come back here once in a while to meet your friends. I believe that could be arranged."

Theresa smiled at last at her father's suggestion.

Chapter 22

ONLY ELAINE AND DEVIN knew what Sandakan looked like. For the other kids, the environment was new and unfamiliar. Theresa, Linda, and Raymond could remember a little bit, but Susan had not been born in Sandakan and had never grown up there.

Before they moved in at the plantation, the company offered Aaron and his family a temporary residence in an old colonial residential area on top of the hill overlooking Sandakan, where, decades ago, Aaron used to walk alone.

He walked toward the location he'd once admired. He noticed many differences. All the town's buildings were now concrete. The clubhouse where he'd met Elaine had been torn down. The government rest house had given way to a new three-star hotel.

Aaron looked up at the sky. It was empty. He waited and waited for anything to appear nearby or beyond the horizon, but he saw nothing. After more than one hour, he finally saw a lone eagle flying and gliding graciously. He waited another hour, but that was the only eagle he saw. Development and businessmen's greed had taken a toll on this magnificent bird.

The next morning, Aaron walked along the open market. Bombed fishes were all over the place. He was disgusted with what he saw. The seafood was contaminated with cyanide due to the underwater explosion, and he couldn't find any that were not caught that way.

"Very cheap, sir! Only twenty cents per kilo. Come buy!" one seller told him. Aaron looked at him. He didn't smile. Slowly, he turned away from the fishmonger.

Aaron noticed there were not many turtle eggs sold on the open market. He couldn't find a single one. Aaron smiled. "At least the government is preventing the sale of turtle eggs," he mumbled to himself.

"I'm afraid that's not so!" A voice suddenly appeared behind him. Aaron turned around and faced a British tourist. "The lack of turtle eggs is because this country has run out of them, not because of the government control. They don't care!"

"My name is Aaron Johnson. I worked here. I do believe that is an expensive camera you have."

"My name is Rupert Chapman. I am a marine biologist working for a Singapore zoo. I travel here every year, partly to do research. But Sandakan is not what it used to be."

"Well, we will be bumping into each other more frequently," said Aaron.

Aaron was completely satisfied with his new job. He had a big house with two maids to help out, a gardener, and two new four-wheel-drive Land Cruisers. He had a big paycheck and other perks, such as medical benefits and insurance. But what Aaron liked most about his new job was the full autonomy to exercise his own decisions regarding how to run the company. The shareholders were only interested in fat profits. He delivered them, and there would be no questions asked. He should have been the happiest man on earth.

However, Aaron was sad. His wife, Elaine, gambled all the time; Devin did not complete high school and spent his time doing nothing despite his advancing age; Linda was going out with a married man; and Raymond spent most of his time at every disco party in town.

Aaron arrived late from work. He had every reason to stay up late. He came to the office at five in the morning, and now it was almost eight. At least work would keep his mind happy.

However, Aaron did have one source of pride that kept his spirits up. He had Susan, and he spent a lot of time with her, helping her with her studies and encouraging her to read. On Sundays, he would secretly bring her to Saint Mary's Church, and he taught her about

Christianity. He couldn't let Elaine know, or else she would be hopping mad at him. After the morning mass, he would bring Susan to a fast-food restaurant, and twice a month, they would visit the orangutan rehabilitation center at a four-thousand-acre jungle park called Sepilok.

"Daddy, why do I always have to go to bed early?" Susan asked her father.

"Well, as the old saying goes, 'Early to bed and early to rise makes a small girl like you pretty and wise!'"

Susan giggled. Aaron looked at his growing daughter. Deep inside his heart, there was sadness but also hope—hope that he would see Susan grow up to be different from the rest of her brothers and sisters.

"Go to sleep now, dear. You have a long day ahead of you tomorrow. Go on! Close your beautiful little eyes." He gave his daughter a hug and a kiss and covered her with a blanket. Susan closed her eyes. Aaron slowly left the room and switched off the light.

Outside, Aaron saw Devin playing cards and smoking. They hardly spoke to each other. Aaron was unable to get through to Devin, and he did not know why. Devin looked at his father but purposely chose to ignore him and treat him as if he didn't exist. He kept playing his cards. Aaron walked toward his son and stopped.

"How's your day, Son?" Aaron said, trying to open a conversation. "I used to play like that." Aaron laughed, hoping for a response.

There was no response from Devin. Then Aaron kept quiet, turned back, and walked away. Devin continued playing and puffing on his cigarette. He suddenly stopped playing, threw his cards away, and walked toward the workers' quarters nearby.

"Will you be needing us any more tonight, Mr. Johnson?" one of the maids asked Aaron.

Aaron looked at his two maids. He smiled at them. Slowly, he walked to the fully furnished but empty living room. He sat down on the rattan sofa. The maids waited for him to give instruction.

"Sofia, please get me a beer. And you, Maria, please do sit down. Please!"

The maids were feeling uneasy about Aaron's request for one of them to sit with him. Maria motioned for Sofia to go get the beer. She reluctantly walked toward Aaron and sat nearby.

"Do you have a husband?" he asked her.

"Why?" she asked. Then, after a pause, she said, "Yes, I used to have a husband." She was surprised at the question. In the ten years she'd worked as a maid, Maria never had come across such a personal question.

"Do you love your husband?" Aaron's weary eyes looked at her.

"I used to, sir. He used to be a good man. He took care of me very well."

"What happened then?"

Maria kept quiet. She turned to the left and right and then looked toward Aaron. Then she looked down at the floor. She held her hands together and then looked up at Aaron once again. "Do you really want to know, sir?"

"Yes, I do want to know."

Sofia arrived with the beer. Aaron took the beer and looked at Sofia, who was much younger than Maria.

"Thank you, Sofia. You can go now. I want to talk to Maria for a while privately."

Sofia didn't know how to react. She stood up, staring, and then turned to Maria. Maria signaled for her to go. Sofia slowly walked away. Several steps later, she glanced back at Aaron and Maria, wondering what their conversation was about. She then moved on.

"You see, sir, though she is young, Sofia is also a widow. We came from the Philippines. We came to this country to seek income. This income is needed to support our families back in the Philippines. As time passes by, more will be joining us, seeking jobs outside our country."

"Sofia is a widow?" Aaron said, puzzled.

"When I was young, Mr. Johnson, I had a loving husband. But you see, sir, he was a handsome young man; he had American blood in him. Many girls went after him. In time, I had to accept the reality that he would be looking for another one despite the fact that he still loved me."

Aaron saw Maria weeping. He felt guilty for asking. "I'm sorry, Maria. I didn't mean to hurt you."

"It's all right, sir," she said while wiping her tears. "I feel very good that I could share my problem with you. I feel relieved. I had such pressure filling inside me from not telling anyone." She stopped weeping. "I am the one who should say thank you."

Aaron took out his handkerchief and gave it to Maria. Maria took it and wiped her tears. She kept quiet. Aaron went back to the sofa and sat down. He opened the beer and slowly drank it.

"You see, Mr. Johnson. I am a qualified nurse, and I graduated from one of the colleges in the Philippines with a degree in nursing. But there are too many graduates in the Philippines and no jobs available."

"So you chose to work here in Malaysia as a maid?"

"The salary you give us, Mr. Johnson, is much higher than what any average white-collar job pays in the Philippines. Thank you for that."

"You should thank the company who employed you. I didn't employ you."

"About my husband—he refused to find a job but instead spent his time drinking cheap alcohol made from rice or coconut and gambling with money he borrowed. Finally, an elderly rich woman helped him out with his debt, and he was indebted to her."

"So it was never a happy ending after all," Aaron said in a low tone of voice. He continued to drink his beer and finished it off.

"I'll get you another one, sir."

"No, no. I think I've had enough already. You can go now, Maria. Thank you for your time."

Maria stood up and walked away.

"By the way, Maria, how many children do you have?"

"I have two girls, sir. The youngest is six months, and all are taken care of by my mother."

Chapter 23

IT WAS AN ATTRACTIVE place, well decorated, and one of the first few to open up in Sandakan. It brought a lot of customers scrambling to pack the limited space available. This place offered cheap smuggled beers and whiskeys, had a room with darts and snooker tables, and served delicious fish and chips. Except for the game room, the place was dimly lit.

"Well, well, what brings you here, Devin?"

"Hi, Drum. Good to see you," Devin responded, and he continued to sip his beer.

"It has been a long time since we have seen each other. The last time I saw you, you were still in your early teens. You have grown up to be a fine young man, now, eh?" He patted Devin's back. He pulled up a chair and sat next to Devin.

"You have grown up to be bold, old, and ugly, Drum!"

Drum kept quiet and looked serious. Devin was laughing, and slowly, he too turned serious and slightly scared. Drum stared at him with furious eyes. Suddenly, he jerked his body and was about to punch Devin, when he stopped and burst into laughter. Devin hesitatingly joined in his laughter.

"I used to be handsome like you, Devin! Remember? Now is the time for me to age, but your time will come. You too will age."

"Come, Drum. Let's have some beer. Join me!"

For hours, they sat and talked about the good old days. Before Devin and his family had left Sandakan decades ago, he and Drum used to be friends, though they were not that close. Drum talked about his life, and Devin talked about the city on the west coast of Borneo that he'd recently left.

"Some more beers, please!" Drum ordered. Devin was looking worried, and Drum noticed. "Don't worry, Devin! I will be paying for all of this."

Devin felt relieved. "Make it two jugs then! Okay, Drum?"

"Go ahead!" Drum approved of the request.

Almost everybody had left the pub, which was located on the second floor of a shop house near the port terminal. Both Drum and Devin continued drinking. Drum signaled to the bartender that they wished to continue. The bartender consented.

"You know, Drum, I hate my father. I hate him so much."

"Why is that? I thought you two got along very well."

"It was never a good relationship. I hate him for coming here to marry that gambling bitch stepmother of mine." Devin poured beer into his throat. He felt high and could not control his emotions.

"Well, life is never fair." Drum shook his head, and he too drank some more beer. Drum looked at his hands, turning them up and down, his elbows resting on the table. "So what do you intend to do about it?"

"Pray that both of them die! On second thought, I don't want them to die. Not until I get myself a business. Then they can die. Yes! I think I will go into business. Maybe as a contractor, because I see that contractors make tons of money."

Drum laughed. "It is not easy to be in business, especially if you do not have experience." Both of them sipped their beers. "Another jug, boy, and it will be the last!"

The bartender nodded. Based on his facial expression, he was tired and wanted to close the pub. It was almost three o'clock in the morning.

"You know, Devin, there are only four ways to make money: sell drugs, run a gambling network, smuggle, or become a pimp. I assure you that you will be rich, but you need guts to do these dirty jobs."

"What makes you say that only these four jobs can bring fortune?" Devin asked with closed eyes.

"Well, Devin, look at me. You know how I make my living? I smuggle human flesh from the Philippines. I bring in young girls and supply them to ready buyers through the pimps in this town and in Tawau. In a couple of years, I can retire as a very rich and powerful man when I go back to my hometown in Zamboanga."

"Where the hell is that?" Devin asked.

"It is one of the biggest cities in the southern Philippines. I will be a rich and powerful warlord, and maybe you can visit me then and be my adopted brother. Huh? What do you think?"

"Maybe, Drum. Maybe!"

The bartender brought the last jug. Both of them quickly finished their drink. Devin was a bit drunk, but the alcohol had not affected Drum at all. After all, he was used to heavy intoxication.

"Drum, is it true? I heard rumors." Devin stopped.

"Go on, Devin. Be open! What do you want to ask me?"

"I heard rumors that you killed two guys, you were caught by the police, you bribed them, and now you are a free man again." Devin laughed loudly.

After finishing his last drop of beer, Drum stood up and walked toward the door. Devin quickly followed him but hardly could walk properly. Drum waited for Devin, caught him, straightened him up, and guided him to the door. He stopped.

"You know something, Devin?"

"No, I don't know anything at all. I'm ignorant. Can't you see?"

"There are many things best kept to myself, especially the question you asked just now. Don't ask me those questions ever again. Other people might not like what you said. Do you hear me? Do you understand?"

"I understand, Drum, and I'm sorry I asked you that question."

The next day, Devin was sitting in a small coffee shop not far from the pub he frequented. He was deeply thinking about his age. He was still unproductive, which was the source of quarreling between him and his father. He also thought about the four factors Drum had mentioned to him in the early morning.

He sipped his coffee, pondered, and looked at the distant horizon, toward the sea. He noticed that one of the coffee shop waitresses looked different from the rest. She was very blonde and had blue eyes and had fair skin. He kept looking at her. He called over one of the other workers and inquired about her.

"Both of her parents are pure Indonesians. She was born like that. She doesn't have a sound mind. We believe she is cursed!" the worker told Devin.

Devin sipped more coffee. He hadn't had any sleep, and he had not recovered from his hangover. He requested more coffee, hoping that would help him to keep sober. He turned his attention to the worker.

"You tell her that I want to know her. Tell her I'll be coming here tomorrow and want to speak to her—not today but tomorrow."

The worker nodded. Drum had given Devin some cash before he left. Devin took out ten Malaysian dollars and gave the money to the worker. The man was delighted and thanked Devin. Devin nodded back at him.

At home, Devin grabbed a dictionary and looked for the term *albino*. He had heard the word before, but at that time, it hadn't stimulated any interest.

"Albino! A rare kind of skin disorder that makes a person or animal very fair."

After several visits to the coffee shop, Devin befriended the albino woman. He persuaded her to leave her job and promised to look after her. To prove his point, he made love to her on several occasions. He found out she was a widow, was slightly mentally disabled, and had a three-year-old son whom she looked after lovingly.

Devin borrowed his father's vehicle and took her around. He brought her to the turtle sanctuary on a nearby island and took her out to an expensive restaurant. Devin had some money because every week, his father gave him an allowance that Devin collected from Maria. Besides, he still had some money left from Drum. In time, the woman loved him.

"Devin, thank you very much for loving me," she said gratefully.

"With pleasure, my love!" Devin gave her a cunning smile.

Chapter 24

Aᴀʀᴏɴ's ᴏꜰꜰɪᴄᴇ ᴡᴀꜱ ᴅᴇᴇᴘ in the estate thirty-eight miles from town. It was a big white two-story building with electricity and water despite its location. Aaron's office was big and spacious, and he had a male secretary who sat outside the office.

Devin slowly approached the secretary. He was wearing his best white shirt and black pants with a bright blue tie. He stopped in front of the secretary.

"Good morning, Mr. Johnson. Can I help you?" the secretary said.

"I want to see my father. Is he in?"

"Certainly, sir! Please step right in."

"Thank you."

The secretary escorted him in. Aaron was sitting at a big desk. On top of his desk were photos of Elaine and all his children, including Devin. When Aaron saw his son, he stopped his work immediately.

The secretary left the room and closed the door. Devin walked toward his father's massive desk and sat in front of him. His father leaned back in his chair. Devin looked around the office. He had never been there before.

"How is your day, Son?" Aaron moved forward and continued his work while giving certain concentration to his eldest son. Devin glanced at the photos on top of Aaron's desk. He grabbed the frame with his picture, looked at it, and put it back. While working, Aaron couldn't help noticing Devin's action.

"Dad, let's get to the point. I need to borrow some money from you."

Aaron immediately stopped his work. "Is that why you came to see me? To borrow some money?" Aaron leaned backward. "I have given you your weekly allowance."

"Dad, you want me to be doing something productive, something for my future, and you always criticize me for not doing anything. Now I am asking you for a small amount of money as a business investment."

"Very well." His father paused. "How much do you need?"

"Fifteen thousand Malaysian dollars."

His father suddenly stood up. He looked shocked and dismayed. He walked away from his chair and moved toward the window nearby. Aaron put his hand on his lips and shook his head. "Where in God's world do you expect me to get that kind of money? It is a hefty sum, I must say. Honestly, you can't be serious!"

"I am serious, Daddy! Real serious! I've never asked any favor from you, sir. Can't you grant me such? Once I've succeeded—and I will succeed—I'll pay you back with interest."

"Don't promise anything, Devin. If I had money, I would gladly give it you. You don't have to borrow from me. The problem is, I can't think of a way to help you."

"Then I am wrong to think highly of you. I am answering your challenge to be productive, but you can't deliver the other end." Devin stood up and began to walk away.

"Stop there, Devin! Please stop! Okay. I'll think of a way to help you out. Maybe I'll borrow from the company, if that will satisfy you."

Devin didn't turn around to face his father. Instead, he turned his back on him and walked out of the room.

Aaron's mind became more clouded than ever with this new burden on top of the existing problems he was already facing.

His secretary knocked on the door and came in. He was a bit confused about what had gone on. He had seen Devin hurriedly walk away from the office. "Is there anything wrong, sir? Can I help?"

Aaron took a deep breath, faced his secretary, and gave a false smile. "There is nothing you can do, Mike. Nothing, I'm afraid. Maybe you can make me a cup of coffee. That will be fine."

"Right away, sir."

Devin went to a motor engineering workshop. He consulted with the owner regarding what he had in mind. The owner looked perplexed. Devin was asking him to build what he never done before. Devin slowly briefed him again.

"Come back tomorrow," he advised Devin. "Maybe I can work out something for you and give you a quote." Devin smiled and handed him the rough design of a crude caravan. The owner called over his welders and mechanics, who pondered the drawing and consulted each other in Cantonese.

"Come back tomorrow, Mr. Johnson. Maybe we can help you."

Devin came back two days later. The owner greeted him with a smile.

"We can help you, Mr. Johnson. But a very rough design like this will cost you some money."

"How much?"

"It will be very expensive. We estimate the price will be about fifty-five thousand."

"Can't you give a better price than that?" Devin said.

"That is the best price I can give you. I don't think anybody can give you a better offer than that. Nobody! You can try to look around at other workshops. I don't mind."

"That won't be necessary. Okay, I accept your price. But I can only offer you a deposit of fifteen thousand. Once you complete the caravan, I will pay you the balance in two months' time after it is completed."

The workshop owner hesitated. He looked at his mechanics, and they nodded, but still, he hesitated.

"Oh, come on, Fung! You know my father. If you don't trust me, surely you trust him."

"All right. I'm sure you are honest like your father. I'll do it."

Devin was happy with his acceptance. He took out the money, all in cash, and gave it to the workshop owner.

"Mr. Johnson, we will start immediately."

Devin traveled forty-five miles away and went deep inside another estate. There were about two thousand male workers, mostly bachelors, working there. Almost all of them came from Indonesia. Devin had established a rapport with one of the foremen, who came from Flores, near the island of Bali.

"Now, Ringo, I am going to help you become rich," Devin told the foreman.

"How, Master Devin?"

"You tell the workers here that I will be bringing in a caravan and placing it under those trees there." Devin pointed to an isolated, shady spot just outside of the estate. "In the caravan, I will assign one beautiful white woman to service those workers. It will be very cheap—for Caucasians, only a hundred and twenty bucks per shot!"

"Wow!" Ringo was intrigued by Devin's proposal.

"For every customer, I will give you ten dollars. Is that understood?"

"Very good, Master Devin! Your idea is number one!"

Devin had a long talk with Raina, the albino. He made love to her and assured her that he would always love her. All she had to do was have sex with the plantation workers. Raina hesitated, but since she loved Devin, she felt she had no choice. Her mind couldn't comprehend the scheme and what she was agreeing to. It took Devin several more days before she finally agreed to his heinous plan. Devin was delighted.

That night, Raina looked at her son, who was sleeping on a wooden bed covered only with two layers of old bedsheets. She approached her son and gave him a kiss on the cheek, and her tears flowed.

"I have to do this, my son. For you, myself, and your future stepfather, Devin." She grabbed a corner of the bedsheet and wiped her tears. She hoped that Devin's plan would succeed and that the future would be bright for all of them.

Devin consulted Ringo one more time to ensure everything was according to plan. As Devin was talking to him, Ringo kept nodding to indicate he understood.

"Okay, Ringo, I will explain one more time. The caravan will be parked there at that location. Inside the caravan, I purposely have the lights dim, and the albino I am dating will be inside the caravan. Remember, she isn't a real Caucasian. Make sure what you say is true—that none of the workers have ever seen an albino."

"I am sure, sir. If you hadn't told me, I would not have known what an albino is."

"Good. But anyway, it's quite dark inside, and I doubt they will notice. So you start campaigning tomorrow, and get as many customers as possible. Do you understand?"

"Yes, sir." Ringo saluted Devin. Devin laughed at Ringo's reaction.

At four o'clock in the evening the next day, Devin cautiously parked the caravan among the thick undergrowth below a huge tree. The vehicle was perfectly concealed, and no uninvited passerby would notice it. Devin entered the caravan and sat next to Raina, who was half naked. She wore a tight miniskirt so short that her red underwear was noticeable. She didn't wear a bra, and the low-cut T-shirt she was wearing exposed the top part of her breasts.

"I'm scared, Devin. You think this is a good idea?"

"Don't you worry, honey. I will take care of you. No matter what, I will always love you." Devin lit a cigarette and smoked. "Don't you trust me?"

"I trust and love you, Devin. After all this, I just want to be with you and go far from this place." Raina put her head on Devin's shoulder.

Suddenly, there was a knock on the caravan door. Devin signaled Raina to get ready, and he stood up and walked to the door. He opened it and saw Ringo. He went out, closed the door, and moved away from the caravan with him.

"Okay, sir, good news. Today we will get at least fifteen to twenty customers." Ringo looked around. "By tomorrow, another twenty or maybe more."

Devin offered him a cigarette. "Cheers to our future, Ringo!"

Ringo nodded. "They will be coming any moment now, sir."

Chapter 25

FIVE WEEKS PASSED, AND Devin was making a lot of money. Ringo too shared his newfound prosperity. However, success didn't come easy for Devin. The management of the plantation where Devin operated his illegal brothel had come to know about his activity, and they were threatening to lodge a police report. Besides, Raina was getting haggard and sickly from servicing all the plantation workers.

Drum paid a visit to Devin at the site. They hugged each other and sat down a few yards from the caravan. Drum took out a cigar, lit it, and puffed the smoke into Devin's face. Devin coughed. For fifteen minutes, Drum kept quiet. He kept smoking his cigar while deep in thought.

"This is so disgusting, Devin! I am a cruel man who has done a lot of bad things in life, but I would not stoop this low and be proud of what I was doing."

"That's business, Drum," Devin answered without feeling any remorse. "You are also a pimp!" Devin said.

"The ladies I bring here are all corrupt and materialistic. They are prepared for any excitement. I would never deceive an innocent girl!"

"Okay, I have had enough of your lecture!" Devin shouted. "Now get out of here!"

Suddenly, Drum grabbed Devin's neck and squeezed it. Devin fell to his knees, struggling to breathe. Tears ran down Devin's cheeks, and his eyes turned red.

"Stop it! Stop it!" Raina came out of the caravan, shouting at Drum. She held Drum's hands and also fell to her knees. "Please stop!"

she begged again, crying. Her customers became terrified, thinking Drum was the police. They quickly left the scene. Drum suddenly released Devin and pushed him to the ground. Devin was desperately trying to grasp some air. Drum cleaned off the dust on his shirt.

"I came here to inform you that you have to stop what you are doing. The police are in the final steps of their preparation to raid you. They told me there is nothing much they can do. As a friend, the best I can give you is a warning so that you have some time to stop." Drum put his hat on and left.

Raina tried to comfort Devin, but he pushed her away. Raina slowly put on her clothes and moved back into the caravan. Devin was still desperately trying to breathe. Slowly, he began to recover from his ordeal as he sat next to a big tree. He stood up and went looking for Ringo.

"Okay, Ringo, another few days, and then we have to stop the operation entirely."

Ringo nodded.

Devin took the risk and successfully continued for another five days without any apparent action against him. He decided not to push his luck any further. He sent Raina home, cleaned up the caravan, and managed to sell it for twenty thousand dollars; all in cash.

Devin quickly packed a bag, deposited his earnings in a bank, and bought himself an airline ticket. He went to the airport early. He didn't inform any members of his family that he was going away, except Linda. But he didn't tell Linda his destination. On the way to the airport in a taxi, he smiled to himself about the money he'd made. *I now have enough capital to start a business in Jesselton,* he thought while visualizing his future.

Chapter 26

RAINA WAS GETTING DESPERATE. It had been three days already, and Devin had not come to look for her. She missed him very much. She had stopped working at the restaurant because of her love for Devin, and Devin had not given her money except to feed her and her son while she was working in Devin's makeshift brothel. Her son cried all the time now because she could not afford to buy milk. One of her neighbors noticed her difficulty and volunteered to look after her son for a while.

"You go look for your husband. We will look after your son while you are gone. Don't worry. We will take care of him."

Raina's tears flowed down her cheeks. "Thank you!" she said with deep appreciation.

She changed her clothes and started to leave but stopped. She coughed continuously and looked at her handkerchief. There was a sign of blood. Her neighbor noticed that she was looking tired and sick. Raina's tears kept flowing. She was desperate to meet Devin.

Ringo was laughing loudly with several of his friends. He had made a considerable sum of money; some of friends knew how, but some didn't. He boasted about his achievement as the group gathered together in a makeshift hut usually used by farmers to sell their fruit.

"You know what I am going to do with this money?" he bragged. "You! You know what?" The man he addressed smiled sheepishly and shook his head. "You! What about you?" Everyone laughed.

"I am going to buy a big piece of land when I go back to Indonesia, and I'm going to marry one of the headman's daughters in my village."

"But you're married already!" the youngest of the congregation cried out, and everybody burst into loud laughter.

"Silence!" Ringo commanded. Everyone kept quiet immediately. "I can have more than one wife, eh?" Ringo laughed, and the crowd joined back in the laughter. While they all seemed to be enjoying themselves, the laughter died out one by one until only Ringo was laughing. He turned around and noticed a woman approaching them.

Everybody recognized who she was, and some of the men left. Raina looked around, recognizing all of them but a few. She coughed and couldn't seem to stop it. She dragged her tired legs toward Ringo.

Ringo looked at her and frowned. Raina ignored Ringo's reaction and stood in front of him. Again, she coughed continuously. Ringo was about to move away, when she suddenly grabbed his shirt.

"Please! I beg you. You are the only person who can help me. Please!" she pleaded. Ringo attempted to avoid her, but her sudden burst of energy enabled her to grip him tightly, and she refused to let him go. "Please! Have mercy on me! I just want to know where Devin is. Please tell me!"

"I don't know where he is." Ringo struggled to loosen her grip but to no avail.

"Listen to me. Please listen to me. I want to find Devin! He said he would look after me. You've got to help me!"

"I don't know where Devin is!" Ringo shouted.

"You know! I know you know!" Raina cried.

Ringo was running out of patience. As his struggle to relieve her grip on him failed, he raised his hand and struck her strongly on her left cheek, but still, she held on to him. He struck her again, this time on her left ear, and Raina wobbled and released Ringo. Slowly, she fell to the ground.

Lying on the ground, she raised her right arm and continued to plead for nonexistent mercy. Ringo shuffled his shirt and suddenly raised his foot and kicked Raina's face. Raina collapsed. Ringo looked around at the remaining crowd and walked away.

As Ringo disappeared, one of the men approached her and helped her to sit. He pulled her away from the dirt and tried to make her sit on one of the boxes nearby. She held him tightly, and slowly, her hand touched his face.

"Thank you!"

"Please try to relax."

Another man went to get some water from a well nearby. When he returned, they cleaned her of dirt and washed the visible wound. They waited with her till she regained some of her last remaining strength.

"Thank you to all of you," she said as she wept from the sorrow of the tragedy that affected her.

"Lady, the only way you can find Devin is to approach him at the plantation several miles from here," one man said. They explained to her where Devin lived and how to arrive at his home.

"Even if Devin fails to help you, at least his father can. We've all heard that his father is a good man."

Raina tried to stand up but collapsed again and again. Finally, a few of the men, some of whom had made love to Raina, helped her to reach the house of Devin. The men didn't stay and went away immediately.

Raina waited at the house's entrance.

Aaron arrived home from work depressed, with pressure on his mind. He expected his house would help to soothe his fatigue and depression, especially the sight of his lovely daughter Susan.

As he arrived home, he noticed a sickly woman waiting outside his house. He stepped out of his car, closed the door, and walked slowly toward his house. The woman kept looking at him. He noticed that she tried to smile but couldn't.

"Can I help you?" he said in excellent Malay.

Raina's eyes looked heavy, and there were black marks around both of her eye sockets. Her head dropped down a little, and she tried to prop it up. Aaron noticed that the woman was about to collapse, and he quickly threw his briefcase and caught her. He shouted for help, and the maid came rushing to see what had happened. Raina had fainted.

When Raina recovered, she noticed she was in a room, lying on a bed. Suddenly, her coughing burst forth again, and she couldn't stop it. The maids tried to calm her down. Susan too was watching her, along with her father.

Aaron approached her and sat beside her. "Are you looking for somebody?"

She nodded and cried. The coughing was continuous. "Sir, I am looking for Devin."

"Why are you looking for Devin?"

"Sir, I am supposed to be his wife. He promised me."

Aaron looked irritated. He rose and stood in front of Raina. Raina didn't look into his eyes. Aaron shook his head and walked away from her. "What makes you think my son will take you as a wife?"

"He said he would marry me! He will take care of me! He promised me!" She cried loudly. "I did everything he asked me to do. He slept with me for many months already, and he asked me to have sex with people. I did it for him!"

Aaron immediately asked Sofia to take Susan away. Aaron approached Raina and begged her to slow down. Maria lowered her head in disbelief. Aaron was both irritated and worried about what was developing.

"Maria, can you go find Devin?"

"I'm afraid I can't, sir!" Maria answered angrily.

"Why not?"

"Devin left Sandakan. He left days ago. He only informed Linda about it. And Linda told me. But Linda didn't tell me where Devin went."

Aaron was speechless. Raina was crying more loudly. Instead of sympathizing with her, Aaron could not tolerate Raina's emotional outburst. Suddenly, the telephone rang. Aaron left the room to answer the phone. While he was answering it, Elaine arrived. Elaine noticed that Aaron was speechless after answering the phone. He brought Elaine into another room and explained everything to her.

"How can my son go after a bitch? A dirty bitch like you? You get out of my house! Get out!" Elaine yelled at Raina.

Aaron tried to calm her down. He brought her upstairs to their room and kissed her. "Calm down, my love! I will settle this matter. You stay here."

Aaron brought Raina to the plantation clinic, and the doctor diagnosed her as suffering from syphilis and gonorrhea. Aaron settled all the expenses, took her to her house, and gave her two thousand dollar.

"That is all I have, Raina. I wish I could give you more, but I can't."

"You are very kind, sir. May God repay your kindness."

"I promise to inform you as soon as I hear of Devin. And take care of your son."

"Thank you, sir, Mr. Johnson. Thank you!" She wept.

Aaron reluctantly hugged her, walked to his car, and left. As he was driving, his mind focused on the phone call. It had been from another plantation firm to discuss Devin's operation with their workers. The information fit the story told by Raina. Aaron couldn't believe Devin had done such a horrible act.

When he got home, two men were waiting for Aaron: Mr. Fung and one of his mechanics, whom Devin had been dealing with. They conferred with him outside the house. Aaron nodded. Mr. Fung patted his back and went away.

Elaine came running out and saw Aaron's gloomy face.

"They told me that they built a caravan for Devin, and he paid them only fifteen thousand dollars. Devin still owes them another forty thousand. I owe the company fifteen thousand. Now I owe the workshop another forty. Where will I get that kind of money?"

Elaine approached Aaron, her loving husband, and comforted him. He smiled, tried to forget his misery, and kissed her. Elaine hugged him tightly. She pulled him up and pointed at their room upstairs. Aaron smiled widely. At least he could forget some of his problems temporarily.

Chapter 27

TEN YEARS HAD PASSED. William had graduated from law school in Singapore. He now worked for a legal firm in his hometown. William remembered the day when he'd had to face reality and study hard, for he had learned one strong lesson: there was no such thing as free lunch.

William pondered the time when he'd been silly enough to try to use supernatural power to pass his test. He smiled to himself and considered himself fortunate that he had come to his senses and realized that the only way to pass was by studying hard.

His memories faded, and he was back to reality. He looked at the stack of files on his desk. He despaired at the sight of all the work, but it had to be done. As he was scribbling in his notebook, he suddenly remembered Theresa. He stretched his arms and leaned back in his chair. "Theresa!"

"What did you say, Will?" His boss walked into his office.

"Oh, nothing, Rick. I'm just thinking of the good old times."

"Yeah, go on with it!" His boss smiled and started to walk out of the room, when he suddenly turned back toward William. "Why don't we join some insurance brokers—high-powered individuals and young like you? We might get something out of this socializing."

"Yes, sir! Eh, what time, sir?"

"Seven thirty this evening—sharp."

As Ricky left, William flipped open some files and began jotting down notes. However, his mind was still with Theresa. He wondered where she was right now. He would love to find out about her. It had been a long time since he had seen her.

William was good at dealing with people. During the dinner, William created a strong rapport with the brokers, and they introduced him to their clients who dealt with real estate. William not only was good at dealing with the high-ranking managers but also didn't miss the chance to establish a personal relationship with the insurance union leaders. Soon William's company was raking in huge sums of businesses from these connections.

"You've got talent, Will," said Lisa, one of William's coworkers.

"What kind of talent? I am like everybody else."

William gulped the Coke in his hand. He looked at Lisa and then looked out the restaurant window, watching cars pass by. Lisa was referring to the rapport William had built for their firm. Last night had been a big hit. They'd gotten multiple sales and purchase agreements from a big-time developer. The boss liked William very much.

"By the way, thanks for this lunch. What a fine restaurant you've brought me to, Will." Lisa had graduated from school in London and was two years older than he. "Don't you want to have a girlfriend, Will?"

"What kind of question is that?" William looked out the window again, hoping to avoid her question.

Lisa looked at him more earnestly. She put her arms on the table and smiled at William. "I am sure you need to find one."

"Not at this moment, Lisa. I am too busy."

"The Chinese used to say, 'High eye to men who are choosy.' Their eye is too high, so they don't notice any admirers right in front of them."

"So? What's that got to do with me?"

William kept looking outside. Both kept quiet and kept their thoughts to themselves. Five minutes later, Lisa felt they should focus on other subjects, especially the one that interested her the most.

"Will, if I were you, I would join politics."

"Ah, that's a boring occupation. Don't you think so?" William replied.

"It's not an occupation, Will. It's a volunteer organization. Like the Salvation Army. If you join a political party, who knows? You could rise to be a leader."

"You think so, Lisa? You think a person like me can be a leader?"

Lisa looked at William. He had grown to be a handsome man, except for his big ear. He had a problem with that, especially when he kept his hair short.

There were a lot of guests coming to the restaurant, because there was a live band of talented Filipino musicians. Like everybody else, Lisa enjoyed the music.

"I believe in you, William. You can be a good leader."

That night, William gave some serious thought to what Lisa had said. He was lying on his bed, looking at the ceiling, with his clothes still on and his tie loosened. His mind kept analyzing the words "If I were you, I would join politics." Suddenly, he rose from his bed and sat down.

He recalled his moment with Ricky just after the lunch with Lisa. Ricky had said, "Well, Will, I don't mind you joining politics. You have brought a lot of business to this company. Why should I mind? But bear in mind that you must continue to keep up your good work."

William stood up, walked out of his bedroom, and went toward the refrigerator. He had become hungry after all of his thinking.

At his office the next day, William was busy attending to his routine. Boredom clouded William's mind, as he had to go through tons of paperwork at his desk. It was seven in the morning, and nobody was at the office.

Suddenly, there was a knock on the door. William stopped doing his work and stood up. He walked toward the continuing knocking sound. *Couldn't be Ricky or Liz, because they have a key,* he thought to himself. He opened the door slowly and peeped outside.

"Hi, Will. It has been a long time."

"Goodness gracious! How did you find me here?"

"Your mother told me I could find you here, and I did."

"I was hoping for a girl, you know!"

"Sorry to disappoint you, Will!"

It was Ramlan Omar, his long-lost childhood friend and neighbor. They went to a stall nearby and had a long chat, with topics ranging from their good old days together to the educational level that both of them had achieved. They laughed and joked and made fun of each other, and both enjoyed the reunion.

"You study law, I can see. Well, I took up public administration at the local college nearby. I didn't have the money to go full-time, so I studied part-time and worked part-time. It took five years for me to finish my studies, but it was worth it. But I intend to continue studying, and I'm thinking law."

"You have to be good with your English to take up law, Ramlan. I'm not belittling your English, but that's a fact. You need to polish it up a bit."

"I know that, Will. Thanks for your concern."

"So where are you working now?" William asked with interest.

"I work with the government four miles from here. I'm actually attached to the Islamic affairs department. Government pay, however, is very low, you know."

"Tell me more, Ramlan."

"I'm also the state government union secretary general."

"The government has a union too?" William raised an eyebrow.

"Of course! We have about eighty thousand active members throughout the state. Cool, isn't it? But frankly, Will, this shouldn't interest you."

William nodded. Ramlan was right. What did his job have to do with William? However, William considered the tremendous influence the Islamic department had on the ruling government. Ramlan could be helpful in the future.

"You want to hear more interesting news, Will?" Ramlan said, tickling William's curiosity.

"I am interested. Tell me more."

Ramlan and Will struggled over who would pay the bill, but eventually, Ramlan won. "I'll pay for a token sum like this, but you can pay for a big sum, like in a fancy restaurant."

William became anxious about what Ramlan was about to reveal. He became impatient. Ramlan could see that William was irritated. Ramlan stood up and began to walk away. William followed him.

"You remember the girl you always talked about? The one you were infatuated with or in love with or whatever? Remember?"

"Theresa!"

"Ah, yes, Theresa."

William stopped Ramlan from walking, hoping to get more information from Ramlan. Ramlan smiled when William held both of his shoulders tightly. Ramlan could see the excitement on William's face.

"Okay, okay! She works at a hotel not far from where I am working. I still remember her face clearly from when you showed me her photos. I'm sure she is Theresa."

Ramlan gave the details and location of where Theresa worked, and William was excited and nervous about the prospect of meeting up with her. Ramlan said good-bye to William and went off. William walked slowly to his office nearby. *Is she married? Is she single?* he wondered.

At the office, Ricky noticed that William was staring out his window as if pondering something. He walked quietly into his office and closed the door. William suddenly jerked from his seat to greet his boss, but Ricky asked him to remain calm.

"A penny for your thoughts?"

"Sure, Rick. Bet on it."

"You're in love!"

William put his hand in his pocket, took out a coin, and tossed it to Ricky.

Chapter 28

AARON HELD HIS HEAD in his hands. He hadn't shaved, his shirt had not been washed for months, and he hadn't bathed for more than three days. Bottles of beer littered the small table in front of him, while a small television set was entertaining him. The room was messy; old rags and newspapers covered the floor.

Aaron was in a shabby shape that contrasted his appearance during his life at the plantation. Now he lived in a two-room apartment in the middle of Sandakan. The place was dim and gloomy.

Aaron turned away from the television, which was showing a live football match between local teams. He walked toward the table scattered with pictures of his children. There was no picture of Elaine. With one hand holding a bottle of San Miguel beer, he picked up Susan's picture, looked at it, and held it close to his chest.

Aaron went to the bathroom and looked at himself in the mirror. He turned his face right and then left, holding his jaw with his right hand. He pondered his appearance for a while and then turned and walked away. Aaron thought for a moment as he approached the door. He had decided to take a walk around town. It had been awhile since he had gotten out of his apartment.

Aaron went to a nearby seafood restaurant on the edge of the sea. Despite his appearance, the manager welcomed him and gave him a seat in the corner, away from the other guests, where Aaron could watch the ships moving in and out of the Sandakan waterway.

Aaron could see the manager instructing the waitress in the distance, and he noticed she was looking at him. Aaron took out his box of cigarettes. He had only one stick left, and it was half used. He looked again toward the sea, trying to capture old memories. The colonel, Sam, the confrontation, Elaine—it all had begun in this town, his second life. His thoughts moved to Colonel O'Brian. The old man had retired decades ago. He'd heard from his friends that O'Brian had died peacefully in his sleep a few months back.

"Sir, are you by yourself?"

Aaron's mind was still on the colonel. He turned toward the voice and looked carefully. The colonel faded completely. He saw a familiar face.

"Maria! How are you?" Aaron tried to clear his groggy voice. He stood up, tried to smarten up himself, and stared at her.

"I'm okay, sir. Can I sit with you?"

"Sure, Maria. It is an honor for me."

As they sat, the manager came and asked Aaron what he would like. Aaron signaled to the manager that he would make the choice for him, and the manager immediately understood. He instructed the waitress to come near Aaron, Aaron whispered to her, and the waitress nodded.

"I hope you two enjoy yourselves. This restaurant is the best!" the manager said.

"Thank you, Mr. Chin."

Aaron looked at Maria. Maria smiled at her former employer. She had liked working for Aaron; she'd felt she had dignity, and he'd been an understanding boss. It was Elaine whom she and Sofia had been unable to tolerate. They'd both stopped working for the Johnsons six months after the incident involving Raina, the albino.

"Sir, if I may ask, what happened to you?" Maria watched Aaron with sympathy.

As Aaron was trying to pull out the slightly broken cigarette stick, the waitress came with two bottles of beer and two packs of cigarettes.

"I didn't order these."

"Well, sir, the manager insists. This is for free."

Aaron looked at the manager, and from the distance, he gave a nod to him. Aaron waved at him to say thank you. Aaron threw away the old cigarette box. Aaron picked up a new cigarette and lit it. He inhaled the smoke deeply, enjoying the fresh tobacco, which was something he had not tasted for some time. Maria kept watching him.

"So, Maria, what have you been doing?"

"I work for a Chinese couple with a three-year-old son, sir. They are rich people who live on top of that hill." Aaron looked toward the hill. It was an exclusive area for the powerful and rich timber tycoons.

"Well, they are nowhere near you, sir. You were my best employer, as far as I'm concerned. There are no two ways about it. But they are also good to me, and they pay very well. But if I had a choice, I would rather work for you—but not for Elaine!"

Aaron squeezed the cigarette into the ashtray. He puffed the remaining smoke and leaned back a little. Both kept quiet for a while, keeping their thoughts to themselves. Again, Aaron was startled when the waitress brought food he had not ordered. He looked at the manager, and again, the manager indicated with his hand that everything was all right and that Aaron didn't have to worry about anything.

That evening, Aaron enjoyed food he had not tasted for a long time: fresh seafood from the Celebes Sea. Maria appreciated dining with Aaron.

"How's the food, Maria?"

"Very fine, sir! I enjoy it. Nobody has ever dined with a maid before, and I am embarrassed about it."

Aaron looked at her. "Don't be. You are special for tonight." He paused. "So, Maria, you asked me what happened to me."

Maria nodded slowly.

"It's a long story, though. It will bore you," he said.

"No, sir. I want to know."

"I knew how Elaine mistreated you, Maria. Both you and Sofia. I don't blame you for leaving. But it made me sad to see both of you go. And Susan missed you both." Aaron continued to drink his beer while he talked to Maria. He had finished five cigarettes already. "When Devin left all of us, he also left behind a huge debt for me to settle. You remember the incident involving Raina?"

Maria nodded.

Aaron took another cigarette and continued smoking. "I was in a state of deep financial difficulty. Elaine didn't want to know about my suffering. She kept insisting that I give her money for her ever-growing compulsion for gambling. But I saved a certain amount of money without the knowledge of anybody, not even Elaine, for Susan's future. I kept it away so that not even I could take it out. I invested in her education. And no matter how difficult my financial difficulty is, the money is secure."

The waitress came and cleaned up the table. Maria continued to listen earnestly.

"Thank you," Aaron said to the waitress. "Then Raymond came up with an idea for a business to supply fish to the workers in the estates. I did not want to venture into that business, but Raymond was sulking. To make him happy, I gave him my support, both moral and financial. The business turned bad, and I ended up further in debt."

"I'm sorry to hear all this, sir."

"That's all right. It's not your fault. Well, since I couldn't come up with any money to supplement Elaine, she kept seeing a man she called her old boyfriend, who she claimed she'd met before me. He is richer, and she could get anything she wanted from him. She openly said she was sleeping with him!"

Aaron wept. Maria too was sad at what Aaron had just said. Tears rolled down her cheeks when she saw Aaron break down.

"And you know, Maria, she even told me her boyfriend enjoyed having sex with somebody's wife while the husband knew! Can you believe that? Do you know how hurtful it is to be treated like that?"

Maria looked around to see if the other customers were noticing the commotion by Aaron. Nobody seemed to notice.

"So, Maria, my enthusiasm for work depreciated, and I performed miserably. Somehow, the management heard about my problem. They asked me very nicely if I would like to continue or to rest for a while. To be fair to them, I told them that I would like to resign immediately. They accepted my resignation, but they supported me to clear my debts, they paid the rent for my two-room apartment downtown, and they gave me some gratuity, which can last me for two years or more if I spend it wisely."

"What about Elaine, sir?"

"Prostituting, I presume!"

"Where are your children?"

"All of them went to Jesselton, each of them with his or her own life. They never bother to contact me, especially Devin. I haven't heard from him since the day he left all of us."

"What about Susan? Mr. Johnson, I've missed Susan so much!"

Aaron finally smiled a little. As Aaron was about to talk, the manager came toward Aaron.

"All of this is free, Mr. Johnson. Before you say anything, please accept all of this. Only this time! Next time, I will charge you. I promise."

"Thank you very much, Mr. Chin!" Aaron said. The manager left. "As for Susan, she is not with me, but she is okay."

Chapter 29

WILLIAM SPENT EXTRA HOURS working for his legal firm. In return, he wanted to take the day off on Friday. He talked to Ricky about his intention, and the boss gladly gave him three days off. "Come back on Tuesday! Have all the fun, and get yourself rejuvenated."

"Are you sure, boss?"

"Yes, I am sure. Go on! Have some fun, and tell me about it later."

"Yes, boss!" William grabbed his coat and his briefcase and left the office quickly. Ricky watched him leave and laughed quietly. Lisa walked toward Ricky, and they both observed William disappear from the office in a hurry.

"I wonder what the young man's up to," said Lisa.

"Something really interesting must have come up in his life," Ricky guessed.

"So, Rick, we have the office all to ourselves. Nobody will disturb us. What shall we do?"

Ricky looked at Lisa. He held her hand and slowly pulled her toward him. Lisa took his other hand and tightly squeezed it.

Suddenly, the door opened with a bang. Ricky threw Lisa's hands away and stood, staring at the door. Lisa straightened herself, turned away from Ricky, and acted as if nothing had happened.

"Sorry, Rick! I forgot my wallet. Can't travel without one, you know!"

"For heaven's sake, Will! Next time, try to be courteous when entering the office."

"Okay, I'll keep that in mind! Ah, here it is. My wallet. Have fun, both of you!"

When William once again disappeared from the office, Lisa coughed and tried to clear her throat. Ricky watched her. Both of them decided to continue their work and think about fun later.

William moved quickly to his car. He threw his coat and briefcase in the backseat, climbed into the vehicle, and sped off recklessly. He almost hit a motorcyclist, and the man put up his middle finger as he stopped.

William stopped in front of a florist and bought a bunch of roses and a friendship greeting card. He hurried to his apartment, washed up, and put on his best attire. As he was about to leave, he took some mail from the post box at his door and scanned the envelopes quickly.

He threw the mail onto the sofa and rushed out of his apartment to his car. As he drove, his mind was thinking deeply. *Will Theresa be surprised and happy, or will she be oblivious?* William hoped for the best and hoped he would not be disappointed.

When he reached the hotel according to Ramlan's description, he walked toward the lobby and asked the door-boy about Theresa. The door-boy pointed and said that Theresa was in the office just behind the reception counter. William thanked the boy and moved toward the counter. He was getting nervous.

Don't screw up, Will! he thought to himself. He approached the girl working at the counter, and the girl asked him to hold on. As the girl moved into the office, William played with his fingers to kill time, which he felt was traveling slowly. William felt that he had waited for ages for Theresa. The girl walked back out, but there was no Theresa in sight.

"I'm sorry, sir, but Theresa is busy at the moment. Is it possible for you to wait for her? Maybe in half an hour? You can wait in the hotel lounge if you like, or maybe you can come back later?"

"I'd like to wait for her in the lounge."

"I'll inform her about it."

William helped himself to coffee and some Danish biscuits served in the lobby. Half an hour seemed like one day to him. He looked at his watch. It already had been forty-five minutes since he had looked for Theresa. He had finished his tidbits, and he was going to ask for another, when he saw the girl he was waiting for approach him.

William stood up, and crumbs dropped to the ground. William looked at his black trousers and cleaned them up. Theresa smiled broadly. Theresa looked gorgeous in a black coat, a white shirt, and a long skirt covering her knees. The dark clothing contrasted perfectly with her fair skin, which was neither Asian nor European but in between. William quickly approached her and offered his hand.

"How are you, Will?"

"I'm fine!" William squeaked like a mouse due to his nervousness. He became more embarrassed. Theresa laughed at him. William joined in the laughter. "I'm fine, actually. How are you?" William said.

"Just okay. Normal and cool."

"It has been a long time, Theresa."

"Yes, Will, a very long time. Very long time!"

"Will you join me for a drink?" William said.

Theresa looked around and shook her head. William was disappointed. He nodded, indicating that he reluctantly understood.

"Actually, I am on duty now. I'm not supposed to sit with customers."

"I'm not a customer. I am your friend."

"I'll tell you what. Why don't you pick me up after work? I'll wait for you here. We can go someplace exclusive."

William smiled. "Yes! I'll pick you up right here on time!"

William watched Theresa walk back to her desk and then turned around and walked away, slowly at first and then quickly. William was delighted. He could feel the blood rushing with excitement in his veins. This would be a great night.

"Thanks for the flowers, Will. They are pretty. I like roses, especially white ones," Theresa said later that night.

"An exceptional beauty like you should sleep in a bed of roses. The gift is nothing."

"Don't flatter me, Will. You make me feel like a balloon ready to blow apart!" Both William and Theresa laughed. William ordered a bottle of champagne. Theresa noticed that William requested a cheap one; nevertheless, she knew it was good. Theresa looked around; she felt comfortable.

"This is a good place, Will. Thanks for inviting me here. Uh-uh! Don't you dare to flatter me some more!"

William smiled at Theresa. As she was eating her appetizer, William gazed at her. She felt uncomfortable and turned away from William.

"What, William Stewart? What? Why are you staring at me like that?"

"You are beautiful, Theresa. I think I am falling in love with you."

William continued gazing at her. The champagne arrived, and William immediately straightened up and looked at the waiter. The waiter poured champagne into Theresa's glass. As he was about to pour some into William's glass, William put his hand on top of it and indicated that he wasn't having any. The waiter understood and left.

Theresa was surprised at William's action. "Why are you refusing the champagne? Why did you order it in the first place?"

The waiter arrived again, this time with the food: butter prawns, mixed vegetables, steamed fish, and sweet-corn soup.

"I can't drink alcohol, Theresa. I have an ulcer in my stomach."

"I see."

They both enjoyed their dinner, and afterward, William took her to her apartment. When they arrived, Theresa thanked William and told him good night. "See you tomorrow, Will!"

As William continued to spend time with Theresa, he came to understand that her parents had divorced; Devin was nowhere to be found; Raymond was running a small business in Sandakan; and Linda was working in Brunei, one of the richest kingdoms in Asia, located on the west coast of Borneo, about 150 miles from Jesselton. Linda was working for an oil firm run by Dutch merchants. Theresa didn't mention Susan.

William was interested to know more about Raymond. He'd considered Raymond his best friend growing up, and he always would.

Theresa did not hide the fact that Raymond was presently married to a Chinese nightclub hostess and had two children with her, one boy and one girl.

"When can I see Raymond?"

"He will be in town soon. I heard he will be giving up his business in Sandakan and coming here, maybe to look for a job. If he drops by, I will inform you."

William nodded, and by his facial expression, Theresa noticed that he was eager to see him. It had been a long time, and Raymond had a lot of wonderful as well as sad stories to tell.

One day William brought Theresa to a McDonald's restaurant that had just opened. It was packed, and they had to share their table with two teenagers.

"What are the names of Raymond's two kids, Theresa?"

"The eldest is a girl. Her name is Janet. The boy is Chris."

Chapter 30

WILLIAM HEARD FROM THERESA that Raymond would be coming to town tomorrow. Theresa informed him that Raymond would see him in a small town just outside the city. William was excited and happy. After ten years, he now could see his best friend.

***

William had been waiting one hour and twenty-five minutes for Raymond to arrive. He waited at a nearby stall, exactly where Theresa had told him to meet Raymond. William's fourth cup of coffee was almost finished, and he had looked at his watch several times.

Another forty-five minutes later, just as William was about to give up, he saw a pickup truck with a metallic brown color park right in front of him. The vehicle's glass was tinted, and William couldn't see who was inside, but he had a feeling it might be Raymond.

A lady got out of the driver's seat, and William was disappointed. He paid for his coffees and stood up. At the back of the truck, the windscreen opened, and he saw two kids inside. He slowly walked away.

"Not so fast, you asshole!"

A man got out of the passenger seat. William looked back. "Raymond! Raymond, where the hell have you been?" William shouted as he rushed to him and shook his hand vigorously.

"Slow down, Will! You are making a commotion. Everybody is looking at us."

119

"So what? He is my friend! Raymond! His name is Raymond!" William continued shaking Raymond's hand.

"Okay, Will! This is my wife, Cecilia, and these are my two kids."

"Hello, everybody. Why don't we sit down? You all must be awfully tired from the long trip. Come."

All of them had a simple dinner at the stall. The food was good, clean, and cheap. William noticed that the kids seemed to be hungry, and they ate a lot. Raymond was not eating much, apparently too shy about his shabby condition. Raymond had long hair and seemed as if he hadn't bathed for a day or two. After the meal, both Raymond and his wife smoked heavily. The kids wanted to go to the restroom, and Raymond signaled for his wife to take them there. Raymond had already smoked a pack of cigarettes in less than an hour.

"Hey, what about the Indonesian girl that you lost your virginity to?" William said.

"Not so loud, you fool!" Raymond turned his head to see if his wife was nearby. She was still with the kids at the washroom. "I dumped her years ago. It was history. In fact, I had forgotten about her before I left for Sandakan. I caught gonorrhea from her. It was my first time having sex, and I caught a venereal disease. It was embarrassing when my father had to take me to a private doctor. But the doctor kept my secret, and none of my family members knew about it."

"Oh boy! What an experience. I thought you said that you would never get married?"

"Come on, Will! That was kids' talk. Cheap talk! Every one of us grows up! Except you, I think." Raymond continued smoking.

"You are right, Ray. Everyone grows up except me. I am among the classmates that are still not married. I have not come across a perfect match. But maybe soon!"

Raymond watched William's face and knew exactly what he meant. "I heard you have been dating Theresa. She is a tough one to crack—I can tell you that. She had many boyfriends before, and she is extremely choosy. But I heard you've been out with her quite often. I think you could beat the odds."

"What have you been doing lately, Ray?"

"Long story. I will tell you later."

"Have you heard about Devin?"

"Again, a longer story!" Raymond finished off his beer and waited for his wife and kids.

William rented a hotel room for two nights for Raymond and his family. While his wife and kids were sleeping up in the room, Raymond and William spent time in the hotel lobby, chatting. It was a long chat.

Raymond began the conversation by talking about his parents' separation, and he seemed to blame the breakup on his mother. Theresa, earlier on, hadn't blamed either of her parents. Raymond also told about how he'd started business young. When he'd followed his family to Sandakan, Raymond had immediately ventured into business and decided against his father's wish to continue studying.

Raymond explained to William that initially, he'd ventured into operating a nightclub with a friend he met in Sandakan. However, somebody had complained that they were operating without a proper license, and the authorities had had to close the place down. He'd then ventured into the fishing industry with the help of his father. That too had collapsed, because of severe competition from the other wholesalers, especially the Filipino immigrants.

"Your parents are separated, not divorced?" William asked.

"They are only separated. My mother left my father. My father still loves her. Why? Did Theresa tell you they are divorced?" Raymond took out another cigarette to smoke.

He talked about how he'd met his wife, about his two children, and about Sandakan, and he and William also delved into the past, talking about when they'd spent time together in school and after school. They laughed and joked while reminiscing. It was an interesting conversation that lasted till close to dawn.

"What about Devin? You didn't tell me about him."

Raymond slid down in his chair, yawning, as if William's question were a boring one that he wanted to avoid. "It's getting late, Will.

Tomorrow you are working." Raymond stretched his arms high and again yawned. "I too need some rest. We'll talk about Devin tomorrow."

William looked at his watch and nodded, agreeing. He called the waiter for the bill.

"See you tomorrow, Will," Raymond said.

"With pleasure, Ray."

Raymond rose and took the stairs to his room. After settling the bill, William walked out to his car and stopped. He thought for a while.

Why did Theresa say their parents are divorced, while Raymond said they're separated? Theresa probably wants to protect their mother. A divorce sounds mutual.

William looked at his watch and was horrified to see that it was already five thirty in the morning. He had never stayed up that late. In a few hours, he had to be back at work. William started his car and drove off quickly.

Chapter 31

WILLIAM BEGAN TO FOCUS on his ability to communicate and build rapports with people. While bringing business to his firm, he also took the opportunity to establish strong networking relationships with many of the public and private employee union leaders and secretaries. He took them out for lunch or dinner, talked about their problems, and voluntarily helped them whenever he could.

William also took the opportunity to mix with student leaders. Doing so made him accessible to the various teacher-parent unions throughout the state. With such a big spectrum of contacts, the firm could not cope with the load of business brought in by William.

Ricky summoned William to his office. Ricky was waiting and sitting in his executive chair behind a big table made of expensive chestnut wood. He didn't look pleased, which made William nervous.

"Sit down, Will," Ricky said, and slowly, William sat in front of Ricky. "I don't know what to do with you. You have spent too much time on social work and politics, I might say."

"Boss, if I may say—"

"Let me finish first, Will. You shut up! As I was saying, you spend too much time with your extraordinary activities, you go out and spend too much time using this firm's funds to entertain people, and you load us with so much work!" Ricky stood up, walked to his small refrigerator, and took out two cans of Coke. He offered one to William. William hesitated but slowly took it.

"Because of all the piles of work you've brought on us, how would you like to be my partner, Will?"

Ricky's offer stunned William. For a while, he'd thought he was going to be unemployed and facing the prospect of looking for another job somewhere else. It was an unexpected offer by Ricky. William looked at Ricky with his mouth open.

"Close your mouth, Will. A fly might make a nest out of it."

William closed his mouth, and he was about to accept the offer, when he stopped and stood up. He walked around the room and then faced Ricky. "Can I have a few days to think about your offer?"

"Why?"

"Because your offer is too good, Rick, and I thank you a million for that. Anybody in the world would jump to accept it, except an idiot."

"Like you?" Ricky said jokingly while drinking his Coke.

"Yeah. Like me. Please give me some time to think about it. Two days at most."

"Okay, Will. That's your choice. But if I were you, I would take this opportunity. Even Lisa highly recommended you to be my partner. So whatever decision you make, please make the best."

"Sure, Rick. I'll take your advice seriously." William drank his Coke but didn't finish it. He put the can on Ricky's table, stood up, and walked away from Ricky.

"One more thing, Will. The wedding cards will be distributed soon. Next month, I will be married."

William turned back to Ricky. "Well, I'll be! Who is the lucky girl?"

"Lisa!"

William looked at Ricky, tilted his head a little bit, and pointed at him.

Chapter 32

A ARON JOHNSON, TWO HUNDRED miles away from most of his children, who were on the west coast of North Borneo, was watching the stars from his apartment. He had opened some of the windows to let the cool night air filter into his home. However, with the nice breeze, his apartment was soon infested with mosquitoes. He closed the windows and relied on the fan to circulate the stale air.

Ever since he'd met Maria, he had made her a companion and shared his problems with her. He discussed with her his life, and Maria had learned to console him, as if she were a psychiatrist being paid by Aaron.

"Mr. Johnson, if you had been born as a Filipino, with a spirit like the one you have right now, you wouldn't have survived to see the world very long. You don't know how much suffering most of the people endure—no food, no money, broken families, abusive parents, not enough jobs, corrupt officials, crime. Compared to them, your problems are nothing! You have to think of the unlucky ones, sir. Think deeply about them, and then compare them to yourself."

Aaron remembered Maria's advice clearly. As he sat alone in his dark apartment lit only by the television, he suddenly thought of taking Maria out. He had washed some of his clothes but had not ironed them. He did so and immediately left the house.

"Maria! Maria!" Aaron shouted in a low voice.

Maria slowly peeped out of the quarters provided by her employer and saw Aaron. She covered her pajamas with a coat, walked toward Aaron, and rubbed her eyes.

"Go out with me, please. I'm bored."

"Right now? At this hour?"

"Please!" Aaron pleaded.

Maria looked around and then faced Aaron. "Okay."

They went for a light supper at the stall of Aaron's former plantation supervisor, Idris. Idris always wanted to give a free meal to Aaron, but Aaron had warned him that if he did that one more time, he would never come to his stall again. So Idris reluctantly charged Aaron, but he gave Aaron a good discount.

After forty-five minutes of healthy conversation, Aaron offered to walk Maria home. Maria asked where Aaron stayed. Aaron hesitated to reveal his address, but with Maria's persuasion, he finally agreed. Aaron walked with her and showed her his apartment.

"Up there," he said.

Maria looked up. "Can I have a look?"

"Oh no! Please don't, Maria."

"Please, sir."

Aaron thought for a while and then motioned for Maria to follow him. Aaron showed her the place, including the bedrooms, kitchen, bathroom, and living room. Maria pinched her nose, and Aaron felt embarrassed.

"Come. Let me take you back to your quarters, Maria," he said, and Maria nodded.

***

There was a loud knock on the door. Aaron was almost naked, wearing only his underwear. He shook his head vigorously and looked at the table clock. It was already 12:35 in the afternoon. As usual, he had overslept. The knocking didn't stop. He covered his lower body with a towel and walked toward the noise. "I'm coming! Please be patient!"

He opened the door. It was Maria. She smiled at Aaron. Aaron rubbed his head. He didn't know how to react.

"Aren't you going to let me in?"

Aaron stood there for some time. "Okay. Come in."

"I have taken a day off from work, and my master agreed to it. So I decided to come here and help clean up."

"Maria, I appreciate what you are trying to do, and frankly, it is very kind of you. However, I would like to do it myself."

Maria looked at Aaron; he was looking at the floor. "I'll help you with it, sir."

"Can't you understand? I said no! I am capable of taking care of myself!"

Maria was shocked. Never had Aaron been so rough to her. She bit her lips and began to walk out of the house. "Sorry for being a nuisance to you!" she said.

As Maria was about to leave, Aaron quickly realized his poor attitude and rushed to stop Maria from leaving the house. Maria struggled to walk out, but Aaron held on to her tightly. Maria burst into tears.

"I'm sorry, Maria. I'm very sorry. I didn't mean to be nasty to you. I promise it will never happen again."

Maria kept crying, but her struggles weakened, and Aaron let go of her slowly. He slowly brought her to the sofa, he cleared the rubbish away, and both of them sat down.

"I just want to help you. You are a nice man, and this is the only way I could repay your kindness," Maria said, weeping quietly.

"It's okay, Maria. I do understand, and I'm sorry for my rude behavior." Aaron slowly lifted Maria's small, oblong face with his massive fingers. Maria looked at Aaron, wiped her tears off her face, and smiled.

"On one condition," he said. "Don't call me sir. Just call me Aaron. Understand?"

"Okay, sir."

Aaron raised his eyebrows, and both of them burst into laughter.

Aaron walked around the town. He approached a newspaper vendor and looked at the latest news coverage. It had been many months since he had abandoned all interest in the world around him.

He tucked the paper under his arm and went to the small grocery store. It offered everything despite its size, including canned foodstuffs, soft drinks, toilet paper, stationeries, and even Scottish whiskeys. Aaron was looking for fresh farm products, and he found them.

At the ground floor of his apartment building, he stopped. He looked up and wondered whether he could carry all the things he'd bought to the fifth floor, because the elevator was under repair. He took a deep breath and used the staircase.

Aaron opened his apartment door slowly. He was bewildered. He walked with a rapid pace toward the kitchen, put down all the groceries, and walked unevenly toward the living room.

The whole place had been brightened up. The floor was clean and shining, the tables were cleared of all rubbish, and the furniture and television had been realigned. Everything looked better. There were no more empty beer bottles or piles of cigarette ashes. He went into his room, and all was tidied up there too. There were no more mismatched socks, smelly underwear, or dirty bedsheets. All had been washed.

"Your clothes will be dry soon, Aaron. It took longer than expected because there isn't much sunlight. After that, I'll iron them for you." Maria crossed her arms, watching Aaron's face, which was full of amazement.

Aaron smiled but didn't say a word. He pointed his finger and then rushed to the bathroom. He closed the door and looked at himself in the mirror. He looked at his unshaven beard, long hair, and dirty shirt.

The whole place is sparkling clean except me, he thought to himself.

Maria looked at the groceries Aaron had bought. She immediately went to work on preparing a meal.

More than an hour later, Maria had prepared food on the clean dining table, but Aaron had not come out of the bathroom. Maria looked toward it and was thinking of giving a gentle knock on the door, when Aaron came out. Maria just looked at him. He was a different man. He was the same man from years before.

"Why are you staring at me like that?"

"Nothing, sir. I'm sorry."

"What did I tell you?"

"Don't call me sir!" They both said the words together and smiled at each other broadly.

Aaron sniffed rapidly. "You know, Maria? Nothing is better than home cooking, and I can smell it already!"

After finishing the meal, Aaron leaned back in his chair, and Maria observed the satisfaction in him. He grabbed a beer and opened it. This time, he poured some into his glass and some into Maria's glass.

"What did you say your qualifications are, Maria? I can't seem to recall. It was a long time ago."

"I graduated from the University of Cagayan de Oro in the southern Philippines. I studied nursing and hygiene."

"That explains this cleanup operation!" Aaron looked around, and Maria giggled quietly. "You don't look Filipino to me. You don't even look Asian."

"I don't know, sir. I mean, Aaron. My parents told me that a Spanish priest raped my father's great-grandmother."

"Really? Raped by a Spanish priest?"

"I find that hard to believe too. But that was what everybody in my town back home said. But one thing I'm sure of is that being somebody different, my grandmother attracted a young American soldier stationed near her place. They were about to be married, but he was killed in action. My grandmother gave birth to my father before marrying a local Filipino."

Aaron and Maria kept quiet. Maria stood up and cleaned the table. Aaron moved slowly toward the sofa and sat down. He saw the newspaper he'd bought and picked it up. He browsed through it. As his eyes were scouting for information, he noticed an interesting article. He took some time to read it. It was about rubber wood, and indeed, it was interesting to Aaron.

"It's time for me to go back, Aaron. I've finished cleaning up the kitchen, but I don't think I can help you iron your clothes unless you can wait for me this weekend."

"That's all right, Maria. You have done more than what you should have. I don't know how to thank you for that."

"I'll go now, Aaron."

"Maria, can I walk you to your place? I don't mind, you know."

Maria smiled.

Chapter 33

"CAN I COME IN, boss?" William knocked on the door of Ricky's office.

Ricky looked up and immediately invited William in. "So? Have you given serious consideration to my offer?"

"Yes, Rick. It took me all night to make a decision, and it was a tough one to make." William sat down. "Your offer is too good, Rick. Actually, I should not have thought about it. I should have straightaway accepted it."

"Then?" Ricky put both his palms up.

"But I have to decline your offer. I thank you very much for the trust."

Ricky was shocked by what William had said. "Is anything wrong? Maybe it's me or Lisa or the firm?"

"Oh no! Not at all. Everything is okay. Don't panic. Rick, I built the connections and networks for this firm, and things have been going on independently. That means that without me, the firm will still prosper."

"May I ask what you are implying?"

"I've decided to decline your offer to be your partner, and I want to quit too. But I swear it's got nothing to do with you or Lisa or the firm."

"Is it about the girl you have been talking about? What's her name? Theresa?"

"Actually, I want to focus on politics, sir. I might be joining a political party soon, and I don't want all of this to affect my work."

Ricky thought for a while. "Can't you work at the same time while being active in politics?"

William stood up and walked around the room. "I can't, Rick."

Ricky reluctantly let William go. However, he gave an option to William: if he did not make it as a politician, he was always welcome to come back to the firm as a partner. Ricky told William he would wait for him no matter how long it took. William once again thanked Ricky for his faith in him, and then he said good-bye to everybody at the firm, packed his things, and walked out of the office. Lisa rushed to him, caught his hand, and gave him a kiss on his cheek.

"I'll come to your wedding," he told her. "Count me in."

"We will be expecting you, Will. Please do come."

Chapter 34

THE MALAYSIAN ELECTION WAS around the corner. Parliament had been dissolved, and the government parties and the oppositions were trading accusations against each other. The government was defending its credentials, which had enabled Malaysia to be deemed a newly industrialized country. The oppositions accused the government of practicing corruption, nepotism, and favoritism.

William did not agree that the government was perfect. It had failed to address environmental issues, and the wages of government staff were still well below average compared to the country's per capita income. That contributed to the government being corrupt. The government tended to protect politicians, even though they committed serious crimes, such as murder. They always found ways to cover up the misdeeds.

However, William agreed that the government had brought stability and prosperity to the nation. Government schools were abundant and almost free of charge. The government even provided free uniforms to poor children and attempted to provide computers to every school. Furthermore, the rate of achievements between rural and urban students had been narrowed. Illiteracy was almost a thing of the past.

The government also had given huge allocations for health and dental facilities. The facilities only charged a patient one dollar to see a doctor. X-rays were free, and so were the medicines. There were enough hospital beds for the sick patients, and even immigrants were given some privileges.

William had established strong networks with many union leaders, school associations, clubs, farmers, and ordinary workers. By his own initiative, he convinced them to support the government and ensure that the government would get a two-thirds majority. William strongly believed that the Malaysians were not ready for a full-fledged democratic system like those in the West, but the time would come.

William did not do the job alone. He was fully supported by Ramlan, who prepared all the paperwork, an activity that would have been taxing for William if he had tried to do it alone. Ramlan handled the correspondence and filing, keeping track of people and their phone numbers and addresses, and he also helped William with his schedule.

The government won and continued ruling. They won with the two-thirds majority required. William was tired of the political scene, and he had spent a lot of his own money and energy campaigning for the government. All he got in return was a letter of gratitude from the deputy prime minister of Malaysia. After he read the letter, he lay on his bed, put the paper on the floor, and slept for the first time in a week.

In the morning, as he was having his breakfast, William read the newspaper that had been delivered to his apartment. When he'd finished his breakfast, he put down the paper and thought, *what am I going to do now?*

Chapter 35

RAYMOND REQUESTED WILLIAM MEET him at the hotel where Theresa worked. William obliged without any hesitation. He could peep at Theresa and see how she was doing. Raymond waited in the lounge with his wife. He'd left his kids with a neighbor who had volunteered to babysit them. He had rented a cheap two-room house on the outskirts of town.

By the time William arrived, Raymond and his wife had helped themselves to two bottles of red wine that were almost finished. William greeted and joined them. Raymond ordered a dozen sandwiches and two packs of cigarettes.

"I saw your name in the news. You are a politician now," Raymond said.

"That's a contribution to society. To ensure our country continues to be stable."

"That's political talk. I could have sworn you were campaigning to us. Frankly speaking, I supported the opposition. The government is very corrupt. It is high time for them to change. However, I still did not register to vote."

"Thank goodness! Maybe if you'd voted, you might have brought down the government."

Both Raymond and William laughed. Cecelia joined them in laughing, but she did not understand a bit of what they were talking about. They hung around enjoying the live entertainment in the lounge.

It was close to midnight. Cecelia tapped Raymond's shoes with hers and gave him a signal. Raymond took a deep inhalation of his cigarette smoke and disposed of the ash on the floor. He threw the cigarette butt and nodded to Cecelia.

"William, actually, I have something embarrassing to say." Raymond took out a cigarette and put it in his mouth but didn't light it. He paused for a moment.

"Go ahead, Ray. Say it. What bad thing can happen to me if you say it?"

"I haven't paid two months of my rental bill. In fact, I borrowed money from my neighbor to pay for the electric and water bills. I would like to borrow money from you."

"How much?"

"Five hundred bucks."

William took out his wallet and gave the money to Raymond.

"What about this food and drink? I can't afford this either, Will," Raymond said with embarrassment. William called for the bill and settled it. Both Raymond and Cecelia thanked William.

"Well, I'm going to go look for Theresa," William said.

"Go ahead. Make a good girl out of my sister. She needs a guy like you."

William smiled and went to look for Theresa. It was already twenty minutes past midnight, and William thought to himself that Theresa might have gone home by now. He asked the girl at the reception counter, and to his surprise, Theresa was still around.

The girl called Theresa on the phone, and within a minute, she came out of the office. Not long after that, a man followed, pinched her backside, and whispered something in her ear.

William felt a rush of blood circulating vigorously around his body. He felt as if a knife were slicing part of his heart, but he kept his cool. He pretended not to notice them, and he took some brochures on top of the reception counter to try to look natural.

William stole a peek and noticed Theresa was looking at him while the man held her hand and then left. Theresa approached William.

"Thank goodness, Will. I don't have a ride. Can you drive me?"

"Sure." William pretended not to be aware of anything despite the fact that it hurt him so much. Theresa went to fetch her things, and

William waited for her outside the hotel in his car. After Theresa got in, William summoned his courage, but the words would not come out of his mouth. He closed his eyes for a second and finally said, "Who is that guy?"

"Which one?"

"The one who was with you just now."

"Oh, that was the marketing manager. We have a lot of things to sort out; that's why we finished our work very late. It happens occasionally. I told him he did not have to drive me home tonight, because I would be going with you."

William felt relieved a little bit, but it still hurt him.

After William dropped her off at home, he drove around town to get his mind off Theresa. When it was almost dawn, finally, he went home. In bed, his mind kept replaying the scene of Theresa with the manager, and he wondered what they'd actually been doing. *Were they doing their work, or were they fooling around?*

The thought bothered William, especially when he visualized Theresa and the manager inside the office alone. He closed his eyes rapidly, shifted to his right side, and forced himself to think of other thoughts that could help him sleep.

Why is she doing this to me, and why am I in love with her? Why am I a fool?

***

Raymond's problem was getting serious. The landlord decided not to let him stay anymore and requested that he leave. He didn't have enough money to stay in a cheap hotel. Raymond had no alternative but to stay in the car with his wife and their two children. He drove aimlessly around town.

Theresa informed William of Raymond's problem, and William came to see him. William could afford to put up Raymond at the cheapest motel, which was fourteen miles from town. It was a run-down place without any air-conditioning, but at least it had a clean toilet attached to each room and a common kitchen for every tenant to use. William could only afford to sponsor ten days, and Raymond quickly accepted.

What happens after ten days? William thought to himself. William himself was running out of money and didn't think he could help Raymond indefinitely. Suddenly, William had an idea. His father's farm thirty miles away needed a hand, and since Raymond had lived on a plantation before, surely he could help out and at the same time get a decent job.

William immediately went to see his father. The strictness of his father had created a generation gap between him and his dad. When he was a kid, his father had run a regimented life for them and had not shown any affection to his children, for fear that his kids would be too pampered and fragile when they grew up to face the world.

William's father had had to pay the price for his beliefs, for as soon as his kids reached their twenties, they couldn't communicate harmoniously with their dad, despite the fact that their father had tried to bridge his relationship with his children.

"I've never asked any favor from you, Dad. I hope you can help Raymond out and please help me out with this problem."

"But this isn't your problem! I have a lot of capable men already working at the farm. Why would I need more people?"

"His father operated a plantation before."

"Yes, but that was not him. His father and he are two different persons."

William's father was signing out payments to his creditors. He never missed paying them longer than thirty days. Many of the local traders liked to deal with him. His father's real estate business was a success, and he had then decided to experiment with agriculture, getting involved in integrated farming, including chicken raising and fruit growing.

"How long have you known this Raymond?"

"More than ten years. He is a Eurasian, Dad. I think he deserves our help."

His father kept doing his work. William felt it was futile to seek help from his father. He slowly walked away.

"Wait a minute, Son." David Stewart Sr. took off his glasses, wiped his eyes, and squeezed his forehead. "All right. Ask Raymond to work on Monday. They can stay at one of the farm quarters meant for the supervisors."

"Thanks, Dad."

"I want you to know I am doing this for you, Son."

William turned away and left. His father stood up and thought, *I hope William knows what he is doing.*

William informed Raymond about the job, and Raymond rejoiced after hearing the good news. William celebrated with Raymond and his family at the hotel coffeehouse. After the celebration, William looked in his pocket and scrambled to search for his bankbook.

He had no more than forty-five dollars in cash in his pocket, and in his bank account, he had enough only to pay for his rent, which was due in a few more days.

"I'd like to take the kids outside for a walk," Cecelia said, and she asked to be excused.

"Sure, honey, go ahead," Raymond said. He and William watched them go. "Can I order one more bottle of beer, Will?"

"Go ahead." William was now worried about his dwindling resources. Raymond called the waiter over and made his request. *I hope this is the last one!* William thought to himself.

"Ray, remember a few months ago, when you promised me the story about Devin? I'm still waiting."

Raymond hit his potbelly stomach, indicating that he was full; leaned back; and burped. "Excuse me, Will. You really want to know about Devin?"

William gave a nod. Raymond lit his cigarette. It seemed to William that the only time Raymond didn't smoke was when he was sleeping. Raymond released several circular smoke rings from his mouth.

"Raymond, the kids want to go back and sleep." Cecelia suddenly appeared from behind William. "I don't think they can stand anymore. They are tired."

"Why don't you drive home?" Raymond suggested.

"So how will you get back?"

"William can take me. Is that a problem, Will?"

"No problem. No problem at all. I'll take him, Cecelia. Don't worry. Raymond and I have a lot of things to talk about."

Raymond searched his pocket, took out a ring of keys, and gave it to Cecelia.

"He was a very loving brother." Raymond's beer was nearly finished. "That's what everyone thought." Raymond paused.

"So what happened?"

"One day he took Theresa for a walk to one of the most remote areas of the plantation. Theresa followed him because who else do you trust except your own father and brothers?"

"Then?" William impatiently asked.

"Devin put a knife to her throat. He wanted the money Dad gave Theresa for her birthday. I should not be telling you this."

William caught hold of Raymond's shoulder and asked him to continue. "Please, Ray. I need to know."

"Theresa screamed. Devin punched her, and Theresa collapsed. He took all her money and left Theresa alone. A passerby saw the unconscious body and raped her. Theresa woke up and found a stranger on top of her. But it was too late. Theresa almost went mad about this incident. Devin disappeared for a while."

"I didn't know that Devin was capable of doing such a thing. He seems to be a very quiet guy." William shook his head in disbelief. "But why did he leave her?"

William was upset that this thing had happened to Theresa. He could not bear the thought that someone had already had sex with her. But he still loved her no matter what happened to her.

"That's not the end of the story."

"What?" William shrieked.

Raymond continued and informed William that nobody wanted to rock the boat, so the secret was kept tightly. Theresa had only revealed the incident to Linda. They didn't want the shame to be exposed, and besides, Devin could be arrested for robbery or charged with assault with a deadly weapon.

"Where is Devin now?"

"Probably in Singapore. After moving away from Sandakan, he came here and opened up a renovation and interior decoration business. He set up a well-designed office, littered the place with magazines, and presto! Business came. As many as twelve rich customers were impressed with Devin, and each of them deposited between fifty to a hundred thousand bucks. He closed his office and ran away with the money. He spent most of his time on the island of Bantam, just few miles away from Singapore."

"Didn't that hurt his clients?" William asked.

"Are you crazy? Many of them kept quiet, but some of them sent a hitman to kill him. But they couldn't find him."

"How do you know where he is?"

"Only Linda knows. And Linda told me. Even Theresa does not know."

After taking Raymond home, William pondered Raymond's family life. It was full of tragedy, and William felt lucky that his family had not broken apart. He thought, *that is probably the reason Dad is so strict.* That was probably why their life had been so regimented. But amid the disciplined lifestyle, his mother had been there to comfort them with love. *Raymond's brother and sisters don't have the love of their mother, Elaine.*

Chapter 36

"WELL, WELL, WILLIAM, so you are coming back after all, eh?" Ricky jumped to meet William as he entered the office. Ricky noticed he was wearing simple, casual clothes and sneakers. Dark glasses covered his eyes.

"Thanks for coming to the wedding, Will!" Ricky shook his hand and pressed it tightly. "So when do you start work?"

"I didn't come to work, Rick. Just to say hello to old friends."

"Oh, I see."

"Where's Lisa?"

Ricky put his arm around William's shoulders and pulled him into his office. "Lisa is on leave. Last night, she had the best time of her life!"

William smiled. They went into the conference room, and Ricky closed the door slightly. They both sat, and Ricky put his hand at the back of his head. "I don't think you came to say hello, Will. There is something else, isn't there?"

William kept quiet. He took off his dark glasses and put them on the table. Ricky confirmed his judgment. William seemed not to have had enough sleep.

"Come on, Will. Don't keep things to yourself. I can see from your face and your eyes. You probably can't sleep because you are facing some problems."

William played with his glasses. "Actually, I came to borrow some money from you, Rick."

Without hesitation, Ricky went out of the room and into his office and closed the door. About two minutes later, he came back and put thirty thousand dollars on the table. He sat down and watched William.

"What's this?" William said, shocked. "I didn't ask for this much. I just want to borrow a couple thousand dollars."

"That's your money, Will. Take it."

"My money?" William replied with apprehension.

"Actually, I saved this money for your commission. I'm supposed to give it to you at the end of this year. New Year's surprise! But since you need it, take it." Ricky stood up and approached William. "The firm is progressing very well. Even though you are no longer with us, you deserve this."

"That's more than enough, Rick. Are you positively sure?"

"Sure I'm sure! Take it. Before I change my mind," Ricky said jokingly.

"Thanks a thousand, Rick!"

William managed to clear his debts, and he paid his rent six months in advance. He continued to be active with several social programs, cooperating with clubs and associations. By now, he had plans to join a political party aligned with the government. He began to build a rapport with them just as he did with nongovernmental organizations.

One day, as he was having breakfast at the coffee shop below his apartment, a man in light-colored batik cloth approached him. The man glanced around, whispered to William, took out an envelope, pushed it toward him, and walked away. William felt uneasy as he watched the man walk away. He dropped his food onto the table and rushed out to find out who this person was, but he had disappeared.

He went back to his seat, pulled the envelope closer, opened it, and peeped inside. He found an airplane ticket to Kuala Lumpur and two thousand dollars. The envelope even contained details regarding which hotel to stay at and what room number.

Kuala Lumpur meant "mud estuary." The city of the mud estuary was located at the connecting point of two major rivers. Once, it was one of the biggest cities in the British East Asian Empire, and the town was a center for the trading of two important resources, tin and rubber, which were thriving on the Malay Peninsula.

Kuala Lumpur rivaled Singapore in terms of beauty and grandeur. Some folks said that if Kuala Lumpur had been an independent country, it would have been richer than Singapore. It was strategically located almost in the middle of the Southeast Asian countries of Indonesia, Singapore, Malaysia, and Thailand.

Long ago, it was a simple Malay village, until Chinese immigrants settled there in large numbers because of the fight to control the precious tin business. Now it was one of the fastest-growing cities in the world and boasted a population of almost three million inhabitants.

William knew the city well. He'd studied there before and had even stayed right in the middle of town; he knew almost every street and road there.

After reaching the airport, he straightaway went to the prescribed hotel, using the airport limousine service. He stayed at the Pan-Pacific Hotel, located near the convention center, a big shopping mall, and the headquarters of the ruling political party.

He put his bag on the bed; took a long, warm shower; got dressed; and immediately rushed to the mall to look for a place to eat. He found an open French-style street café and ordered a tuna sandwich, chicken soup, and coffee.

William looked at his watch. He had an appointment precisely two hours from now in his hotel room, and he still did not know what it was about.

William waited impatiently. Time was moving too slowly for him. *I wish it would go by faster! I want to get whatever the problem is over with,* he thought to himself. The unknown was disturbing his concentration and his schedule.

At last, there was a knock on the hotel door. *Right on schedule!* he thought. When he opened the door, he found a man holding a mixture of fruit.

"Are you the man I am waiting for?"

The man, unsure what he meant, locked around. "The manager requested I bring this fruit, sir. I am just a bellboy. Did you order this, sir?"

"No, I didn't order anything."

"But the manager insists you have this. May I come in?"

William let him in and looked around outside his room. There wasn't anybody. "Place them on the table, and thank you very much."

The man waited at the door. He smiled.

"Oh! Sorry!" William handed some small change to the man.

"Thank you, sir," the man said, and he left.

William became frustrated. Still, there was no sign of the person scheduled to see him. He jumped onto the bed, switched on the television, and waited. He closed his eyes tightly and listened to the noise created by the television.

"William! William!" She held him tightly. William opened his eyes and smiled. He responded and held her tightly too. He kissed her passionately, putting his hand inside her clothes, and she held her arms around his neck. "I love you, Theresa."

"I love you too, Will."

Suddenly, the doorbell rang. They ignored. It continued ringing. William opened his eyes and looked around. "Theresa? Theresa?" he called out. The doorbell still rang. There was no Theresa around.

William went to the door, opened it, and saw another man. "Are you a hotel employee?" William said.

The man laughed. "No. I am here to meet you, as promised."

"You are late. Very late! I dislike broken promises, especially dealing with time."

"Sorry. A lot of unexpected things happened."

"You should not have come at all. You interrupted my dream." William regretted that his dream had come to an abrupt end. "A wonderful dream," he continued. "You can come in now."

"Thank you."

The man came in, walked toward the desk next to the window, and sat. Then he stood up again and offered his hand to William. They shook hands.

"My name is Andy Murray." Just as William was about to introduce himself, Andy asked him to relax. "I know all about you. I know your name, Mr. Stewart."

"Have you been spying on me? Are you a freelance tabloid journalist, or maybe you are a private detective? How come you know about me?"

"Be patient, Mr. Stewart."

It was getting dark. There was a growing thundercloud developing outside the hotel, and they both looked out the window. Andy put his hands in his pockets as he watched the falling rain hit the hotel.

"I parked my car very far away. If this rain doesn't stop, I'll be soaking wet."

"Why didn't you park in the hotel's parking lot? And why didn't you bring an umbrella?"

"The parking is full downstairs, and I forgot to bring my umbrella." He watched the rain develop into a heavy storm. Andy shook his head. He turned to William and asked him to sit down. He sat on the bed.

"As I said, my name is Andy Murray. I am like you—a half-breed pariah. My father is Irish, and my mother is a Baba from Malacca. I work with a consultant firm that advises the government on many matters. It is a big firm, and I am one of the salaried men. Listen to what I have to say, and please take my advice. Are you ready?" he said, and William nodded. "Good! Can I call you William?"

William looked at Andy. "Sure. Why not?"

"Okay, William. We are a profit-motivated consultant firm, and we advise the government on a lot of matters. We gather information on international trade and potential investors from the United States, Europe, Japan, and even Singapore. We give analyses of the Malaysian as well as the world financial and market situations. You name it. It is big, William. Huge! But despite the size of our involvement, our role is only to grease one of the tiny gears in the machinery of the system."

"What does this have to do with me?" William didn't get the point Andy was trying to convey.

"You see, Will, we also advise the government on a lot of political matters. We heard about your role in East Malaysia, and word reached the top that you are indeed a good help for the government." Andy rose, stretched, and looked out the window, as if he could stop the rain. "It's raining all the time here in KL. Do you have a lot of rain in East Malaysia?"

"So what are you trying to tell me, Andy? Can we get straight to the point?"

"You are impatient, my friend." Andy sat again on the bed. "We, as well as the government, see that you have big potential ahead of you, Will. They are impressed with your dedication, and they know you sacrificed some of your own money. We came to know that you want to get involved in politics. But I strongly advise you not to."

"Why not?"

"We are different people, Will. As I was saying, we are half breeds. It is sensitive for us to get involved in politics. People will question our colors, ideology, religion, and loyalty. They will question everything, especially if we have enemies."

"I don't have enemies," William said.

"You will if you get involved in politics. Believe me! Enemies will look for your weaknesses. Politics means the art of bringing people down. The best thing for you to do is work behind the scenes. Like me. You will succeed more, Will. Trust me. You don't have to spend money. They pay you money, but you still can contribute to society. And it is more effective this way."

On the plane going back home, William pondered what Andy had said. It was a sickening situation, but what he'd said was true. The turbulence and the pilot's warning for crew members to be seated didn't bother him. He looked out the window, seeing only darkness and the rain splashing against the glass. Occasional flashes of lightning brightened the sky for a fraction of a second.

"Can you hold my hand?" said the lady next to him. "I am extremely scared. I don't like flying."

William turned toward her. He hesitated, but the woman was filled with panic. He smiled at her, held her hand, and tapped it. "Don't worry. Planes are extremely safe."

Chapter 37

Aaron was looking for an old friend, an acquaintance he'd known a long time ago. But the problem was that every time he looked for him, he was out of the country, most of the time gone for a few months. He would be in the United States, England, or the Middle East, building up his international clients while his factory in Sandakan churned out the goods.

However, this time, Aaron was lucky. The man's secretary called Aaron and fixed an appointment. Aaron had just installed a house phone in his apartment. He dressed in his best and left for the meeting.

The office was on the top floor of a building near the harbor. Aaron looked up and counted twelve floors. He walked into the building, and a security guard asked him to sign a logbook. He complied and signed his name in it. As he waited for the lift, he wondered what his friend looked like.

Aaron hurried into a narrow corridor. As he approached a big room, the secretary greeted him. She walked right to Aaron and showed him the way.

"This way, Mr. Johnson. He is expecting you."

"Thank you," he said. The secretary opened the door and let Aaron in.

"Fucking son of a bitch! Al! You've changed a lot! Look at you!"

Aaron approached Sam, and they hugged. He hadn't changed. His hair was still dark and slightly masculine. He had some wrinkles, but they were hardly noticeable.

"Sam, how are you, old chap?"

"Never felt better! Even if you have a big problem, don't think about it. That is the secret to a healthy lifestyle."

Sam led Aaron to a big cupboard filled with wine. Aaron noticed that all of his furniture was made of fine timber that looked like temperate pinewood. Sam poured some wine into Aaron's glass and then his.

"This calls for a celebration. A happy reunion between two lost friends."

They toasted and drank. Sam noticed that Aaron kept looking at the furniture in his room. Sam smiled and sipped his wine.

"This is all made from rubber wood. My factory made them, Al. The texture is smooth, isn't it? Listen, pal. Why don't you accompany me to my factory about thirty-three miles from here? On the way, we can talk as much as we like."

Aaron raised his glass of wine. "That is indeed a good idea."

Sam explained to Aaron that British planters had brought rubber seeds to North Borneo in the early 1900s. They planted the seeds, and soon the place was filled with rubber plantations. Rubber became important because of the car boom in the United States. Even though the plant originated in Brazil, Malaya and British Borneo became worldwide producers of rubber.

Now the rubber trees were old and produced less latex. Latex was used to manufacture tires, but the price of rubber was far too low because of the competition from synthetic rubber made from oil. The price of crude oil was also dropping like ripe apples. However, most of the trees were almost a century old, and if properly treated, they could be shaped into beautiful furniture.

Sam took his time and drove no more than thirty miles per hour. He was grateful that Aaron had come to look for him and agreed to visit the factory. Aaron enjoyed the ride and didn't mind the speed. Sam slowed his Land Cruiser some more as he approached the end of the asphalt road.

"We will be traveling another twenty miles on dusty gravel road. You won't mind, eh, Al?"

"Not at all, Sam. I am used to traveling on gravel roads." Aaron looked at Sam.

Suddenly, Sam sped vigorously as he approached a group of workers unloading oil palm fruit at the grassy corner of the road. Sam laughed loudly. In his rearview mirror, he could see that the workers were covered with zero-visibility dust created by the speeding vehicle.

Aaron looked back and was surprised at Sam's sense of humor. The poor workers were covering their faces as the dust began to settle. Sam immediately slowed his car again. Aaron turned toward the front and shook his head in disbelief. Sam was still laughing, and Aaron couldn't help but smile.

Then, suddenly, Sam was about to change his gear for a short speed, but Aaron held the driving wheel. "Please, Sam. Don't do it again. That was fun we left behind. But in front, that's a woman with a baby."

Sam nodded and agreed to drive reasonably. "How did you know where I was, Al?"

"I read an article about rubber wood, and it mentioned your name. I inquired from a friend who had a rubber estate, and he told me how to get to you." Aaron paused for a while. "Are you still with the oil equipment sort of things?"

"I used to be involved in that stuff. I made a huge fortune just after the Indonesian confrontation was over. But the American buddies of mine smelled blood, and in no time, they were swarming all over Indonesia. There was a cutthroat price war, and bribery was a way of doing things. Some wise guys got to know a better way of doing things. They built a rapport with the Indonesian president's children, and they got themselves a good bargain. So I had to close my business and venture into producing rubber-wood furniture."

"Is it lucrative?"

"Not as good as the oil business, but at least it kept my investment going." Sam stopped his vehicle next to a depleted jungle that was actually a forest reserve. He stared at one of the big trees remaining. Aaron looked at Sam.

"Shhh!" Sam said, and both kept quiet. Aaron and Sam kept their eyes fixed. A furry red mammal slowly came out from the undergrowth. It kept itself partially hidden, and Aaron couldn't make out what it was. Sam snatched a bunch of ripe bananas from the backseat, opened his car window, and threw it toward the creature. The animal waited for a few seconds, dashed out, grabbed the bananas, and then went back into the jungle. Sam slowly drove off.

"You know what that was, Al?"

Aaron turned around and faced Sam. "An orangutan?"

"You're absolutely right. Every time I pass this road, I make it a habit to stop there and feed her."

"A female orangutan?"

Sam nodded. "Yep! A female orangutan. She knows the timing of my arrival, I think. That jungle was supposed to be protected. But some tycoon jerk played golf with the forest authority, gave them a lot of Christmas presents, and splashed them with cash, and the orangutan is now homeless."

In the distance, Aaron could see smoke coming from Sam's factory. The traveling had made him tired but not bored. Aaron felt his body ache because of the bumpy ride. However, he was used to this sort of traveling from his time working on the plantation.

"I'm a pro-environmentalist, Al. I hate people cutting down natural forest."

"But you yourself are doing the cutting," Aaron said.

"You see, Al, the trees I am cutting are rubber trees. It is an introduced species, and it is cultivated. As I said before, the price of rubber latex is going from bad to worse. The price is extremely low, and the government wants to plant a newer breed with a higher yield, so the government is willing to subsidize businessmen to cut the old trees. There are thousands of acres of old rubber trees that need to be brought down. So I came in to cut the old trees, process them, and market them as rubber-wood furniture."

They spent three hours at the factory. After the visit, Sam and Aaron sped back to town. This time, Sam drove fast, and Aaron became nervous. When they reached town, it was almost night time, and straightaway, Sam brought Aaron to an exclusive clubhouse in the same building as Sam's office. It was on the third floor.

They enjoyed their dinner and drank wine throughout the night. They talked about every topic they could think of: international affairs, the United States presidential election, the environment, the world economy, and so on. Soon they had nothing to talk about. Sam just stared at Aaron.

"Elaine left me, Sam. You know Elaine. Remember?" Aaron looked down at the table.

Sam kept staring at him. He turned his face away and nodded. "I heard about that. Sandakan is a very small town. News travels fast. I'm sorry it happened to you, Al."

"No problem at all. But my kids. Their whole life wasted without the care of a loving mother." Both of them again kept quiet, each feeling dizzy from drinking too much, but neither was seriously drunk.

"So what have you been doing lately?" Sam asked.

"Nothing, Sam. I stay at home and watch TV and let the world pass by."

"Why don't you work for me then?"

"You can't be serious. I am nothing but bad luck, Sam. If you hire me, I might bring your company down under."

"Oh, come on, Al! What more bad luck can happen to me, huh? My wife just died of cancer, one of my smaller factories in Surabaya burned down, and my sister is seriously ill back in the States."

"I'm so sorry, Sam."

"It's not your fault. Everybody's got problems, Al." Sam rubbed his eyes and shook his head slowly. "I loved my wife, Al. But there are things in life you can't control. And now she is gone. If I go home, there is emptiness in the house. That's why I don't like to go home. Every time I do that, I sense the presence of her."

Sam looked deeply into the bottle of wine, but his mind was blank except for the desperate attempt he made to get a clear vision of his lovely wife. "Let me send you home, Al. We will talk again tomorrow."

Aaron was satisfied that his home was now clean. His clothes were all washed, there were no more dirty dishes, there was no more rubbish indiscriminately thrown around, the toilet was clean, and the bedsheets were clean. What better place was there than home?

He jumped into his bed with his clothes on, too drunk to take off his shirt and pants. But he still could think. He closed his eyes, and the thoughts still came. He shifted his body to the other side, but the vision persisted.

"I am going off with my old boyfriend. He is richer than you, richer than most. He can give me anything I want, unlike you! You ask too many questions. 'What do you do with the money? Why isn't there enough to eat? Why this, and why that?' I am leaving you, Aaron. For good!"

Aaron suddenly opened his eyes and struggled to stand up. He walked with an unsteady motion toward the living room. He threw himself onto the sofa and pushed his head backward.

Aaron observed his surroundings. This apartment was almost perfect to him. He didn't need an expensive house, big car, or big salary. What he had was already reasonable, and it had been a token from his former employer for free. However, his home had something missing. It was filled with loneliness, and he did not know how long he could stand that. The company couldn't compensate for that. He had to figure out how to solve the problem himself.

Chapter 38

WILLIAM WAS SATISFIED WITH his new job. He was appointed as the director of the New Growth Consulting Firm, in charge of East Malaysia. He was paid handsomely, much more than he'd earned at the law firm. He was also given generous traveling allowances. His duty was to maintain good relationships with union leaders, teachers, students, and farmers. He also was to establish good rapport with the politicians, but he himself could not be openly involved in politics.

William had to write extensive reports covering his activities and his opinions about the East Malaysian situation, especially politics and trade. He had to give an accurate assessment and predict the potential paths that the country was taking, especially concerning Borneo.

William employed two staff members, a secretary and an assistant. He rented eight hundred square feet of office space in the middle of town, renovated it, and bought a secondhand fax machine and computer. He requested three phone lines: one for the general office, one for the fax, and one for his own. The company paid all expenses.

His secretary was to attend to all matters involving his schedule and appointments, including details such as getting his plane tickets. His assistant was to follow up with all of their established contacts. He also helped William with the report preparations, for both he and the secretary were university graduates. With his new and powerful position, he also acted as a lobbyist for interested parties.

Union members were more likely to get higher wages through their connection with William; parents and teachers communicated effectively through him when they wanted more computers for the schools; and with his help, farmers could get more grants and subsidies to ensure continued productivity.

William flew to Kuala Lumpur at the end of every month, unless there was an emergency situation that required him to travel twice. He was required to submit his report, almost a hundred pages, to Andy and to brief him personally on the current situation. Andy would bring it up with their organization's department in charge of compiling all the assessments from all over the nation. Reports also came from places outside Malaysia, especially Indonesia, where Malaysia had sizeable investments.

"Boss, there is a phone call for you from your father. He says it is urgent, and he needs to see you," said Moses, William's secretary. His glasses were low on his nose, almost below his eyes, and his left hand was holding the telephone apathetically, while the other hand was on his waist.

"Tell him I am in the middle of an important meeting," William said slowly.

"I did," Moses said with a loud voice.

"Goodness gracious! What can be so important?" William rose from his chair and went toward Moses. Moses gave William a lazy look and passed him the phone. William jokingly snapped at him, and Moses walked away.

"Yes, Dad? What is it?"

"I have something to talk to you about, and it is important. It's about Raymond."

"Can we find some other time—perhaps tomorrow?"

"This is important, Will! You have to meet me today. Please!" His father hung up the phone.

What can be so important about Raymond? William thought to himself.

William went to his father's office, but the staff there told him that his father had not come to work that day and probably was at home. He walked hurriedly to one of the tables and grabbed the telephone. His mother answered and confirmed that his father was at his house.

William drove to his family's residence, which was twelve miles south of the state capital, located between the express highway and the vast South China Sea. It was a fifteen-acre estate that his father had bought forty years ago. At that time, it had been extremely cheap, but the purchase had tightened the belt of his family for years afterward.

It was a single-story bungalow modeled after an English cottage, with slight improvisation. Since William's mother liked flowers, the land was lavishly landscaped with imported and local ornamental plants, fruit trees, and vegetables. The house had a swimming pool, which was located near the beachfront.

William parked his car outside the garage. He looked at the house and remembered his mother's words: "Your father wants you to stay here. Since you are the eldest son, you will inherit this property." However, William wanted to work out his life alone, without outside help as much as possible.

He walked slowly into the house and approached the old piano. He tapped the keys and found that the piano was well tuned. One of the housemaids saw him and bowed slightly. William gave a quick nod.

"There you are, my boy! It has been a long time. How are you?" His mother approached and gave him a strong, long hug.

"I'm fine, Mother. Is everything okay?"

His mother caught him by his hand and pulled him toward the garden chairs facing the sea. As they sat down, his mother instructed the maid to get a jug of lemonade and two glasses. William took off his dark glasses and put them into his pocket. He watched the sea waves break as they hit the sand. The rhythm was soothing. William closed his eyes for a few seconds and then opened them again.

"Mom, lemonade? You still threat me like a baby boy," he said with a smile.

"You are my baby boy, aren't you?" His mother laughed and then paused for a while. "So how is everything? How are your job and your financial situation? When do you intend to get married? I am longing for grandchildren, you know."

"As I told you over the phone, I have a new job, and I like it very much. My financial situation is now okay, maybe some small bumpy situations once in a while. And about marriage, you have to be patient, Mom!"

Both suddenly remained quiet. Then the maid arrived with the lemonade. After she put the jug and glasses on the table, she again bowed a few times. William again nodded.

"Why does she have to bow every time she sees us?"

"She came from one of the poor provinces in Indonesia. She cried the day she was given the opportunity to work here. Maybe she is very grateful." They both watched her disappear into the kitchen.

"How are my three little brothers?"

"You know very well they are studying. Murphy is studying to be a lawyer like you. He obtained a degree in child psychology. James and David are studying to be civil engineers, and they are graduating soon."

William was pleased to hear the progress of his brothers. "So where's Dad?" William drank his lemonade and finished it quickly. It was good, and he poured another glass. Still, he couldn't quench his thirst, and he had another glass. His mother laughed at his action.

"Your father is expecting you in the study."

"Why do you want to see me, Dad?" William asked a few minutes later.

"Oh, Will! Please sit down."

The room was a small library. He sat in front of his father.

"I want to discuss Raymond." His father closed the book he was reading and faced William.

"What about Raymond?"

"Tell me very frankly, Will. How long have you known Raymond?"

William tilted his head to the right and leaned forward. "What?" William was feeling uneasy about the question. He looked his father straight in the eyes.

"How long have you known Raymond? This is important, Will. Please, for once, let's communicate. I beg you."

William felt funny that his father, for the first time in his life, had to beg for a conversation. "Well, I have known him for almost twenty years, I guess. Why?"

"Who is his father?"

William paused for a while. "He used to be a soldier for the British army. Then he got a job here and later in Sandakan as a plantation manager. That's all I know."

"What do you know about Raymond?"

"He is a smart person. He always claimed he is smarter than others," William said with a smile. "He didn't finish high school, but he is sharp enough to converse like graduates." William paused and then continued. "He is a graduate on his own terms, if you know what I mean, Dad. He ventured into business, but he was not successful due to bad luck and also because he was always cheated. Maybe he is too honest—that's why."

"So that's what you think about Raymond?" His father played with the pen he was holding and then deliberately dropped it onto the floor. His father stood up and walked toward the bookshelves. "You know what I think about Raymond? He is a bloody crook! That's what he is!"

William almost jolted from his seat upon hearing his father condemn his friend. *Why is Dad doing this to me?* he thought to himself.

"Keep away from him, Will! Hear my advice. He will bring you down if you are not careful. I think he knows your soft spot, and he is exploiting that to the fullest."

"No! It can't be! Why, Dad? Why?"

His father cleared his throat. He stood upright and straightened his shirt. "At the plantation, Raymond seemed to be hardworking, offering to do marketing and deliver the farm products. He traveled frequently, and everyone thought he was doing good things for the company. But reports came in, especially from Jafar, the farm supervisor, that Raymond sucked out the gasoline from the pickup truck and sold it cheaply. He came back to the farm, filled the tank up full again, and went back to sell the gas again and again. True enough, the company's expenses on fuel were extremely high, unprecedented in the company's history ever since Raymond arrived."

"You trust Jafar? The immigrant? You take his word?"

"Of course I do!" His father raised his voice.

William became upset at what he'd heard. He was about to leave, when his father gestured for him to sit down. William's mother came rushing into the room to see what had happened. His father looked at his mother, and his mother slowly left.

"That's not all, Will. He even siphoned some of the money from the cash sales business. Look, Will, if I hadn't considered your feelings, I could have reported this matter to the police, and there would be an investigation on him. However, I am willing to overlook this. But what I can't tolerate is that he instigated the workers to strike and talked badly about Jafar and me, saying that Jafar and I conspired to exploit him and the workers."

William shook his head in disbelief.

"I am worried for you, Son. He is using you. Maybe he knows something about you that enables him to take advantage of you. Please be careful."

"I've had enough of this nonsense for today!" William stood up and walked out of the room. This time, his father let him be.

"Be careful, William! I will not sack Raymond without your permission, despite what he did. Do you understand?"

William didn't turn back to hear any more from his father. He rushed to his car, ignoring the maid bowing in front of him as he passed her by.

"Will! Will!" his mother desperately called out. But William slammed the door of his car and immediately drove off. His mother's face sank. She too was upset that such an incident had occurred. William's father came out of the house and comforted his mother.

"Do you have to be so nasty to him?"

"I have to tell him the truth."

"You didn't make up the story, did you?"

David bit his lip and walked away.

Chapter 39

WILLIAM HAD A TIGHT schedule ahead of him. Moses informed him that tonight he would be attending a dinner at the Shangri-La Hotel, organized by the insurance agents' union. A few hundred members would be attending. Tomorrow morning, he would be attending the Farmer's Day celebration in a remote village in Beaufort. The function was to last the whole day, and the day after tomorrow, William was supposed to meet an environmentalist group.

"And you asked me to fix a time with the National Front politicians tomorrow," Moses reminded William.

William, who was perfecting his tie, suddenly popped out of his office. "But you said tomorrow I have an appointment with the farmers."

"You tell me, sir. I've briefed you on your schedule for weeks, and suddenly, you insist you want to meet the politicians tomorrow. So I don't know."

Moses was a fussy secretary. He spoke his own mind and was not easily pushed around. He had worked with several companies, and they'd all fired him in less than a month. However, despite his feisty attitude, Moses worked hard, was full of initiative, and was able to solve problems, and that was what William wanted in a secretary.

"Take it easy, Moses!" William straightened his tie and looked at himself in the bathroom mirror. "You'll figure it out."

"Yeah, I'll figure it out," Moses grumbled. Moses went straight to his room.

"Boss, the report you needed!" Ramon, his assistant, came running toward him as William was preparing to leave the office.

"Thank you, Ramon. Is this all?" William put the report in his briefcase.

"That is all, sir."

William looked at Ramon and smiled at him. *Indeed, I have an excellent team,* he thought to himself.

That night, William persuaded Theresa to accompany him to the dinner function and act as his temporary consort. William was tall, and his coat suited him well. The black suit contrasted nicely with his white shirt. Theresa was equally tall and elegant. She wore a dress that matched his suit. As they entered the hotel dining hall, everybody stared at them, especially the men, and William felt proud. He smiled at Theresa as they sat down at the table with the union's committee members, including the chairman himself.

Later that night, as William was driving Theresa home, he said, "Thanks for spending time with me, Theresa. You have been a great help to me."

"Don't mention it. I do that because of your kindness to Raymond." She turned toward William and held his temple, caressing it slowly. William felt the greatest pleasure when Theresa touched him, even though she was only touching his hair.

Suddenly, he received a phone call. William picked up his cell phone. "Hello?"

"Boss, how was your dinner?"

William laughed and turned toward Theresa, who was watching him. "I've never enjoyed it so much, Moses. It was a good one. Why are you calling in the middle of the night?"

"I've figured out how to fix your schedule tomorrow to fit in both the farmers and the politicians. Since the politicians need exposure, I figure you can bring them to the Farmer's Day celebration. What do you think?"

William thought for a few seconds. "That's an excellent idea, Moses. I'm so proud to have you as my secretary."

"Good night, sir. And take care."

"Good night, Moses."

"Who was that?" Theresa asked.

"My secretary—and he is a man!"

Theresa smiled and continued touching William.

***

Despite William's disregard for his father's accusation against Raymond, the words still bothered him. Night after night, the words rang in his ears: *He's a bloody crook!* William woke up in the middle of the night, trying to shake off the memory.

The next day, he informed Moses that he would like to have a day off. He requested Ramon handle his routine, despite the fact that Ramon was overloaded with his own work. Ramon did not hesitate, but William saw the reluctance in his facial expression. William could not blame Ramon for his apparent apathy. He did not say no, but William feared that in his heart, he was angry. The workload would put tremendous pressure on Ramon, and it might break him.

Suddenly, William remembered Ramlan. Ramlan was more than willing to help him out and always did. Ramlan came to his office at William's request. William called for a meeting with Ramlan and his staff, and they sat and discussed in the conference room. Ramlan agreed to help out, and he encouraged William to take two days off. He was willing to work under Ramon.

William noticed there was sadness in Ramlan's eyes. "Are you okay, Ramlan?" William asked, almost whispering, as he held his shoulder.

Ramlan smiled at him. "I'm very okay, Will. Why do you ask?"

"You look very sad."

"I'm okay!"

Ramlan paused and continued to collect the paperwork he'd been assigned. He turned; looked at William, who was watching him; and laughed. "Really! I'm okay! You go ahead. Take your two days off. I will help out."

"Thanks, Ramlan!"

William called Raymond and asked him to take the day off. He said he wanted Raymond to come to town as soon as possible. As a matter of procedure, William requested permission from Jafar, the company's farm supervisor, to release Raymond only for the day. William wanted Raymond to come alone.

William waited at the beachfront where he and Raymond had first met. Memories flooded his mind when he looked at the sea in front of him. There at Tanjung Aru, he'd met Raymond and Linda, and his most wonderful memory was of watching Theresa play.

The beach was no longer what it used to be. Massive development had taken place within the area. The beautiful, tall decades-old casuarinas trees had been cut down and replaced with imported acacia, a simple, hardy plant. Rubbish littered the beach, a sign of a growing population, and squatter settlements mushroomed nearby. The sand was muddy due to the silt accumulating from the massive forest clearance near the source of the river that came out into the beach.

William needed the day off. Even if he had not intended to meet Raymond, he needed to relax and take his mind off his work. After all, he had not taken any leave for a long time.

William looked at his watch. Raymond was ten minutes late. He stood up and walked toward several hawker stalls. He got himself a Coke, came back to the same spot, and sat down.

Rather than getting anxious about waiting, William took out his notebook and started scribbling his proposed plan for next month. He sipped his Coke slowly and jotted down ideas.

"What the hell are we meeting here for?"

William turned around and looked up. "Hi, Raymond! You are one hour late."

Raymond sat down. "What do you expect? The farm is forty miles away, and I am traveling in your father's farm junk. In Singapore, that vehicle would be banned from traveling on roads."

"What happened to your pickup?"

"I sold it off. I needed the money badly, so I sold it cheaply for cash. I reckon I'll travel around with this old junk after all."

William kept writing in his notebook. He had almost finished his plan by the time Raymond arrived. *Might as well finish it off and then have a long talk with Raymond,* he thought.

"So what's up? What did you summon me here for?"

"Relax, Ray! Just for a while. Let me finish my work."

After he'd finished, William and Raymond went to a nearby food stall along the beach. It had not been there back when William and Raymond had first met. The food was cheap and good, and they enjoyed their early dinner. In the distance, they watched the sun go down.

Not many people patronized the place, despite the tasty food. William counted only three occupied tables. He wondered how the owner could survive for another month with only a handful of customers. All the attendants were sitting, bored, with nothing to do. A new batch of customers arrived, and the waitress suddenly became excited and buzzed around.

Raymond tapped at his stomach. It was already bulging and didn't correspond to his age. He shouldn't have had a belly like that for another ten years. But William knew that Raymond drank a lot of beer, which likely contributed to his odd body shape.

"You should do something about your potbelly. Besides, you're growing fat."

"Well, as the Chinese say, it's a sign of prosperity!"

"Remember, Ray, when you said Eurasians were good for nothing and had no place to consider home? Do you still stand by your words?"

"Sure! Eurasians have no country. They are outcasts. Neither East nor West."

"But I think they are lucky, Ray. They have advantages. They can be Asian, and they can be European. They have both continents to themselves!"

"Yeah right! And you think you're smart?" Raymond gave William a sarcastic look. William called over one of the attendants and asked him to bring the bill and clear the table as well. William asked for a glass of orange juice. Raymond settled for a thick black coffee.

"How was your date with Theresa?"

William looked at the floor and smiled. "We had a wonderful time at the dinner function. She was elegant, Ray. You should have seen your sister graciously move into the dining hall. Everybody looked at her." Both of them paused to think about what else to talk about.

"So why did you call me here? You said there was something important you would like to talk to me about."

"Yes, Ray, very important. And I don't know where to begin."

"Okay, shoot."

"All right. I hope you don't mind me asking you this, Ray. It has been troubling me since my dad called me up. You don't mind, do you?"

Raymond shook his head, indicating that William should continue. William paused in thought.

"Come on, Will! We haven't got much time. Go ahead. Say what you want to say."

"My father believes you stole gasoline from the company, Ray. He also believes that you siphoned off some of the cash sales. And then you instigated the workers to strike and go against Jafar and my father. Is it true?"

Raymond thought for a second. "Nope!" He spoke confidently and shook his head. "Will, if I wanted to cheat or steal, I wouldn't go for this petty crime. I would hit the jackpot, like robbing banks. And why should I instigate workers, for heaven's sake? It would serve me no purpose. Unless I could take over the farm. Then it'd be worth it."

William felt relieved at Raymond's explanation. He took a deep breath and released it, feeling the pressure let off. His father was wrong after all. When he got the time, he would meet up with him and explain what Raymond had said. That might convince him.

"You wouldn't rob a bank, would you?" William asked jokingly.

"If I had the means, why not?" he said, and William looked at him. "No! I'm just pulling your leg, Will! Do you honestly believe I could pull that stunt? When did your father speak to you about me?"

"Weeks ago, I think."

"Well, I don't blame your father for the accusation. I blame it on Jafar!"

Chapter 40

WITH THE RAYMOND ISSUE out of his mind, it was back to business for William. Instead of two days, he had taken one week off, and he'd had a good rest. With new vigor and enthusiasm, he was back in full form.

During his absence, Ramlan, who'd assisted Ramon, had done a fine job. His work was beyond William's expectations; there wasn't any slack to pick up. Appointments were attended and on schedule, and their clients were satisfied. There had been a good synergy among Ramon, Ramlan, and Moses.

As soon as he went back to work, William asked Ramlan if he would like to join his team permanently. Ramlan made a decision on the spot: he would like to be part of William's workforce. William was delighted.

That night, William tried to work out roles for his subordinates. Moses would carry out his usual tasks without any changes. Ramon would focus more on building rapports with nongovernmental organizations, or NGOs, as well as private-sector unions, while Ramlan would receive a new assignment. Since he was presently working with the government, he would be assigned to government union members, teacher-parent associations, farmers, fishermen, and politicians. Some of William's and Ramon's workloads would be assigned to Ramlan when he joined the team.

As for William, he could now focus more on the businessmen and environmentalists.

William was a strong advocate for business growth, and he valued relationships with businessmen. However, William also believed that the growth of business should not be at the expense of sacrificing the environment. Not many people in Malaysia or Asia shared his idealism, but he was prepared to make the public realize the importance of business and the environment growing together in parallel.

Ramlan gave one month's notice to his employer of his impending resignation, and then he could freely join William's firm. William called for a meeting and briefed them on their new responsibilities. William's immediate focus was on writing reports that were already three months late. Piles of paperwork flooded his desk, and Andy had been barking at him over the phone, calling from Kuala Lumpur. Once, he was on the line with William in Zurich, and again, he lectured William for half an hour about the backlog.

William, Ramon, Ramlan, and Moses cancelled all appointments for a few days and worked together to finish the reports. Without much sleep, they worked for a full forty-eight hours. It was a marathon for them.

"Boss, there is a call from your boss!" Moses yelled from the other room. "He wants to talk to you now!"

William snatched the telephone, instructed Moses to put the other one down, and sat on his table. "Where are you, boss?"

"Don't *boss* me! I am now in Paris. The government is screaming at the chairman, the chairman is screaming at his directors, one of the directors is putting me in the frying pan, and what am I supposed to do? Kiss you? He just screwed me a few minutes ago!"

"Don't get paranoid, Andy! I'll submit the work once you're back. It's finished!"

Chapter 41

"CAN I SEE YOU now, Will? Please?"

"It's three o'clock in the morning. What's up?" William rubbed his eyes and put the alarm clock back on the bedroom table. "Just hold on, Theresa." He rose from his bed and put his feet on the floor. "Okay, where were we?"

"I want to see you, Will. Now!"

"Sure. Why not? But I have to get dressed first. Where do we meet?"

"There is a twenty-four-hour convenience store behind the place where I work. I'll wait for you there."

"Wait!" he said, but she hung up. William was feeling groggy, for he'd had only a few hours of sleep. He went to the toilet, washed his face, and looked in the mirror. "I don't think I have time to shave."

As William was driving, he spotted her waiting. There was a slight drizzle, and Theresa didn't have an umbrella or a raincoat. He slowly approached her, parked, and opened the car door, and she rushed inside. She was a bit wet.

"Please drive, Will! Drive now!"

"Where do we go?"

"Drive anywhere! Take me anywhere you like!"

William thought for a while. Theresa kept quiet and looked out the left window. She put her right hand on her mouth. William saw that she was trying to control her emotions, but he could tell she had been crying. William felt lost. He didn't know how to react or where to go. He drove around town from north to south and east to west without any destination in mind.

168

He drove for hours. The sky brightened as the sun rose over the mountains in the distance. Theresa hadn't said a word. Neither had William. He didn't want to interrupt her. William saw an ideal spot to stop close to the seafront. There was ample space near the sea. He parked his car and looked at Theresa.

"You haven't said a word."

Theresa raised her left hand, asking William not to talk anymore. She still faced the window, away from William. William slid back in his seat and looked straight ahead.

Slowly, Theresa turned toward him. She took some tissues from her bag and wiped her eyes. William tried to look without turning his face toward her. She turned away from him and, like William, looked straight ahead.

"Thanks for accompanying me."

At last, she speaks, William thought. "What happened, Theresa?"

"Remember the man you saw at the hotel with me? The marketing manager?" She continued wiping her tears. "To tell you the truth, he was my boyfriend. We've had a special relationship for the past two years, and I love him very much."

William felt as if his heart had melted. The news was painful. He turned away from Theresa, hoping to hide his feelings from her. Theresa looked down and kept wiping her tears. She shook her head slowly.

"Go on, Theresa." William pretended to be calm.

"But now it is over!" Theresa burst out crying suddenly. William slowly took her in his arms. "It is over, Will!" she said.

William did not know whether to be relieved or disappointed. "Be patient, my lady," William said, trying to comfort her.

"He told me he can't divorce his wife, because he still loves her and his children. But earlier on, he said he would." Theresa was weeping while talking.

William took her home and carried her in his arms into her room. He brought her to the bed, laid her down gently, and helped her take off her shoes. Slowly, her eyes got heavy, and finally, she slept.

William walked out of her house slowly. He closed the door gently and moved away. In the car, William felt like crying himself—not because of Theresa's plight but because of the way she treated him.

Why didn't she tell me she was in love and going steady? Why didn't she refuse to meet me or at least tell me off? At least then I would not have been hoping for the moon. The thoughts created blisters in his soul.

William drove alone in the jammed streets. The traffic was heavy, as it was almost noon, and he hadn't gone back to work. He was in no mood to go back to the office, but he wasn't tired enough to sleep either.

William hung around at an isolated coffee shop. He didn't bring his cell phone, and there was nobody to bother him. For the first time in his life, he drank beer, and after half a glass, he was almost drunk.

By the time the hangover feeling was gone, it was almost midnight. The shop was closing, and William paid and left. He went to his apartment and took a hot shower. He hadn't eaten the whole day, and he consumed a light supper that he made himself.

God in heaven! Why is this happening to me? he thought.

"Why?" he suddenly shouted. He placed a pillow over his head as if it could get the problems out of his mind. He felt as if the devil were celebrating and whispering in his thoughts.

William jumped out of his bed, rushed to the bathroom, and took a quick shower. He brushed his teeth and haphazardly shaved. After dressing, he didn't stop to have breakfast, nor did he have time to pick up the morning paper. He rushed to his car and looked at his watch. It was a quarter past eleven; he was already late.

The door slammed open as he entered the office. There was nobody there except Moses, who was shocked by the loud noise. His right hand was on his chest, and another was holding a file.

"That was rude, Mr. Stewart!" Moses straightened his body.

"The reports! I have to submit the reports! Oh God! I was supposed to submit them yesterday! Prepare my ticket right now, Moses!"

Moses didn't budge. He just stared at William.

"Where the hell are the reports?" William turned to Moses, who was still staring at him. "Why are you looking at me like that? Why aren't you preparing my flight?" Moses turned away from him and went to his desk.

"Moses! Moses?" William watched him sit down, and his temper began to boil at his disobedience. "I'm asking you one more time!"

"The reports have been submitted already! Andy was screaming like a lion, asking for them. Where were you yesterday?"

William was taken aback. Moses opened his laptop and started doing some work.

"I had some urgent things to settle yesterday. Who submitted the reports?"

"Since you were not around, Ramon, Ramlan, and I decided that the reports had to be submitted and somebody had to fly to Kuala Lumpur. We all decided Ramon should do the job and brief Andy on any important developments. We told Andy you were in the ICU with severe appendicitis."

"You said what?"

"Appendicitis!" Moses continued with his work while talking to William. William turned toward the door, which was still open, and slowly closed it. He sat next to Moses. Moses ignored him for a moment and then said, "Andy said after the briefing, he wants to fly down and see you at the hospital." William shook his head and laughed as Moses continued. "But we told him you don't want to be disturbed, and only family members can visit you."

"So when will Ramon be back?"

"He will be back this evening. You know Ramon. He had never been to Kuala Lumpur. In fact, he never travels outside the state. So I don't blame him if he decides to take the day off and tour the city."

William kept quiet as he watched Moses working. Slowly, he walked away toward his office. Then, suddenly, he turned around and walked toward Moses. "Thanks, Moses. I don't know what I'd do without all of you." Moses ignored him and continued his work.

As William was doing his work, there was a low tapping noise on his door. William put his pen down and looked up. He could see Ramlan outside, asking for permission to come in. William waved his hand, and Ramlan entered slowly.

"Good afternoon, Ram!"

"Afternoon, Will. Can I sit down?"

"Of course, take a seat."

As Ramlan was about to sit, he suddenly remembered that the door was still open. He requested permission to close the door, and William consented. He sat, paused, and then spoke.

"There is something I want to ask you."

"Go ahead, Ram. Say anything you like. We are always open with each other."

Ramlan continued to hold his words. He was reluctant to speak out.

"Is everything all right?"

Ramlan took a deep breath. "Be open with me, Will. Tell me the truth."

William was getting anxious and a bit worried about what Ramlan had on his mind. William nodded.

"After you introduced me to Raymond, we occasionally met with each other. Once in a while, he came to town from your family's farm; I usually stumbled upon him." Ramlan paused again.

William pushed away his paperwork and put his arms on the desk. Ramlan seemed to be summoning the courage to continue talking. He turned left and right and then faced William.

"One time, Raymond asked me to sit with him in one of the cafés inside a shopping complex. We had a long talk."

"What did you talk about?"

"We talked about a lot of things, boss. But what disturbed me the most was that he told me you said to him that I was an idiot. All Malay-Javanese boys are idiots! Easily manipulated! You were even amazed that I'd managed to get my degree!"

Ramlan's revelation startled William. Cold sweat suddenly appeared on his head.

"According to him, you told him my stupidity is in my genes. That's why Java, with a big population, was easily enslaved by a handful of Dutch for more than three hundred years." Ramlan paused again. "Tell me, Will! I'm very loyal to you, and I obey you—not because I'm easy bullied but because I admire you and believe in your idealism. Tell me—is it true that you said such nasty words? Did Raymond make up those stories?"

"That's a lie, Ram! That is an absolute lie. I don't know why he said those things to you."

"Thank you, Will. At least I now know you didn't say such bad things about me. I know you very well. Maybe Raymond is jealous of me or you. But I'm glad you didn't say those words." Ramlan stood up. "Will you excuse me? I've got a lot of things to do."

William looked up at Ramlan. "Sure. Go ahead, Ram."

William walked around the room, feeling upset and angry. He was disappointed in Raymond. He felt like speeding all the way to the farm and confronting Raymond one more time.

He sat down and thought about what Ramlan had just said. Unfortunately, it was the truth. Raymond hadn't lied. William had made the mistake of condemning Ramlan, and he hadn't deserved it.

It was supposed to be a joke. Eurasians usually would tolerate it if their race was made fun of, but not Asians. They tended to take this sort of humor seriously. William should have been more sensitive to this. Another disappointment was that William had lied to Ramlan in order to save himself. William was embarrassed. This mess was all because of Raymond, who'd breached his trust.

"Will, a call for you! It's your father again!" Moses shouted.

William picked up the phone. "Dad?" William said politely.

"Jafar had a freak accident. He is reported to be in stable condition at the city hospital. The car he was driving—the brakes didn't work, and he banged into a stationary truck. But he was lucky. You should have seen the vehicle. Totally condemned! And we can't claim from the insurance because it is a third party. I have to find a new vehicle to replace his once he goes back to work."

"Goodness, Dad! I'll drop by to see him at the hospital today. Bye! And take care of yourself."

William doubted his father. *Freak accident! It must have been deliberate!*

William looked at the business card Raymond had given him for Red Dragon Sawmill Industry. The owner was Mr. Chia Swee Kow. It was located at Mile 32 on Sandakan Road.

When Raymond had given him the business card months ago, he'd said, "You know, Will, this Mr. Chia is the one Chinaman who brought my downfall. No doubt it was the fishermen who conspired against me and made my fish business collapse, but this Mr. Chia! Oh yes! He is the one who made me suffer heavily and made me what I am now."

William looked at the card, gripped it, and stared straight ahead. *Maybe I'll pay Mr. Chia a visit to see what he has to say about Raymond,* he thought.

William had other reasons to be in Sandakan. He had built strong ties with the small but vocal unions around there, and he enjoyed cultivating his relationships with the powerful barter traders who had extensive businesses ongoing between the town and the southern Philippines. William occasionally had lunches with big-time construction companies, who were pleased to entertain him.

However, William unintentionally had developed a strained relationship with the timber industrialists. Most of them were plunderers who had no respect for the environment, and their greed had resulted in forest destruction and the endangerment of many animal species in the Borneo jungle. These people had no qualms about encouraging corruption among the poorly paid government officers. Some of those who resisted the temptation and tried to carry out the law were being threatened and even murdered. As usual, these heinous crimes were either resolved with a token compensation or deliberately forgotten, as if the victims had never existed in the world.

This time, William had reason to meet one of the hundreds of them with a different intention and purpose—not to discuss the environment, timber, or corruption but to discuss Raymond.

After meeting with some teachers and farmers' union leaders, William went back to his hotel room and called Mr. Chia at his office. He put the receiver in between his chin and shoulder and held the business card in one hand. The phone rang many times. Finally, Mr. Chia's secretary answered. She told William that her boss could be located at his factory—not at Mile 32 but at Mile 48. William sighed.

Forty-eight miles from town! William thought. *Is it worth going? What the heck? I'll just get a cab and solve the problem once and for all.* William wrote down the address the secretary gave him and called a taxi.

At his destination, William slowly opened the car door. "Wait for me no matter how long it takes," he instructed the driver, who gave William a nod. William entered the factory. A cloud of sawdust was floating around, and the high-pitched sound of saws cutting the timber was deafening. It echoed all around. The workers seemed to be immune to it.

William approached an employee. "Hello. My name is William. I'm looking for Mr. Chia."

The worker didn't say a word but pointed to a location not far from where they were standing. William thanked him and move toward another worker, who was manning a huge machine. Beside him was Mr. Chia.

"Hello. Are you Mr. Chia?"

"What? What did you say?" the man said, putting his right hand on his right ear.

"Are you Mr. Chia?"

"Sorry! I cannot here you!" He pointed at the machine and shook his head. Then he pointed to a room not far away. He asked William to follow him. William agreed. They walked quickly and entered the room, and Mr. Chia closed the door.

"Now it is better. What did you say just now?"

William brushed off the dust from his clothes. There was dust everywhere on his body, especially in his hair. Using his hands, he rubbed the sawdust from his head.

"My name is William. I am looking for Mr. Chia. How can I see him?"

"I am Mr. Chia."

William stared at him. "In that case, I've found him."

Mr. Chia sat on the table and asked William to sit down in a chair nearby. William sat down. He was still attempting to clean his hair.

"So, Mr. William, what is it you want from me? I hope you are not a salesman. I will throw you out immediately."

"No, Mr. Chia, I'm not a salesman. Actually, I've come to talk about your former partner, Raymond."

Mr. Chia kept quiet. He turned away from William and proceeded to a cupboard full of files. "Raymond? He is okay. His father is a very good man."

"I'm not talking about his father. I want to know something about him."

"There is nothing to know about him. He is a good man and hardworking and, as I said, just like his father." Flipping through the files, Mr. Chia did not look at William.

William felt that his journey had been a waste. He was about to go home empty-handed. He slowly stood up and began to walk away.

"Wait a second! Wait a second! Why do you ask me about Raymond? Is he your friend?"

William stopped at the door, turned around, and faced Mr. Chia. "Yes, he is my friend. And he used to be my best friend."

"Sit down. Please sit down. He was not my partner. He never was. I know he told everyone that, but believe me, he was just my employee. I was doing his father a favor because his father is a good man. When he worked with me, no doubt he was hardworking and intelligent and full of initiative." Mr. Chia took a deep breath and continued. "But later, what he did to me was terrible. He pretended to deliver my wood to Jesselton, saying that he had a buyer who was paying a very good price. So I let him handle the marketing. It turned out he sold these products in cash and pocketed the money. He started buying beautiful cars and gold chains for his wife and spent lavishly, staying in hotels for months with his family."

William leaned forward.

Chia dropped his chin to his chest. "I lost a few hundred thousand dollars trusting him. If not for his father, I would drag him to prison."

"What about his fish business?"

"I heard he went around in Semporna, the biggest source of fish in Borneo, and convinced the fishermen there that he would help to get a better price than what the Chinese middlemen were offering and that he would buy all their products lock, stock, and barrel. But he needed to be given on consignment. He sold the fish first and promised to pay later. In the end, he sold all the fish at a very low price back to the middlemen and pocketed the money that was supposed to be paid to those poor fishermen. That is what I heard. It was the news of the town several months ago."

William thought about what he'd said. He stood up and shook hands with Mr. Chia. "Thank you, sir. You have been a great help to me."

Back at his apartment, William thought about how to confront Raymond. The case involving Ramlan was the most serious for William. Then there were the trouble at the farm and the so-called freak accident involving Jafar.

If he confronted Raymond directly, it would affect his relationship with Theresa. If he did not confront him, Raymond would be like a cancerous cell within the healthy body of a sound and stable business entity.

The next day, William went to his father's home and had a long discussion about Raymond. He apologized to his father and accepted his mistake of thinking wrongly of him. His father accepted his apology but assured William that it was not his fault, because no one could anticipate such a thing, especially from his best friend. William asked his father's opinion regarding how to face Raymond and ask him to quit. His father advised William not to rush. His father promised to arrange a good time to remove Raymond while making sure no blame would fall on anybody, especially William.

"The past few months, the farm has been doing very badly. The farm prices are spiraling downward, and many of the workers are getting redundant. They know about the situation, and so does Raymond. Everybody knows it is a matter of time before somebody will be retrenched, and nobody will blame anybody for it. That's a good opportunity to sack him without getting the blame."

"Are you sure it's going to be okay, Dad?"

"Absolutely. I am positive about it. I met Raymond at the farm a few days ago. He told me that the farm is facing overcapacity both in production and manpower. He is a smart guy, Will. But for a different purpose."

Chapter 42

Aaron Johnson had been spending time with Sam since their reunion months ago. Aaron had declined the job Sam offered. He'd told him that he was not in the right spirit to work. However, he always accompanied Sam to his factory, and at least twice a week, they would spend time at the pub, drinking and talking.

Aaron had had no problems with his life ever since he met Maria at the restaurant. He'd found a new, recently built three-room apartment not far from town, and his former security employer had paid for it despite Aaron's objection. He still received a pension from the British government for his outstanding service in the 1960s, and he still had part of his gratuity that the plantation firm had awarded him.

The only thing bugging him was that he missed his children, and he also missed Elaine. The loneliness was affecting him. To kill time, he would hang around in Sam's office, but Sam spent a lot of his time overseas, marketing his furniture.

Aaron would walk around the town; climb up the nearby hills, as he used to; and watch the orangutan at the Sepilok Rehabilitation Center. He also traveled to the nearby islands, especially the turtle island of Selingan, where he watched the eggs hatch and observed the baby turtles instinctively rushing to the sea to survive. However, he had done all these things a dozen times.

"Maria, would you like to go out with me tonight?"

"To the same old place, Aaron?"

"No! Some place different. This time, it will be a surprise."

"As usual, surprises." Maria smiled.

"Would you, Maria?"

"Yes, I'd love to."

Aaron asked Maria to dress in her finest dinner gown. Aaron now had access to Sam's vehicles and could use any of them at any time. For the first time in years, Aaron dressed well to fetch Maria. She was waiting outside her quarters. Maria noticed that her female employer was watching her from the window of her house. Maria ignored her curiosity.

Aaron climbed out of the car and rushed to open the door for Maria. Maria laughed at Aaron's action. Now the male employer joined his wife in watching Maria and Aaron as they drove off to the surprise Aaron had promised her.

"Why are they looking at you, Maria?" Aaron asked, as he too had noticed them looking from the window. "They seem very unhappy. But they can't stop you, because it's after working hours."

"I don't know, Aaron. But they are busybodies. Maybe they don't like the idea that a maid like me is taken out by a handsome white man like you. Who knows? Maybe the wife is jealous because you didn't take her out."

"Do you think I'm handsome?"

"There are thousands of ladies who would be in line waiting for your response, Aaron. They'd all line up, and at the end of the line, the last girl at the edge would fall down into the sea and die!" Both of them burst into laughter. "Where are you taking me?"

"Just wait. In a few more minutes, we will be there."

"I can't wait any longer," Maria said in a slow, sexy tone. Aaron looked at her and smiled. They stared at each other for a while. Aaron liked to look at her light brown eyes.

Aaron stopped in front of the Renaissance Hotel, the only five-star hotel in Sandakan. It was a resort hotel catering to tourists who wanted to watch the orangutans and proboscis monkeys, monkeys only found on the island of Borneo.

Aaron parked the car and got out to open the door for Maria. Then, slowly, they walked toward the lobby. Maria held Aaron tightly, for she had never been brought to a place so exclusive. Aaron tapped her hand, which was clutching his arm, and stopped near the entrance.

There were tourists all around. Most of them wore casual clothes, and Maria felt out of place. However, none of the people noticed or watch them. She felt slight relief. They walked toward the swimming pool, where a buffet of Italian food was served. In an isolated corner was a table with candlelight, a bottle of champagne, and Filipino entertainers—a singer and a guitarist. They were waiting for Aaron and Maria.

Maria felt delighted, and she enjoyed the dinner and the music. She watched Aaron munch the final bits of food on his plate. Maria noticed that some of the tourists were sitting by the pool close to them. They too were enjoying the music, which was supposed to be exclusively for Aaron and Maria. However, Aaron and Maria didn't mind their company.

"Ask them to play any music you like, Maria. Go ahead! They can play anything under the sun."

Maria looked at the singer, spoke Tagalog to them, and smiled. "Can you play the song 'Anak'?"

The singer smiled. "Sure, ma'am! It has been quite a long time since anyone has requested such a song. Okay, here goes." It was a beautiful song, and the entertainers sang brilliantly. Maria closed her eyes to enjoy the music. She was enchanted.

After the song was finished, the other guests applauded loudly, and their numbers swelled around Maria and Aaron. Maria turned around and smiled. She looked at Aaron with heavy eyes. "Thanks, Aaron. This was indeed a surprise. I will never forget it."

As Aaron was driving her back to her quarters, Maria unconsciously put her head on Aaron's shoulder and held his arm. She closed her eyes, and she felt that the moment was too short. She hated the idea of going back. She wanted Aaron to take her round and round indefinitely.

When Aaron parked the car in front of her home, she said, "Don't bother, Aaron. Please." Aaron was about to get out to open her door again. Maria kept holding his arm. "Can't we go around town once more?"

"It's getting late, Maria. You have a job to do early tomorrow."

"I don't feel like sleeping."

"Don't worry, Maria. I'll fetch you tomorrow again."

Maria looked at Aaron. "Are you sure?"

Aaron nodded. "I am positively sure."

Maria opened her door, closed it, and walked toward her quarters. She turned around and saw Aaron still looking at her. Reaching the front door, she turned one more time and waved at Aaron. Aaron smiled and drove away.

That night, Aaron thought about Maria. He too had enjoyed the evening at the hotel, and for once, he had no feeling of loneliness. He felt satisfied with the surprise he had given to Maria. He closed his eyes and slept on the sofa.

Chapter 43

WILLIAM'S FATHER WAS WRONG. David Stewart met Raymond at the farm and told him that the business situation was getting worse. Revenue was declining rapidly, and there seemed to be overproduction, including manpower. Mr. Stewart told Raymond that he had no choice but to retrench him and several others. At the farm, Raymond accepted those facts.

Back in the city, Raymond was angry that he'd been laid off. He said nasty things about the Stewarts, including William, who was not spared Raymond's criticism. Raymond told the fellow workers who'd been retrenched that William and his father didn't like him and had conspired against him. They didn't like the workers, he said, and only wanted to exploit them for their own benefit.

Without a job, Raymond spent most of his time with former classmates, neighbors, and acquaintances he met at the pub or in hotel lobbies. Raymond bragged about saving the Stewart farm when it was almost going bust and claimed that after business had progressed because of him, the Stewarts had decided to throw him out.

"William and his father did that?" a former classmate asked in surprise.

"Of course! These people are ungrateful bastards! They only want to exploit people. Those poor workers were squeezed until they were dried up!"

One night, in a small, secluded karaoke lounge just outside the city limits, Raymond was drinking with one of his neighbors, a Korean restaurant owner. For any acquaintance, Raymond was a pleasant guy with an enjoyable personality to hang around with.

Raymond also managed to mesmerize people with his convincing arguments. He always had incredible stories to tell, especially about his tragedies in life, his business failures, and, most of all, his uncensored version of his sex life. He bragged about how many women he had made love to, the positions he favored, the types of girls he enjoyed most, and where the best prostitute den in town was.

"Have you tried anal sex?" he asked Mr. Pak Jee Mon. The Korean shook his head. Both of them drank beer. At the same time, they were enjoying the music in the background. "That's the best sexual act I have ever encountered."

"Really?" The Korean became interested.

"But it's the most disgusting act I have ever encountered too! After having fun, you have to immediately clean up. It was full of shit!"

Mr. Pak closed his eyes firmly, disgusted. Then they laughed uncontrollably.

"Once, I made love to a young prostitute. She had to be hospitalized for two months!" Raymond said.

Mr. Pak again shook his head. "How can you be so cruel?" he said with remorse.

"Well, my Korean friend, variety is the spice of life!"

"Didn't they arrest you for that?"

"It happens in Sandakan. Once a month, the chief of police and immigration will have a go with all the prostitutes in town. Of course, they are taken care of by the pimps. So they made a pledge not to harass or arrest either the customers or the girls."

The Korean nodded, indicating he understood. "So, Mr. Raymond, what do you intend to do with your life?"

"I don't know, Pak. I have such bad karma. I always have bad luck."

"How would you like to work with me at the Korean restaurant?"

"You mean that? But I have such bad luck, and your business will go bust."

"I have faith in you, brother! I want you to show this David and William that you can be a better person under good care. Am I correct?" Mr. Pak said, and Raymond nodded. "I want you to show them that oppressed people like you deserve a happy ending. You know, Mr. Raymond, when I think about those people who mistreated you, I get angry. If these things happened in Korea, I would send gangsters after them to kill them and throw them in the junkyard!" Suddenly, he was mumbling in Korean. "You begin tomorrow, Mr. Raymond. Work with me."

Mr. Pak, out of sympathy, as he liked Raymond, offered him a free room in his house, free food for him and his family, transportation, and generous pay of $1,000. Raymond's duty was to be his assistant at the restaurant.

It was a good job. His wife nagged at him, though. She reminded him that she could not tolerate any more moving around like nomads. This time, she wanted to stay put. She had witnessed many unhappy endings in Raymond's career, and she knew their cause. She had never blamed anybody for Raymond's failures, including the Stewarts. She had learned years ago that no matter how convincing her husband's argument was, it was always a lie.

For the first several months, Raymond worked with dedication. He woke up early in the morning to buy seafood and vegetables and get things organized at the restaurant. He drove Mr. Pak around and accompanied him to the bank. He was so involved that the staff thought Raymond was Mr. Pak's new partner.

At home, Raymond's wife cleaned up the house, washed the dishes and the clothes, and beautified the garden. For Mr. Pak, Raymond was the best employee. Raymond's wife also helped out at the restaurant, and Mr. Pak didn't hesitate to pay an extra five hundred dollars a month to Cecelia.

While Raymond was sitting in the garden after work one day, he saw Mrs. Pak quietly leave the house. She saw Raymond, smiled at him, and moved on. Raymond smiled back. He shook his head and thought to himself, *she must be a crazy woman, smiling for no reason.*

Raymond continued smoking and enjoying the night's coolness.

Chapter 44

WILLIAM WAS NERVOUS. THERESA had called him and asked to see him. She'd said it was urgent. Why would Theresa want to see him urgently? William thought maybe Theresa wanted to confront him about the sacking of Raymond. How could he face her?

Theresa had requested he meet her in the Palace Hotel lobby. William waited there, cracking his fingers over and over again. Suddenly, he saw Theresa walking toward him, and he tried to clear his dry throat.

Theresa sat down in front of him. She kept quiet for a while, and William couldn't tolerate her silence. He noticed she was trying to say something, but the words seemingly wouldn't come out of her mouth. *Raymond has put both of us in an awkward position,* he thought to himself.

A receptionist rushed to Theresa, bringing a document. Theresa browsed through it and put it on the table. She checked it carefully, took out her pen, and signed it. Raymond's fingers couldn't crack anymore, so he put his hands in his pockets. The receptionist left.

"Will, I need to ask you something," she said slowly.

Here it comes, William thought. Still, Theresa could not find the words, or maybe she'd found them but couldn't say them out loud. Finally, she spoke.

"Can I borrow some money from you, Will? I'm very embarrassed to ask you this; it's just for a few days. Once I get my pay—"

William raised his hand, asking Theresa to say no more. He was relieved, and Theresa's request felt like an obligation to him.

"Theresa, you know I will do anything for you. How much do you need?"

Theresa could not say anything more. Tears rolled down her cheeks, and she wiped them. She pressed her legs together and put her hands in her lap. "I have to settle my debts. I haven't paid my rent for three months. In fact, coming up on four months in a few more days." She took a deep breath. "If it's possible, I'd like to borrow six hundred dollars."

"How much is your rent per month, if you don't mind telling me?"

"Seven hundred. But I do have eight hundred bucks with me now. It will be enough to pay two months first and the other month maybe at the end of next month." She inhaled some more air and expanded her chest. "I'm really embarrassed! Please forgive me!"

"Come on, Theresa. There is nothing to be shy about. I will help you. Don't worry."

"You will?" Theresa wiped her remaining tears and tried to smile. Her eyes were red. William took out his checkbook and scribbled on it.

"Thanks, Will! I'll make an effort to pay you back."

"Please, Theresa. You don't have to pay me back. I'm helping you willingly. I'm expecting nothing in return." He signed the check and passed it to Theresa. Theresa took the check but was still too shy to look at it. William put the checkbook away, tucking it in his pocket. William looked around. More people were coming and filling up the hotel lobby's seats. Slowly, Theresa peeped at the figure written on the check. She was shocked.

"Twenty-four hundred? No, Will! No! I can't!" She attempted to give him back the check. "I only want to borrow six hundred."

William held her hand and pressed it against the valuable paper she clutched. "Please take it, Theresa. I just want to help you."

Theresa pulled her hand back and looked at what she was holding. "Thank you, Will. Thanks!" Her tears began rolling again.

Chapter 45

RAYMOND HAD HEARD THAT William was a high-profile person. He had strong connections everywhere and was building stronger relationships with the businesspeople. Occasionally, William appeared in the press, sometimes making a headline. Jealousy flowed with his rushing blood inside his veins when he learned that William flew to Kuala Lumpur every month. It seemed William lived a lifestyle of the rich and famous—William, the person he used to call a lamebrain, birdbrain, and dumb asshole.

Raymond became restless and frustrated. What did he have? He was stuck working at the Korean restaurant with a pitiful $1,000 pay. It seemed that he was working like a slave, waking up at five in the morning and going home at eleven every night. He had no days off, including Sundays, when he was needed the most. Too busy with his work, he was losing touch with his friends and had no time for entertainment, except with the boring Mr. Pak.

Mr. Pak had enviously kept Raymond to himself. He was without a friend in his life, and he thought Raymond was an ideal person to be with, though he was not gay. He expected Raymond to be grateful to him, and he was sure Raymond was feeling indebted.

Raymond began calculating his potential future compared to William's. The Korean restaurant attracted a lot of customers, and it seemed it would continue to exist successfully for the next ten to fifteen years. His life was stable—too stable. It was becoming routine and boring. While he was stuck with his stationary occupation,

William would be climbing higher and higher. Three years from now, William would be beyond his reach.

The more Raymond thought and compared himself to William, the more impatient he became. Every night, Raymond couldn't sleep until one o'clock in the morning. He was smoking five packs of cigarettes daily. *Son of a bitch!* he thought to himself.

One day, as Raymond was manning the counter, a group of businessmen entered. Raymond and Mr. Pak escorted them in, and Mr. Pak knew that a fat profit for today was possible. There were twelve of them. As they were sitting down, a man smartly dressed came in and joined the group.

It was William. Raymond suddenly felt as if his feet were stuck to the ground. William saw Raymond. He immediately rose from his seat and went to greet him. Raymond pretended not to see him.

"Hi, Ray! It's good to see you. I've been looking all over for you. Even your sister doesn't seem to know where you are."

"Hello, Will! I've been looking for you too," Raymond said, pretending to sort out some invoices and put them back in the drawer. "Boy, it's good to see you, Will."

"Are you working here?"

"Actually"—Raymond motioned for William to come closer— "I'm his partner now."

"Good for you, Ray!" William looked around. "And business is good, I see. You will be rich soon, Ray!"

"Who are these people?" Raymond asked.

"Who? Them?" William turned his head. "Oh, they are a consortium of contractors, mostly road builders and electricians. There are proposing to build seventy miles of new highway running from the north to the south. At the same time, they want to propose underground cables parallel to the highway."

"Why are you with them?"

"They have the experts and financial strengths, and I do the presentations." William turned to walk away. "Good to see you, Ray. We should get together once in a while."

Raymond watched William join the high-flying corporate figures. Mr. Pak approached Raymond. "Who is that?"

Raymond's eyes narrowed. "That, Mr. Pak, is William Stewart."

The Korean turned toward Raymond. "The one who sacked you?"

"Not so loud!"

Mr. Pak turned toward William and then faced Raymond again. "Sorry! But he doesn't look too bad. Anyway, we cannot judge a book by its cover."

Raymond smiled, but his blood was boiling. *Yes, Mr. Pak. Don't judge a book by its cover!* he thought to himself.

Since that time, William became a frequent customer of the restaurant. He brought all sorts of people—businessmen, politicians, environmentalists, and other NGOs—and they liked the restaurant. Mr. Pak began to like William. He had been bringing good business to his restaurant. His bank account was getting fatter as William introduced other contacts and dined with them there.

"You know, Ray, when I thanked William for what he has done for us, he told me not to thank him. He said he is doing it for you! You see, you don't have bad karma after all. Maybe William is just trying to clear his guilty conscience. Maybe he is making up for his sin to you."

Raymond kept quiet. *William is probably just trying to show off. He probably is challenging me,* Raymond thought. Raymond noticed his boss was laughing.

"Ray, I am too tired to go to the bank every morning. Why don't you help me out? I want you to bank the money for me, starting from today onward. I also want you to hold my savings account."

"With pleasure, sir. I'll do the best for you and your company. Trust me."

For the next six months, Raymond deposited the cash sales without failure. The account was beautifully flowing, and Mr. Pak's personal bankbook was getting fatter. Raymond patiently watched it grow. When he first gained access to Mr. Pak's personal account, it contained only $25,620.22. Now it had grown to almost $100,000.

As he walked toward the bank one day, Raymond felt his knees getting weaker. He cleared his throat almost nine times before stepping into the building. He watched the customers sitting down with numbers, waiting for their turn. An officer spotted him and called him into his office.

As he entered the room, the officer asked him to sit down. Raymond looked around and then faced him. The man looked familiar, but Raymond did not want to think about it. He wanted to carry out his job.

"Do you remember me, Mr. Johnson?"

Raymond shook his head.

"Your father is the one who recommended me to work in this bank. He and my father were good friends. My name is Norman Liew."

Raymond still didn't know who he was.

"I saw you come in with a Korean owner the other day. Remember? But I didn't have the time to talk to you. Is he your employer?"

"Employer? No! He is my partner!" Raymond said, pretending to be annoyed.

"Sorry, Mr. Johnson. So sorry! Anyway, what brings you here?"

"I come to the bank almost every day. Haven't you noticed?"

Norman thought, holding his chin. "Oh yes! I'm quite busy lately. I am so sorry not to notice you."

"Actually, there is something I want to discuss with the bank. I'm lucky to meet you."

Raymond explained at length that business was getting slow and bad. There weren't enough cash sales, and he showed Norman that today's income was a meager $200 instead of the usual daily deposit of $3,000 or more. Raymond elaborated that his partner had issued a lot of postdated checks, and there wasn't any money left in the current account. He consulted with Norman to draw the money from the savings account to cover the shortfall in the business account. Raymond held his breath as Norman explored the reasoning.

"Why doesn't he come personally?"

"He is much too busy."

Norman said, "I'll call him. I don't mean not to trust you, but it's the bank procedure. I think I have his number. Ah yes! Here it is."

Raymond felt a chill run down his spine. He felt as if he were about to urinate on himself. His legs and hands were trembling. "My God! What have I done?" he whispered to himself as he bent down.

"Mr. Pak? Ah! This is Norman from Public Bank. I just want to check out a few details."

Raymond slid down in his chair, waiting for the world to collapse around him.

"Is Raymond handling your account? I mean, did you give him permission?" Before he could finish, Raymond could hear Mr. Pak screaming in the telephone receiver. "Okay, Mr. Pak! If you say so!"

Norman looked at Raymond. Raymond dared not look at him. Raymond pretended to write something on the banking slip. "Mr. Pak says he has entrusted you to handle his account. So I guess everything is okay."

"*What?*" Raymond said, thinking aloud, and he felt sudden relief in his body. He was surprised. For a moment, he'd thought he could end up without a job or, worse, jailed for years for breach of trust, which was a crime according to Malaysian law.

"How much do you want to deposit to the current account?"

"Make it two thousand three hundred dollars."

"From his savings account, right?"

Raymond nodded.

"Okay, Ray! You can go wait at the counter. I'll inform them what to do."

As Raymond walked out of the bank, he couldn't believe his luck. He'd escaped a seemingly impossible situation.

He realized that Mr. Pak must have cut Norman off because he thought Norman was only asking whether Raymond was authorized to deposit the money. *What a damn lucky one!*

From that day onward, Raymond was keen in depositing money to Mr. Pak's account—but only a quarter of the daily deposit at a time.

Every day, Raymond pocketed the balance and managed to get the bank to transfer the shortfall from Mr. Pak's savings account.

Raymond bought jewelry for his wife, purchased new clothing for himself and his family, and deposited money to buy a brand-new Honda Civic. With his new toy, he took some time off to pick William up and take him out for dinner at his own expense.

"My time has come, Will! Cheers for prosperity!" Raymond had brought William to one of the most expensive restaurants in town. They toasted together.

"Congratulations, Ray! You are fantastic."

"It takes a brilliant mind to be successful, Will."

Chapter 46

AFTER BEING JILTED, THERESA felt she could no longer stand the pressure of continuing with life. She felt betrayed and used, and she had no one to turn to but William. The man she loved still worked with her at the same hotel. She saw him every day, she knew his footsteps, and she knew he was seeing another girl, a waitress working in the hotel lounge.

The man did not want to have anything to do with Theresa anymore, not even as a friend. Now she was back to being just his subordinate, and it was compulsory for her to follow orders. That was how the man who'd once promised her happiness treated her.

She smoked, got drunk, and took ecstasy. She used marijuana and skipped work more and more. She wanted to forget about life, her career, and love. She spent her time mostly alone in the park, at the pub, and at home. With friends and colleagues, she was temperamental, and a small mistake could cause her to scream at the top of her voice. Theresa's mild attitude was gone.

William watched with sadness as Theresa fell to pieces. Once in a while, he discussed the matter with Raymond, when Raymond came to pick him up and go somewhere. William noticed that Raymond didn't seem disturbed by his sister's problems and didn't want to be bothered.

"Who is it?" Theresa was startled by the knock on her front door one day.

"It's me—William. Can I come in?"

"What do you want?"

"I just want to talk to you."

"There's nothing to talk about," Theresa said as she put her chin on her knee.

William scratched his head. He thought for a while and slowly withdrew from the door. As he was walking away, the door opened a little. William turned around and saw Theresa looking through the opening. William slowly turned back toward her. He put his hands in his pockets. "How are you, Theresa?"

"Not fine!" Theresa reluctantly let him in. "You are not working today?" she asked, looking away from William. She was standing next to the dining room wall, resting her fragile body.

"I took the day off," William answered.

"Sit down," Theresa said, and she leaped into a chair. William slowly sat next to her. She was wearing a tight T-shirt and shorts. William couldn't help noticing her beautiful thighs, and she wore no bra. Her tired green eyes made her seductive. However, William was sure she was not in the right mood for romance. William and Theresa kept quiet for a while.

"Theresa, I would like to propose something to you."

"It's not the time to talk about proposals, Will! I'm not in the right state of mind."

"Theresa, I know I should not interfere in your life—"

Theresa jumped up and headed for her room. "Then don't! Don't interfere!" She was in her room for a moment and then came out covering herself with a jumper. She sat in the chair she'd left a moment ago.

"Why don't we go for a holiday?" William said. "All expenses paid. I managed to get some free tickets and a hotel for six nights in Singapore."

Theresa brushed her hair away from her eyes. She remained quiet. She smiled at last.

***

Singapore meant "city of the lion." According to legend, a prince named Paramaswera saw a lion emerge from the jungle as he was exploring the island. Singapore eventually became the hub of the Asian trade center. Its strategic location allowed it to become one of the biggest ports in the world. Singapore was also one of the world's biggest financial centers. As a city-state, it did a lot to beautify the country to attract tourists. It could be considered a modern version of the Hanging Gardens of Babylon because of the massive landscaping project. Free of crime, it was the cleanest city in the world. These were among the reasons for William to bring Theresa there for a holiday. William knew his way around because he'd graduated from the university there.

William checked in at the Goodward Park Hotel, located close to an attractive boulevard in the city, Orchard Road. It had taken some time for him to convince Theresa to come on a holiday. William asked her if it was all right to have only one room with one big bed. She didn't say yes, but neither did she say no. So he got only one room.

Theresa had never been outside Malaysia, and the beauty of Singapore fascinated her. William noticed that she seemed to have forgotten her problems. It was a good sign, and William was happy about it.

While he dealt with the receptionist, Theresa walked around the lobby. The hotel was built in the early 1900s, and it brought back a nostalgic image of the British Empire. William filled out the forms and signed them, and the hotel charged the payment to his credit card.

Theresa kept quiet throughout the day. In the hotel room, every time he approached her or tried to be close to her, she would move away, keeping her distance from him. Most of the time, keeping tight lips, she would stand by the window, looking at the busy street below.

William pretended to watch television while sitting on the bed. The CNN live news coverage of the bloody civil war in Sierra Leone didn't matter to him, as it usually did.

Theresa moved away from the window and walked toward the wardrobe. She took out black jeans and a light blue blouse and went to the bathroom. In ten minutes' time, she came out wearing them and slid her feet into her shoes.

"I'm going for a walk. The street looks exciting," she told William.

William jumped off the bed and straightened his body. "Great! I'll join you."

"Alone, Will. I want to go out alone."

"I don't mind accompanying you. I don't want to be alone by myself. We can sit together at the street café. Wouldn't that be nice?"

"Are you deaf, Will? I said I want to go out alone!" She slightly bent her body and tilted her head a little. Her temper was volcanic. Before William could say anything, she walked out of the room and slammed the door in his face. William stood still, shocked and disappointed.

"I love you, Theresa," he murmured quietly. He slowly walked toward the window and stood there. A few moments later, he saw her walking on the street. "She is there. I am here. What did I do to make her so mad?"

I love you, Theresa. The words played silently in his mind while he fixed his eyes on Theresa in the distance. William noticed that Theresa slowed down, stopped, and turned back, looking up toward him. Then she quickened her pace and walked away until she disappeared among the crowd.

***

It was twelve o'clock at night. William woke up from his interrupted sleep. He was in between light sleep and slumber, and every hour, he automatically opened his eyes to see whether Theresa had come back. She hadn't.

Then there was a knock at the door. William felt relieved. He jumped up and rushed toward it. When he opened it, Theresa was standing there with another man—a tall, handsome Caucasian. She was hugging him.

"Will, meet Julian. Julian, this is William Stewart."

Julian offered his hand to William. William just looked at him straight in the eyes. Julian realized something was not right and pulled back his hand.

How many times must she hurt you? Humiliate you? William could feel his soul speaking to him deep in his heart.

"Julian is a friend I met in the hotel back home. At that time, he was a tourist looking for his cousin," she said, smiling. Julian smiled. William could no longer hide his feelings. His torment was written all over his face.

"Cousin? What cousin?" Julian asked in surprise. "Isn't the orangutan your cousin? That's why you pay so much to see them?" They laughed. William was not prepared to share their sense of humor.

"Julian is currently attached to the Simon Andersen Consultancy here in Singapore. It deals with venture capitalism."

"I'm impressed! Very impressed!" Finally, William managed to speak with sarcasm, but his voice was filled with emotion. Theresa walked into the room and packed her belongings in a bag while Julian and William stood watching her.

"Where are you going, Theresa?" William asked with a depressed voice.

"I'm staying with Julian. He has a big condo apartment at Woodland. He will be taking me around. Won't you, Julian?"

Julian nodded with a smile.

"Thanks for bringing me to Singapore, Will. I appreciate that. I think I'm much better now. I'm forgetting him!"

When they left, William felt devastated. He stared at the closed door. He tilted his head upward and cried.

Chapter 47

RAYMOND COULDN'T HIDE HIS newfound wealth. For one thing, he was too cocky to keep it quiet. Everybody noticed his new lifestyle. The Korean was getting worried about Raymond's achievement. He was worried that Raymond might leave him to focus on whatever else he was doing.

However, Raymond strongly assured him that he would not abandon him. He would stand by him, help him out with the business, and continue to be his only companion on the misty, humid, and isolated island of Borneo. He would work extra hard for Mr. Pak. Mr. Pak was so delighted with Raymond's reassurance that he increased his pay another five hundred dollars.

Raymond told everybody that he had recently invested a small amount of money sent by his father on an illegal gambling syndicate. It was a fruitful venture, and Raymond was now reaping the gains. Everybody believed him and thought he was smart.

Some of his friends wanted to join in, but Raymond informed them that since the company was dealing in illegal activities, they wanted to have as few shareholders as possible. With luck, Raymond was one of them.

Raymond even got himself a driver. The man was a former employee of the Stewart family farm. He was one of the sacked workers who seemed to be dedicating his loyalty to Raymond. His name was Mamat. He was the one who'd carried out Raymond's schemes to make the workers hate Mr. Stewart and Jafar. Wherever Raymond went, Mamat would be there with him as his driver cum bodyguard.

While Raymond was instructing the workers to sort out the vegetables at the restaurant, a call came in from the bank. It was Norman. After the call, Raymond replaced the telephone receiver and thought deeply. Norman had asked him to come to the bank because an urgent situation had just cropped up.

"Anything wrong?" Mr. Pak asked Raymond.

Raymond shook his head. "Everything is fine!" he assured his boss.

Mr. Pak kept staring at him. He had just returned from Seoul from a holiday. He had not been to his hometown for nearly two years, and he'd spent sixteen weeks there while trusting Raymond to handle his business. "I sense you are having a problem. Are you okay?"

"Don't worry, Mr. Pak. I am more than okay!"

Raymond rushed to the bank, as he always did, hoping for a good result in his favor. However, this time, he sensed that something was wrong. Norman wanted him in his office before eleven in the morning. Raymond usually had an attitude that enabled him to ignore the future as if the present would last forever, but now the future was breathing down his neck, and he couldn't ignore it anymore.

"Please sit down, Raymond."

Raymond pulled the chair out with his nervous hand. As he sat down, hope was deceiving him that this problem could automatically be solved one way or another. Norman looked at the computer in front of him. Raymond rubbed his nose vigorously with his right hand. He always did that when he was tense.

"Wait for a minute, Mr. Johnson. I want to check things out with the clerk for a while."

Raymond nodded. He also felt restless because he could not smoke in the bank.

Norman came back and sat down. He again checked his computer, caressing his throat. Raymond was hoping for a miracle. He hoped that things would be fine and that he could go back to work as usual.

"Mr. Johnson, Mr. Pak has issued several checks. However, there aren't sufficient funds left in the current account. Can you inform him and top up the balance? It's only nineteen thousand and seven hundred dollars—more or less, as I have rounded the figures, and I think it should be more than enough."

"What about money from his savings account?" Raymond asked impatiently.

"Let me check the account first. Oh, I don't think that is possible."

"Why not?" Raymond started to bite his fingernails.

"The account has only five hundred dollars and thirty cents left. You have been requesting to transfer money all the time to cover the shortfall, remember? Wow! Business is so bad that he had to use his personal money." Norman stared at the computer while talking to Raymond.

"No problem, Norman." Raymond said after thinking for a while. "I'll inform Mr. Pak about this. He can rectify the problem. There is no time to waste." Raymond stood up and walked toward the door.

"Mr. Johnson! Money must be in before three o'clock. Otherwise, I can't help you."

Raymond looked at Norman. "I understand," he said in a low voice.

Raymond rushed outside the bank and stopped for a while. His mind was murky, and he couldn't think properly. People passing by noticed him stammering meaningless words. He walked round and round in the parking lot near his car.

"William! William! He could help me out! Yes. He could!"

Raymond looked at his three-thousand-dollar gold-plated watch. He had only five hours left.

When he pushed open the door to William's workplace, Moses held his chest, shocked. Raymond walked straight toward William's office, but Moses stopped him.

"You are a very rude man! I cannot tolerate rude people!"

"I cannot tolerate people like you, you son of a bitch!"

Moses, despite his weakling appearance, pushed Raymond hard, and Raymond fell backward a few steps. Raymond rushed forward and was about to hit Moses, when suddenly, William came out.

"What's all this commotion?"

"This man just busted in!" Moses panted. William slowly tapped his shoulder and whispered to him, and Moses quieted down. In twenty seconds, Moses walked away. William looked at Raymond, who seemed annoyed and worried.

"Come in, Ray!"

Raymond clenched his fists as he watched Moses, who was still looking at him. He slowly released his grip and followed William into his office. There were three people inside. William whispered something to them, and they nodded and left the room. William pointed to the sofa, and both of them sat down.

"I can't help you with that amount, Ray!" William responded after hearing Raymond's whole story. This time, Raymond had told the truth. "Why did you do such things? There'll be a severe criminal case against you if Mr. Pak finds out and decides to lodge a police report. If it's a few thousand, maybe I can help."

"I believe you have the money, Will! You're so successful. Please! I'm begging you!"

"Nineteen thousand is a hell of a lot of money, Ray! I can't afford it."

Raymond slowly stood up and walked away. William watched Raymond leave. William was tempted to help out, but as he pondered what Raymond had done to him, including the slander he'd brought against him and his father, William decided there must be a limit to helping out. However, deep inside his heart, he pitied Raymond and his family, and he wondered why he had done such a stupid thing. However, he also pitied the Korean, the victim of Raymond's foolishness. Most of all, he pitied Norman, the bank officer. Clouds of uncertainty were hovering over him.

Mr. Pak was watching Raymond. Raymond was driving the company's van today, but he was staring straight ahead without speaking. Mr. Pak was sitting next to him, and they were heading home after a busy day.

"Very quiet today, Raymond. I sense that you have a big problem. You didn't tell the truth this morning when you said everything is okay. Surely something big is bothering you." Raymond remained quiet.

"You know, Raymond, if you have problem, you must learn to share it, especially with a friend like me. Is it about your family? Or maybe William and his father are being nasty to you again? Please tell me, Ray. I want to help."

Raymond held his breath and then said, "I have a very big problem, Mr. Pak."

"Please share your problem with me. I am more than willing to help you. Just tell me."

Raymond inhaled deeply again. "I used up all your money! I never bank enough money from the cash sales, and I used your savings account to cover up any shortfalls."

Both Mr. Pak and Raymond kept quiet as if nothing had happened. Both seemed relaxed and cool and kept their thoughts to themselves. Raymond felt a sense of fear and relief. He was relieved because he had told everything to Mr. Pak. However, the Korean's face was red and almost black despite his silence. It said everything.

When they got home, Mr. Pak went straight to his room without greeting the children and Cecelia, as he usually did. Cecelia was puzzled when Mr. Pak passed her as if she didn't exist. The children rushed to him, expecting some gift from him. This time, there were no gifts.

Raymond took off his clothes to cool his flabby body; he was sweating profusely. He sat down and took the last cigarette from his sixth pack of the day. Cecelia approached him.

"What happened? Why is he in a nasty mood?"

Raymond kept quiet.

"Is there any problem with him?"

Still, Raymond didn't utter a single word.

Suddenly, they heard loud noises coming from Mr. Pak's room, including things being smashed, thudding, kicking, and screaming. Cecelia panicked, rushed to her two kids, and held them tightly. They were trembling, as they had never seen or heard Mr. Pak angry. Raymond continued smoking, pretending to ignore the commotion.

Mr. Pak kicked open his door, screamed in Korean, and walked quickly to his van. After he started the engine, the vehicle suddenly jerked forward and smashed into a shoe cupboard in front of it. Mr. Pak ignored the accident and reversed at top speed. Raymond continued to remain calm. Cecelia was terrified. She quickly took the children to their room.

A moment later, she approached Raymond. She stared at him with her hands on her hips. "Mr. Pak has been very good to us. What happened now?" Cecelia said, demanding an explanation.

"You want a life of luxury!" Raymond broke his silence and screamed back at Cecelia.

Cecelia shook her head in disbelief. "Are you blaming me? You mean to say you are blaming me?" she barked. Raymond didn't answer her. He walked away from Cecelia and went outside.

Using his cell phone, Raymond called William.

"Will, can I meet up with you now? It's very important!" Raymond rushed into his house, got dressed, rushed back to his car, and drove away. Cecelia came out of her room to catch up with Raymond, but he was already gone.

Raymond and William met at a McDonald's not far from where Raymond worked. Raymond told him again why he was in trouble now. William continued to listen. This time, his story was more detailed.

"I need your help, Will!"

"I told you, Ray! I don't have that kind of money."

"No! No! This is not about money. This is about my wife and children. I have a feeling deep inside me that I'm going to jail, maybe for a long time. I want you to look after them. Can you do that for me, Will?"

"I don't know, Ray." William thought about this funny request.

William watched him smoke nonstop. It was a marathon. If there had been a *Guinness Book of World Records* title for chain-smoking, Raymond could easily have won it. He smoked practically one stick per minute. Raymond was on his way to the ninth pack.

"Why did you do it, Ray?"

Raymond flipped his cigarette and dropped the ashes onto the floor. It was supposed to be a nonsmoking area, but Raymond ignored the rule. "Do what?" he said, pretending not to understand William's question.

"Why did you take his money? You must have known that one way or another, the problem would catch up to you."

"Who asked him to be dumb? He volunteered to trust me. I didn't ask for it. He is the one who gave me the responsibility of looking after his account. 'Raymond, do this! Raymond, do that! Raymond, bank the money for me! Raymond, look after my account!'"

William shook his head in disbelief.

"Why do you do that?" Raymond asked, feeling insulted.

"Do what?" William asked.

"Why did you shake your head?"

William moved his body backward a little. He noticed that the crowd around them was not happy with Raymond smoking. The smoke was congesting the stale air-conditioned air.

"Ray, I'm very sad that I cannot help you with the money," William said. However, in reality, William thought it was unbelievable that Raymond could be so ungrateful to Mr. Pak. That was why he had shaken his head.

"Can you look after my family if I go to prison?"

William looked at Raymond. One of the other customers approached them. "Can you please not smoke? It's affecting us," the man said.

"Fuck off, you asshole! I don't care if all of you have cancer!" Raymond shouted at the top of his voice. Everybody inside was silent. The man stared at Raymond, and Raymond stood up and stared back at him.

William quickly pulled the man away from their table and begged him not to retaliate. He convinced the man that Raymond was under tremendous pressure and promised he and Raymond would be leaving soon. The man slowly retreated back to his seat. William sat back down. "Come. Let's go somewhere where nobody can disturb your smoking, Ray."

They went to an open stall not far from William's office. William assured Raymond that nothing would happen to him if he just trusted God and apologized to Mr. Pak. Raymond said he didn't believe in God, nor did he want to apologize.

"In that case, Ray, I will try to look after your family if anything happens to you."

***

The next day, Mr. Pak woke up early. He was prepared to lodge a police report against Raymond. He compiled all the available documents, and he would be going to the bank to get more details. His heart was burning with fury, and there was no mercy stored in his memory. As he walked outside, Raymond children's ran to greet him.

"Good morning, Uncle Korea!" they called out.

He pretended not to hear them. Then, suddenly, his feet became heavy, his anger cooled down, and he stopped. When the kids reached him, they held his hands tightly.

"Uncle Korea, will you be buying us some toys today? Last night, you didn't get us toys," the boy said.

Mr. Pak's anger was gone. He held them tightly.

"Uncle Korea, why are you crying?" asked the girl. Mr. Pak wiped his tears. Now there was extreme sadness in him.

Cecelia approached them. She caught up with the children and slowly pulled them away from Mr. Pak. "Uncle Korea is a busy man. He has work to do."

Chapter 48

WILLIAM WAS TOO DISTRACTED to think about his work or about Raymond's problem. He was facing a bigger problem. William rushed to the office and asked Moses to arrange for an immediate flight to Kuala Lumpur.

"You aren't supposed to be in Kuala Lumpur until the end of this month. Besides, you have ten important appointments to handle today," Moses reminded William.

"Just do it, Moses! Ask Ramon and Ramlan to handle them! I want to fly now!"

Later, William slowly walked toward Theresa at Kuala Lumpur's Subang International Airport. She was going away—for good. She had quit her job and intended to immigrate to Australia.

"Don't leave me, Theresa. Please tell me you are not going."

"I'm going, Will. There is nothing to stop me."

"I love you, Theresa! I want to marry you!"

Theresa smiled and held William's face. A few female companions accompanied her. They watched Theresa discuss with William, but they kept their distance, for they knew it was a private matter.

"Theresa, I should not be saying this, but I gave you all of my attention and all the support. When you are down, I am the one who consoles you. I'm the person you can express your feelings to, no matter how hurtful it is to me. I even helped you with your rent, remember?"

"I didn't ask you to give me that money, Will! Did I? I only wanted to borrow a small sum, but you insisted on giving me the money. Who asked you to be an idiot?" Theresa put her left hand on William's shoulder. Her right hand was squeezing William's cheek. "I'll tell you what, Will." She wiped the tears rolling down William's face. "You will forget me once I'm gone. I cannot love you, Will. I just feel that you are like my younger brother."

There was an announcement about the flight for Sydney, Australia. Theresa turned away from William and joined the girls. William had a hunch that Theresa was joining Julian in Australia.

"What a fool I was to take her to Singapore!" he cried aloud to himself.

Theresa shook hands with and hugged the girls. She looked at William from a distance and waved at him. William's heart sank as if it were the *Titanic* as he saw Theresa walk toward the departure hall. She turned around and waved one more time. William watched her wait at the immigration checkpoint, and finally, he could not see her anymore.

William found a spot to sit down. The world had collapsed. He was in no mood to work anymore or even to continue living. *What's the point? Life is meaningless without Theresa!* William closed his eyes, cried silently, and held his head in his hands. He refused to notice anything surrounding him, and he didn't care what people thought of him.

"Uncle William?" a voice said.

He ignored the voice.

"Uncle William?" The voice persisted. "Uncle William, do you remember me?"

William slowly raised his face. His hands were still holding his head. It was a girl, one of the few who'd sent off Theresa. She wore a light green blouse that was soothing to the eyes.

Her hair was light brown, her eyes were light blue, and her skin was slightly tan. A few tiny freckles spotted her cheeks, and like Theresa, she had a sharp nose. She resembled Theresa but was much younger. She had Caucasian features with an Asian frame. She held her hands together in front of her stomach as she waited for William to respond.

William's eyes were still blurred because of the heavy tears, but the tears were starting to dry up. He rubbed his eyes to clear his vision but still couldn't see properly.

"Theresa!" He stood up slowly, and he could hear her laughing. William smiled a little, hoping Theresa had changed her mind and returned to him. William's vision became clearer. It was not Theresa.

"Don't you remember me? You took care of me once at a party my brothers and sisters organized. Remember?"

William slowly shook his head. "No. I don't remember you, I'm afraid."

The young girl bent a little. "Look into my eyes! Maybe that will remind you."

William again shook his head. He thought for a while. His memory still didn't serve him well. He rubbed his remaining tears and looked at her one more time. "But you look like Theresa."

"Do I?" She stepped a bit closer to him.

The distant past suddenly hit William like a rock. He looked up again. The girl he thought he knew smiled at him. It was a smile with a thousand meanings. He was speechless. At last, he sighed. "Susan! Is that you?"

"It's me, Uncle William!" She moved closer again and put out her right hand. William took it, and they shook hands. William was still saddened by Theresa's departure and was still in no mood to talk to anybody. However, it consoled him a bit that Susan was there representing her sister. While he shook hands with Susan, William contemplated following Theresa and immigrating to Australia. But after a while, William realized that would be a waste of time, as he knew Theresa well.

"Are you okay, Uncle William?"

William kept quiet. Again, he sighed. "How old are you, Susan?"

"Eighteen and coming to nineteen in a few weeks' time."

"What are you doing here?"

Susan looked around. "Sending my sister!"

William took out his handkerchief and wiped his face. "I mean in Kuala Lumpur."

"Oh! I am studying to be an architect. I study at the University of Malaya. I will be graduating in two years' time." She smiled. "I hope!"

William remained silent. He loosened his tie and took off his coat. "It was a pleasure to meet you, Susan. I'm very happy indeed! But I'm in a bit of a hurry to go back to work. I hope you don't mind if I make the move. I can ask the taxi to take you back."

"It's okay, Uncle. I'll be following them." She pointed to the other girls, Theresa's friends who had sent her off. They were waiting impatiently for Susan. "By the way, Uncle William, here is my number if you want to contact me, just in case."

Susan scribbled her number on a piece of paper and handed it to William.

"You already have a cell phone at such a young age?"

Susan looked at William. "Dad bought me the phone so he could contact me every week. He is afraid I might get lost in this big city. It is not for other purposes."

William put up his hand immediately. "No, no, Susan. Don't get me wrong. It was just a question."

"Don't worry, Uncle William! Don't be so sensitive! I've got to go now. Feel free to contact me anytime. Bye!" The girls were signaling to Susan to be quick. Susan walked slowly, turned back, smiled at William, and then joined the girls.

Back in his hotel room, William thought about Theresa. He thought again of joining her in Australia. But again, he knew that Theresa would not accept him. In fact, Theresa would not appreciate him coming all the way from Malaysia to follow her. It would interrupt her relationship with Julian, if it was him she was going after. She would be mad at him. Even if Theresa accepted him and recognized his devotion in seeking her out in a distant country, he would forever be at her mercy. She would continue to hurt his feelings, and what would stop her from going out with another man? He had to find some sort of distraction. He would work harder or maybe get involved with politics again just to forget Theresa.

William spent three nights alone at the Star Bug Outlets at the Bintang Walk. He watched people moving in the streets. There were many tourists among the local shoppers there. It was a shopping paradise on par with Orchard Road in Singapore. William sipped his bitter coffee without sugar. He felt helpless and hopelessly devoted to love. He stayed up all night with his fifth cup.

For two midnights, he stopped over at the pub and drank heavily. In the morning, he became sick and threw up whatever he ate. He went to the doctor, and the doctor advised him to rest. However, the problem persisted. He still could not forget Theresa.

As William was sitting in his room, watching TV, he received a call. He ignored it and continued watching. The ringing stopped. Then the phone rang again. William continued to ignore it. Then everything turned quiet. William felt relaxed, but the wounds in his heart hurt. Suddenly, the phone rang again, and William jumped up and grabbed it.

"Andy! For heaven's sake, stop calling me! I am in no mood to talk, okay?"

There was a giggle on the other end.

"Hello?" William cooled down his tone. "Who is this?"

"It's me—Susan. I just felt like calling you."

"How do you know where I'm staying?"

"We exchanged phone numbers at the airport, remember? You gave me your business card. I called your office back in Jesselton. Moses was so kind to give me your hotel."

"What do you want, Susan?"

"I've never been around KL. I am all the time stuck on my university compound. I was wondering if you could take me around, Uncle William."

William thought for a while. "I'm sorry, Susan, but I've got no time to take anybody around. I've got so much work to do, and I have so many things on my mind."

"That's okay, Uncle. I understand. Good-bye."

"Good night, Susan."

William held the telephone close to his chest. He thought for a while. Maybe he could talk with Susan about Theresa. Maybe she could reveal more secrets that would unlock a way for him to get close to her sister. He called Susan back and told her he would fetch her tomorrow morning and would show her around.

It was early in the morning on Friday, and Susan was happy that William had taken the trouble to show her around. They went to Cameron Highland and Fraser Hill, which resembled places in temperate England. On Saturday, William took her to the National Zoo, and they visited the Hindu temple at Batu Cave close by. It was the most enjoyable day of her life.

However, she could not stand that William kept talking about Theresa. It bored her. Susan knew that William was trying to find out information from her, but she pretended to enjoy his conversation about Theresa.

William took Susan out for a candlelight dinner that evening. Everyone in the restaurant could see a mismatch. William was well dressed in a coat and tie, as if he were handling a BOD meeting, while Susan was in a T-shirt, jeans, and sporting shoes, as if she'd just come from a college library.

Susan had never been to such an exclusive place, and she enjoyed the food. William told her that he never drank wine, but for this special occasion, he was willing to partake along with Susan. He advised her that the wine was only meant to make the food tasty. It was not supposed to be a habit.

After sipping their last drink, they looked at each other. Both smiled. Susan took out a single beautiful rose from the vase on the table and sniffed at it. William watched in amazement. Susan noticed that William was about to speak, and she knew it would be about Theresa. She quickly put her hand on his mouth. She then sat back. William nodded and smiled. On the way back to her campus, Susan looked at William and then kissed him on the lips. William was too surprised to respond. Susan pulled back and smiled. "Fetch me tomorrow morning at six."

Susan's gesture shocked William. But one thing was for sure: it totally blocked Theresa from his mind—at least for now. Back at his hotel room, William could not wait for tomorrow. Suddenly, he had a deep fear that Susan was pulling his leg, just as Theresa had done to him.

The next morning, William woke up early and rushed to pick up Susan. She was already waiting. After she got in the car, she pulled William close and kissed him. This time, William responded.

"I like you, Uncle William."

"Please don't call me Uncle, Susan. It sounds weird!"

"Okay. Can I call you Will?" She looked at him.

"Better!" he replied.

William took Susan for a simple breakfast at a stall in Pudu not far from a church. This time, William didn't talk about Theresa. This time, all his questions were about Susan. Susan also talked a lot about her father. William noticed she had high regard for him. She had promised her father that she would graduate to make him proud. William watched Susan as she kept looking at the church.

"Come on, Will. Let's pray together there. It's been a long time since I've prayed."

"How do I pray there? I've never prayed in a church. Besides, I am a Muslim."

"I am a Buddhist. What's the problem with that?"

William looked at Susan and moved his head back a little. He smiled. "Okay. I will accompany you there and sit with you."

After he paid for the food, Susan grabbed his hand, and they quickly stood up and left. As they walked, Susan stopped and hugged William tightly. William responded, ignoring the passersby.

Chapter 49

WILLIAM SPENT ALMOST TWO weeks instead of two days in Kuala Lumpur. Moses scolded William from home. Under pressure, that was how Moses usually reacted, and William had come to accept that.

"It seems I am the boss here! Why am I worrying so much, while you are there? I don't know what for! I'm just your employee, Mr. Stewart. Many of the people here are jumping up and down trying to meet you, and I am the punching bag for their frustrations."

"Moses, that is why I hired you—because I can count on you. I promise you that in a few more days, I'll be back. Please give me a break just this time."

Moses continued screaming on the other end. William put down the phone and laughed about it.

At the hotel compound, William reluctantly let Susan go as she dragged her feet. Tonight they had to part. William informed her that he had to go back to Jesselton but would be back in Kuala Lumpur before the end of the month. Susan blew a kiss to him. William was petrified and happy.

"Good morning, gentlemen!" William said the next day. "Isn't today a very beautiful day? And I hope all of us are itching to work!" William smiled. "Let's go to the conference room."

"What happened to him?" Moses whispered to Ramlan. "He was always moody and gloomy. What a change!"

William was energetic with his work. Both Ramon and Ramlan briefed him on the developments of their jobs, while Moses read out the schedules. After the briefing marathon, William held his face in his hands, rubbed it, and stretched his arms.

William took great interest in a particular environmental group. The group was small but vocal. They did not hesitate to condemn the government openly through both the local media and the foreign press. The government accused them of being opposition tools and anti-development. Often, they were accused of being subversive agents planted by foreign elements who wanted to re-colonize Southeast Asia. William instructed Moses to fix an appointment with the group and make it a high priority. He wanted to meet them that afternoon.

"You have meetings with the manufacturers this afternoon. I've prioritized that, for heaven's sake, boss!"

"Moses, next time, I will follow your priority. But this afternoon, please!"

William met the group at the Hyatt Hotel. Frederick Chong, the president of the environmental association; his secretary, Maniam; and Bonus Yap, the treasurer, represented them. William took them to an exclusive room where the hotel served gourmet French cuisine.

"When I was young, after it rained, my house would be swarmed by millions of frogs, big and small. It was like a plague of Egypt," Frederick told William. "Nowadays, I have to search thoroughly, leaving no stone unturned, just to find a few small frogs. It's a catastrophe, Will!"

"That's because the government didn't stop the developers from clearing and filling the wetlands," Maniam added.

"To them, wetlands are wastelands. These areas are turned into real estate developments. How many local and endemic species, which might be unique and endangered, will be lost forever due to the damage they create?" Frederick said. "They cut timber as if it were grass, especially those businessmen coming from the neighboring Sarawak states. They have exhausted the resources in their place, and now they come here and plunder this state. The rivers are polluted, the plains are flooded, and the weather patterns are changing, all because of these greedy bastards!"

William thought for a while. *There is sense in what they are saying, and I totally agree with them,* he thought. He took out his notebook and jotted notes on their grievances. After a while, he closed the book and turned toward Frederick.

"Gentlemen, this is a sensitive matter that we are discussing. I'm not promising anything, because you are such a minority. The government can overlook you. The best thing I can do is write reports sympathetic to your cause. Be patient."

Chapter 50

M R. PAK LEFT MALAYSIA and went back to his hometown of Seoul. He sold off his restaurant and his van at a loss to another South Korean businessman. He went back penniless and for good. He divorced his wife because he'd found out Raymond had made love to her.

Mr. Pak didn't take action against Raymond. He didn't lodge a police report and didn't demand Raymond pay him back. He chose not to because he loved Raymond's kids and didn't want anything to happen to them, especially if Raymond went to prison.

Raymond didn't feel guilty about what he had done. In fact, he felt relieved that Mr. Pak had left him alone. At least he'd succeeded in having a grand lifestyle for several months before he was caught. It didn't bother his conscience that Norman had been kicked out of the bank and was now unemployed with a bad record because Mr. Pak had complained to the bank manager about the incident. To Raymond, that was Norman's problem. And it didn't bother him a bit that Mrs. Pak was now single. Raymond believed he had done nothing wrong, because Mrs. Pak was the one who had come looking for him.

Mr. Pak had given up renting the house, and Raymond had to look for another place to stay. He sold off his Honda and his wife's jewelry and moved into a small house not far from where they used to stay.

"Papa, why don't we stay with Uncle Korea? His house is big, and this house is very small," one of the kids said to Raymond.

"Papa, last time, we had color TV. Why don't we have it now?" asked the other one.

Raymond squatted down and held his children. "Uncle Korea is just going away for a short while. He will be back soon, and then we can go back to the big house with color TV." His children smiled and ran outside to play.

"Why do you lie to the kids? Why don't you tell them the truth?" Cecelia sneered at Raymond as she smoked. This trouble was unbearable. She had given up smoking a few years ago because she'd wanted to start a new life.

Raymond ignored her and walked away. Cecelia went after him, pulled his shirt from behind, and forced him to face her. Cecelia looked into Raymond's eyes. Anger was burning inside her, and Raymond dared not look at her.

"Why, Raymond? Why?"

"I did it so that I could give you and the kids a life of luxury," Raymond answered.

"Luxury?" Cecelia shook her head in disbelief. "You know, Ray, before I met you, I had my own car. I had so much jewelry that I couldn't keep track if something got lost. I had many beautiful clothes, and I had thirty thousand bucks in my savings account. What do I have now after marrying you?"

"That's why I'm trying my best to get everything for you."

"By becoming a hustler? You are nothing but a hustler!"

Raymond scratched his head. Cecelia was now crying. Raymond slowly walked away and drove off. Raymond went to a public phone and called William. William told him that he would be free at eleven o'clock that night and could meet Raymond at the basketball court next to Raymond's new home.

"Make it eleven forty-five. I'll be there," William said.

"Okay, Will. I will be waiting for you."

***

"How long have you been waiting for me?" William asked.

"Since eight o'clock."

"My God! That is long."

"It's okay. The game finished at ten thirty. I spent time watching the basketball match."

William joined Raymond and sat next to him.

"Are you gay? Sitting so close to me?"

"Sorry, Ray." William sat a little bit farther away. "Will this do?"

As usual, Raymond discussed his problems. He told William that he was running out of money fast and asked William if he could give him some sort of loan.

"How much do you need this time?"

"You said that if it was one or two thousand bucks, that would be no problem, remember?"

"What do you need the money for?"

Raymond kept silent for a few seconds. "I need to start a new life in Kuala Lumpur," he suddenly answered.

William thought for a while and then gave Raymond a nod. "Okay, Ray, I can give you two thousand, and you don't have to pay me back." William was expecting some sort of gesture of gratitude from Raymond, but Raymond seems unmoved. He seemed to take the offer as if it were an obligation on William's part to help him out.

"When can you give me the money? Can I have it tomorrow morning before nine?"

"Come to my office then," William responded.

Chapter 51

AARON JOHNSON MADE A point to call Susan every month. Sometimes he even contacted her three times a week. Aaron missed Susan very much. To him, she was the only one with a promising future. After all, Susan was the only one among her brothers and sisters who'd ended up in a university. Aaron had heard that Theresa had moved to Australia. Susan had told him about it after she left. Aaron was disappointed Theresa hadn't informed him of her intention so that he could send her off.

As for Linda, Aaron had heard she was living in Brunei. She had a boyfriend who happened to be member of the royal family. Once in a while, Linda managed to write Aaron a letter and inform him about her well-being. Aaron heard rumors that Linda had become one of the man's several concubines, but he dared not think further about it. He hoped the rumors were wrong.

As for Devin and Raymond, he had not heard about them, nor about Cecelia and his two grandchildren. He was totally in the dark, which made him worried, especially for the two innocent young kids.

Aaron drank his beer and dwelled on his children's and grandchildren's futures. He sat on the couch, watching the rainy day outside his apartment. His somber mood was darkened by the monsoon lashing at the concrete surrounding him. The deafening thunder didn't bother Aaron. He didn't switch on any lights, and his mind was far from calm. Suddenly, Aaron's cell phone rang. He picked it up and listened without saying hello.

"Daddy! It's me—Susan!"

Aaron felt suddenly rejuvenated. He jumped up and switched on the light to brighten the room. "Hello, my butterfly! How's Daddy's little girl doing there?"

"I'm very okay, Dad. How about you?"

"Never felt better hearing your voice, Susan, my little angel."

"You are not telling the truth, Daddy. I can hear from your voice. You can't hide from me, remember?"

Aaron cleared his throat. "I'm all right. Okay, maybe a little bit sad. That's all."

"About what, Daddy?"

"Your siblings and your mother."

"Say no more, Daddy. I'll finish my studies as fast as I can, and then we will be together."

"No, sweetheart! That won't be right. Your husband will throw me out!"

"He is okay, Daddy! He—" Suddenly, Susan stopped.

Aaron was not happy with what he'd heard. "What did you intend to say, Susan? Can you complete those sentences for me?"

Susan kept quiet.

"You have a husband?" Aaron said.

"No, Daddy! Absolutely not! I don't want you to add some burden on yourself just because I made a slip of my tongue. What I'm saying is I'm in love with someone, Daddy."

Aaron kept quiet. He shook his head, praying that no bad news would overcome him. "Susan, dear, don't you think you are too young to have a lover? It will affect your studies. Can't you start loving someone after you graduate?"

"He is okay! I promise you."

"I know this is your first encounter with love, sweetheart. I know how you feel. But it will affect your education."

Susan kept quiet.

"Honey!" Aaron tried to get her talking.

"He is not around in Kuala Lumpur all the time, Daddy. He only spends a few days here once a month. Besides, when he visited me, he took me to meet his architect friends. They gave me a lot of new experiences, Daddy. He is involved with my studies."

Aaron felt a little bit relieved at his daughter's new revelation, but he was still worried for her. "Who is the man?"

"William Stewart. Have you heard of him before?"

Aaron thought for a while. "Oh yes! He is your brother's friend, isn't he? Don't you think he is a bit too old for you?"

"Wasn't Mummy too young for you when you married her?" Susan laughed.

Susan assured him that William was a decent man who operated a consultant firm in Jesselton. Susan went on trying to convince her father, and after a while, Aaron felt partly reassured.

"Good-bye, sweetheart!"

"Good-bye, Daddy!"

Aaron sat down and pondered what Susan had just said. *Susan is big enough to look after herself. Oh God, please protect her from harm,* Aaron prayed.

As Aaron was sitting, he heard three knocks on the door. "Maria, is that you?" Aaron cried out.

"Yes! It's me."

Aaron quickly ran to the door and opened it. There was Maria, soaking wet. She was slightly shivering. Aaron quickly pulled her inside.

"Say no more, Maria. Go right to the bathroom and get yourself a hot bath. There are plenty of towels; you know where to get them."

Maria tried to smile, but her shivering prevented her from doing so. She quickly went into the bathroom and closed the door. Aaron smiled cunningly. He watched the bathroom door without moving. Half an hour later, Maria opened the door a little bit and peeped outside. She saw Aaron standing there. Maria giggled.

"Aaron, I've forgotten to take the towel! Can you help me get one?"

Aaron laughed. "Why should I?" he answered.

Maria closed the door and waited. Five minutes later, she yelled from inside, "Aaron! Did you get the towel for me?" There was no answer. "Aaron, this is not funny anymore! I want to go out!"

Again, it was quiet. Maria slowly opened the door and saw towels on the floor a few feet away from her. Aaron was nowhere in sight. She quickly rushed out and then rushed back into the bathroom. A few minutes later, she came out dry wearing only two towels, one covering her hair and one covering her naked body.

Maria looked around and didn't see Aaron. She moved out a little bit and then saw him standing on the balcony, watching the storm subsiding. She walked toward Aaron and stood next to him. Aaron didn't say a word.

"Why are you outside, Al?"

"Why do you call me Al? That is not my name."

"Well, I heard Sam call you Al, and I thought it was nice, so I call you Al too."

"Must you follow people, Maria?"

"I can't think of a better nickname than Al."

Aaron smiled and shook his head. Then he looked toward the horizon. They watched the storm subside, but it was still raining and thunderous. Aaron looked at Maria and pulled her closer to him. Then he looked back at the storm.

"Look at the storm, Maria. For several hours, it was as fierce as ever, with darkness in every corner. But then, after some time, it was all over. Look at the sun's rays shining through the black clouds. It's just like life, Maria. For years, you can have darkness in your life. Then the time comes when you see hope."

Aaron turned toward Maria. He watched her carefully, admiring her. He took her hands and held them tightly. He pulled her closer, took off the towel on her head, and let loose her wet hair. Slowly, he moved closer to her and finally kissed her. Maria felt shocked and wonderful as she responded. She too held him.

Chapter 52

For weeks, Raymond and Cecelia were involved in a heated argument about whether to go to Kuala Lumpur or not. Both were adamant, and both wanted their way. Their children watched and cried as their parents battled it out. Finally, they came to the conclusion that they had to separate. Cecelia decided to go back to Sandakan, while Raymond would pursue his dream of building a business empire in West Malaysia. The two kids were to follow their mother, and Raymond agreed.

After selling everything he had except his clothes, Raymond managed to raise $4,000, including the $2,000 he'd received from William. He gave Cecelia $2,500 and kept the balance for his one-way ticket to Kuala Lumpur and any contingencies that might arise.

By now, every one of his friends had heard what Raymond had done to the Korean. Raymond decided to keep his departure a secret. The only person he told was William. Raymond asked William to send him off, and William did.

"I'll never come back to North Borneo. This place is a shithole!" Raymond checked his ticket to make sure of the flight schedule. He watched the many passengers hanging around the departure entrance hall. "You know, Will, Kuala Lumpur has a big population. I could make tons of money even by operating a hawker stall. I'll be successful this time. You'll see!"

William smiled at Raymond's words, but he was not concentrating on Raymond, because he was too busy noticing satisfied Japanese tourists saying farewell to their tour guides.

William called over one of the tour guides. He told William the tourists loved this place and would be returning again with more friends. The Japanese liked the highest mountain in Southeast Asia, Mount Kinabalu, and they also liked scuba diving around Sipadan Island, near the border with Indonesia.

"It's one of the best diving spots in the world. Two hundred different tourists from all over the world come to this island every day," the tour guide told William.

"Remember to remind your boss that the Tourist Association has an appointment with me tonight," William told him.

"Don't worry, Mr. Stewart. I'll remind him," he answered, and he moved back to the crowd of Japanese.

"You know those people?" Raymond asked while he smoked.

"I know most people, Ray. It's my business, remember?"

"Yeah. Your business." Raymond inhaled deeply and puffed smoke out.

Then the announcement came for the flight to Kuala Lumpur. Raymond put out his cigarette, took out his boarding pass, and lifted his bags. He approached William, and they shook hands.

"Remember what I told you. I will only return as a multimillionaire." Raymond looked into William's eyes.

"Millionaire in Indonesian rupiah?" William joked.

Raymond grinned. "No, Will! Millionaire in US dollars or British pounds!"

"So what about Cecelia?"

"If I make it, she'll come back to me begging! You'll see."

Raymond released William's hand and moved toward the crowd of passengers lining up for the security clearance. William continued watching him until he moved to the immigration counter.

William's cell phone rang. He picked it up. "Yes, Moses? What is it this time?"

"Don't forget, Will, that you have an appointment with the Tour Association tonight."

"Don't worry, Moses. I remember."

William had had several meetings with environmental groups and the Tour Association for the past three weeks. He traveled with them, looking into potential sceneries to promote, but only saw rainforest devastated by illegal logging. He dived with the professionals to see the waste created by illegal fish bombing. He pondered the future of the 10 percent of undisturbed natural beauty.

"Will, are you serious? You want to raise this matter? I think those guys in Kuala Lumpur will not like to hear what you're writing," Ramlan said as he looked at William's report. William tapped the conference table with his pen. He thought deeply.

"Why don't we just give them what they want and not create any controversy?" Ramon said, reinforcing Ramlan's argument.

"Guys!" William broke his silence. "Let me do my part. You all will continue the routine activities. After all, we have been performing very well not because of me alone but because of our teamwork. I slacked for months, remember? And you guys delivered and covered my ass."

William's remarks flattered his subordinates. They all smiled. For the first time, William saw Moses smile, but he immediately pretended to yawn and looked serious.

"You guys continue to produce the work they are expecting. I'll focus on these controversial matters, and I'll deal with Andy directly. This is a matter of principle."

Chapter 53

RAYMOND ARRIVED IN KUALA Lumpur with $700 in his pocket. The Kuala Lumpur International Airport was far from the city, and Raymond was unsure whether he had landed at the right place. All around him were thousands of acres of palm oil, and the airport was the only building.

Where the hell is the big town? he thought to himself. *Can this be Kuala Lumpur?*

"Taxi, sir?" A man approached Raymond.

"I would like to go to the city," he answered.

The man twisted his head. "You mean KL?" he asked, and Raymond nodded. "One hundred dollars," the man said.

"A hundred? Why is it so expensive?"

"KL is seventy-miles from here, sir. Everybody charges this rate." The man pretended not to be interested and walked away slowly.

Raymond picked up his bag and followed the man. "Okay then! I'll pay one hundred bucks."

The man directed him to a fleet of ordinary cars that didn't look like taxis. He kept quiet about it and continued to follow. The man led him to a small, dirty old locally made Proton Saga. *Hundred bucks for this?* Raymond thought to himself.

Outside the terminal, a tourist approached one of the airport limousine counters for a trip to the city. The attendant took out a list and smiled at him. "It is fifty dollars to the city, sir."

The tourist looked perplexed. "But those men charge one hundred dollars," he said with amazement.

"Oh, those, sir, are pirate taxis. Do be careful in dealing with them!"

Raymond counted his money when the taxi dropped him off in the center of a busy street in the middle of the city. He shook his head. *Hope this will be enough,* he thought to himself. He walked aimlessly for a few hours, but time didn't affect him, as he was amazed at watching the towering buildings mushrooming all over the place. He enjoyed watching the many people moving around, unconcerned about their surroundings and keeping matters to themselves.

Raymond sat by the sidewalk and watched the cars passing by. There were many Mercedes-Benzes and BMWs. He counted eight Porsches in fifteen minutes. Raymond had seen only one Porsche in his life when he was in North Borneo.

I will own that in two years' time. I promise you, Ray, he told himself.

He began to get worried. He knew no one except Susan, and he knew Susan couldn't help him. Besides, he had lost touch with his father and forgotten Susan's address. It was getting dark. He continued to drag his belongings around. In one of the dark alleys, he saw stairs. Outside was a signboard: Room for Rent. As he walked up, he made every effort to carry his bag, because urine and human excrement covered the steps. Raymond held his breath and walked up as quickly as he could. At the second floor, he saw two youths consuming drugs with syringes. They were too preoccupied with themselves to notice the presence of Raymond. Raymond stopped for a while to take a deep breath. As one of the drug users was about to raise his head and face him, Raymond quickly continued moving upstairs.

Finally, he reached the fourth floor. A fat Chinese man sat at the entrance, watching a small TV set and fanning himself with an old magazine. Raymond approached him and spoke to him politely. He didn't smile.

He continued watching his TV. Raymond waited next to him, still panting heavily. The man looked at Raymond out of the corner of his eye. He stopped fanning himself and tried to stand up with difficulty.

He signaled to Raymond, and Raymond followed him into one of the available rooms. It had only one light bulb, and when lit, it was dim. The windows were broken, and the door lock didn't work properly. It had one small bed with an overused mattress.

The man then showed Raymond the bathroom and kitchen, which were shared with the other four tenants.

"It will cost you one hundred and eighty a month," the man said at last.

"For a lousy room like this?"

"If you don't want it, you can go find another place!" he screamed at Raymond.

Raymond leaned against the wall and thought. "Okay," he finally said. "I'll take the room." He immediately paid the rent in advance and threw his bag inside his room. It was noisy outside, and he couldn't do anything about it. Another menace was the harassment of mosquitoes, and Raymond despaired.

Raymond noticed that all the tenants had small children. This would be a serious nightmare for him in terms of sleeping at night. Sweat covered his body, and he felt hot, but he couldn't take off his clothes. because the marauding insects would feast on him. He just slumped onto the bed and waited for tomorrow.

I have to find a job tomorrow. I have to get out of this hell! Suddenly, Raymond heard a loud bang, followed by the crashing sound of broken glass. He covered himself with the pillow to escape the commotion outside.

Chapter 54

ANDY SUMMONED WILLIAM IMMEDIATELY to Kuala Lumpur. The tone of Andy's voice was not soothing. William went through the documents he had prepared months before and tried to summarize them in his head. He had a feeling that the bombardment of questions would pertain to these reports.

William stayed at the Hilton Hotel not far from where Raymond stayed. However, neither of them knew of the other's presence. In his hotel room, William rehearsed the points over and over again.

There was a knock at the door, and when William opened it, there was Andy with a sour face, as if he had put vinegar all over it. He walked in and went straight to the desk.

"Can you tell me what you are doing?" he immediately said to William.

"Documenting a report, sir," William answered confidently, though he was filled with nervousness.

"Why the talk about the environment? The chairman and the directors don't like this sort of report. Word reached the top man about your activities with the environmental group, and I can assure you, Will, he is not too happy about it."

"Look, Andy, we just can't turn a blind eye to this matter. The concerns are growing among the people, especially among the younger generation."

"Your job is to straighten things up!" Andy screamed. "The documents you submitted spell it out clearly, Will! You are behaving like you are one of them!"

"It's principle, Andy!" William screamed back.

Andy kept quiet. He was shocked that William had fought back. William suddenly realized he'd been rude to Andy, and he softened his tone.

"I agree with you that our firm wants to make money from the government, and we must give them what they like to hear and recommend solutions to problems. Yes, I agree to that. But we must care about our environment. A lot of rotten shit is happening in East Malaysia, Andy! Sometimes I think Bruno Manser had his points and did the right thing to instigate the Penan natives in Sarawak."

"Be sensible, Will!" Andy spoke with a slower and more composed voice. "Soldiers have to be sacrificed in battles. Resources have to be extracted from the earth. We eat meat that we slaughter every day. To animal lovers, that's bad, and they say, 'Those poor animals!' The same goes for the environment. That's the price of development. You can't have a good environment and rapid development for a country at the same time. It's impossible!"

"It's for our future generations, Andy. We are obligated to protect them."

"I say we speak about the present. Let the future look after itself. When the time comes, men will know what to do." Andy pleaded for William to understand.

William sneered at Andy. He walked toward the window and carefully arranged his thoughts. "I work well with you, Andy, because we share a lot of things in common. But regarding the environment, we are poles apart." William paused. "I will continue to fight for this issue until the government sees my point."

Andy shook his head vigorously. "The government will flatten you, Will. They will not hesitate. They will steamroll you. Mark my words." Andy slowly left the hotel room, feeling disappointed.

William started to have doubts about his struggle. He knew that the government would not tolerate dissidence and would not hesitate to use the dreaded Internal Security Act, or ISA, to arrest anybody who criticized them. His fight for justice would be lost and forgotten once he was arrested for raising a sensitive issue like the environment. But somehow, somebody had to fight. William looked at his watch.

I'd better meet Susan! he thought. *Only she will understand my struggle.*

That night, William poured out his problems to Susan. Susan was too raw to understand the real world, but the least she could do was listen to William. William noticed that Susan was not paying serious attention after he'd been bragging for half an hour, and he didn't blame her for being disinterested.

"I have a friend who is a top architect, whom I met in Jesselton during their association gathering." William spoke slowly while writing a point in his notebook. He noticed that Susan's interest was rejuvenated. "He is the best. He is an American graduate with a contemporary American style of architectural thinking."

"I love that, Will! When can we meet him?"

"Unfortunately, he is quite far from KL. We have to travel all the way to Singapore. He has offices everywhere, including here, but he spends most of his time there. Interested?"

Susan stretched her arms and yawned. It was late. Nobody was around in the university's canteen hall, and it was closing.

"I guess not," William said as he stood up and took Susan by her hand.

They walked slowly to the outer limit at which guests were allowed.

Susan kissed William quickly, trying to avoid being noticed, especially by the religious extremists, who were common in the Malaysian universities. William was about to turn around, when Susan called to him. "I love you, Will!"

William smiled and blew her a kiss.

Chapter 55

For days, Raymond had been scouting around to get a job. He made friends easily and told them about his tragedy back home, claiming he was a victim of being cheated. A pimp gave him $300 because he liked Raymond.

Raymond was reading through the newspaper's help-wanted column, when he suddenly saw a small notice board outside a car-rental office: Immediate Vacancy for Office Boy. Raymond walked in. He glanced around and saw several staff members, mostly women. Raymond went straight into the manager's office and sat in front of him. The manager was talking on the phone, and Raymond waited patiently for him to finish. The manager replaced the receiver and looked Raymond up and down.

"How many languages can you speak?" the manager asked with a coarse voice.

"Three. No! I think four. Make it five!"

"Are you trying to pull my leg, man?"

"I can speak English, Malay, Hokkien, Cantonese, and a little bit of Mandarin."

The manager, who was Chinese, tested him. Raymond spoke well in all of the languages, including Mandarin. The manager asked him a few more questions, which Raymond answered with confidence. Finally, he asked about cars. Raymond was employed in less than fifteen minutes.

"How much is my pay, sir?"

The manager put his index finger on his lips. "Oh! I almost forgot. You start with eight hundred basic. However, there is a lot of overtime, and if you are hardworking, you can make a thousand bucks monthly." Raymond smiled.

Raymond worked hard. He took on any task assigned to him. Sometimes he used his own initiative to complete a job, even if it was not his. He didn't complain about an overload of work or any extensive overtime. What better than to avoid going back to his pitiful room?

Occasionally, when a driver protested going on a long-distance assignment, Raymond voluntarily and eagerly offered to replace him. When the general manager or any of the clerical staff were too lazy to go out and buy lunch outside the office, Raymond would take the trouble to help them.

The witty Raymond seemed to be open-minded and have a wide spectrum of knowledge, which made people want to get close to him. His usual modus operandi was to talk about his unfortunate life, and the man he blamed the most was William.

Raymond worked for Million Dynasty Car Rental Service, which was a subsidiary of a larger company called Jade Dragon Holding Company. Jade Dragon had an extensive interest not only in car rentals but also in plantations, property, travel and tourism, construction, and commodity brokerage. Every six months, the company's chairman would call for a gathering at their main headquarters, which was not far from where Raymond worked.

The chairman was a young, bustling Chinese entrepreneur whom they called Mr. Chuan. He was about Raymond's age, and he had become a multimillionaire six years ago through hard work and a stroke of luck. He'd borrowed money from banks and friends to buy a plot of apparently worthless former tin-mining land filled with huge cavities. He'd worked hard with the civil and soil engineers to solve the problem of developing the land.

He'd succeeded, and his 1,300 houses had sold like hotcakes. From there on, he had begun to build his business empire. He was an engineer by profession.

About four hundred staff members were invited to the meeting, and Raymond was one of them. Raymond watched the crowd as they seemed to unconsciously congregate into several groups, each with its own leader. Raymond walked toward the table filled with alcoholic beverages and food. He walked slowly along the table and helped himself to beer and tasty sandwiches.

Raymond couldn't help noticing that the conversations were mostly gossip among the girls and office politics among the men. The girls seemed to take notice of every detail—what dress someone wore, where someone got her earrings, how fat someone was. The men were more interested in power struggles and cliques.

"Mr. Johnson?" someone said.

Raymond turned around. He suddenly put away his beer and his sandwich and immediately cleaned his mouth with his hand.

"Take it easy, Mr. Johnson."

"I'm very sorry, Mr. Chuan. I didn't notice you."

Mr. Chuan patted his back and pulled him away from the busy crowds who were observing them. "Call me Michael. I'm not officially a Christian yet, because I'm still unbaptized. But I like to be called Michael."

"As you wish, Michael. The name fits you a like hand in a glove."

Michael was flattered. He straightened up a little bit and smiled broadly. "I've heard a lot about you, Mr. Johnson."

"Call me Raymond, sir."

Michael again smiled broadly. "Right! Raymond!" Michael helped himself to some cakes on the table.

"I've heard a lot of good things about you. We will be meeting more often, Ray."

Chapter 56

Ramlan, Ramon, and Moses looked solemnly at William. They were sad. For years, they had worked hard together as a team, and none was dispensable. They all needed each other.

William called them all into his office. As they sat, they tried to console themselves in an anticipation of what William had to say. William looked at their faces and nodded gently. He held his breath, inhaled deeply, and released the air in his lungs.

"Guys!" William pretended to be cheerful. "This is not the end of the world. I can still fight another day. The most important thing is that we must continue our struggle in what we believe in. It's no use working for something or someone if you know they are doing the wrong things." William stood up and walked toward the small refrigerator nearby. He took out four cans of Coke and walked back to his table. He opened the cans and gave one to each of them.

"Actually, the boys in KL wanted to close our branch here. But I told them you guys are not involved in what I am doing, so it's unfair to penalize you all just because they are pissed off at me. So basically, they saw my points and decided to retain you boys but sack me."

"We'd rather go along with you," Ramon said.

William smiled. In his heart, he was appreciative of their loyalty. "No, you must not follow me. I want you all to continue working and producing good results. If you are still working here, at least you can feed me some information, especially since one of you will be meeting Andy in KL."

William continued to brief them about the necessity of maintaining the office in Jesselton and insisted that he had to fight for the cause he thought was right from the outside.

"Cheers, boys! May this firm succeed!"

The national election was eight months away, as the term of the Malaysian Parliament would expire within that period. William and the environmentalist group made every attempt to explain to the people the importance of ecological balance and preservation of the flora and fauna of the state, and they also touched on the subject of pollution.

They went from one town to another and from one village to the next and showed the people their reasoning. William and the environmentalist group were not alone. William gained a lot of sympathy from parents, teachers, and students who saw and understood his points.

William made an effort not to directly blame the government, but the authorities insisted otherwise. The government claimed he was an ungrateful renegade and accused him of being greedy. He was subjected to a lot of challenges, including the government trying to make his father's business suffer.

William's father had a one-on-one talk with him about the tremendous implications he had created. He told William that he had four blocks of shop houses the government had rented as a medical department storehouse for the past fifteen years, and the government was threatening to cancel the contract. However, William wouldn't budge from his struggle despite his father's pleas.

The government was not the only source of harassment for William. The timber tycoons also joined the fray of condemning him, and they were more ruthless in executing their attempts to stop him. They employed gangsters and thugs to pressure him and had prostitutes try to seduce William and then blackmail him.

William persevered. Even though only a small section of the public accepted his view, many supported his cause—not because of his principles but because of William himself. The government felt it was a nasty risk to pick a fight with him. However, according to their intelligence reports, William had not made much impact. The public was still not yet aware of the value of the environment, because they were still engrossed in their daily struggles to raise their standard of living.

William was lecturing at a small hotel just twelve minutes' drive from the center of town, when he suddenly got a call from Moses. He requested permission to leave for a while.

"Moses! Wow, it is so good to hear your voice. Just like old times."

"Listen, Will. Andy instructed me to inform you to fly to KL— now. There is a flight scheduled to depart in three and a half hours, and I think you can make it. I'll bring your ticket to the airport and will meet you there."

"Wait a minute, Moses! Why does Andy want to meet me?"

"I don't know."

"If I don't want to go?"

"Please, boss! It won't harm you. The worst that will happen is Andy scolding you. You can scold him back. Please go."

William kept silent, thinking for a while.

"Hello? Boss? Hello? Are you still there?" Moses was desperately trying to maintain contact with William.

"Yes, Moses, I'm still here. Give me time, okay?"

"We have no time, boss. Please."

"All right. By the way, why do you call me boss? I am no longer your boss."

In Kuala Lumpur, William stayed at the same hotel he'd stayed at last time. It had been awhile since he'd been there, and he was getting impatient. He wanted to see Susan. However, he had to face Andy first. He had no idea why Andy had summoned him. *What is it about this time? I wonder.*

William looked at his watch. Andy hadn't arrived, and the passing of time was making William nervous. He walked around his room and then lay on his bed and watched TV. He went to the bathroom for the fourth time in two hours. Finally, the knock came. William let Andy inside. Andy kept silent, which added to the pressure William felt.

"So, Andy, let's not waste time. What do you want from me this time?"

Andy smiled. He flipped a coin in his hand several times and still kept silent. Finally, he said, "The board of directors wants to reinstate you, Will. Good news, isn't it?"

"Are they trying to bribe me, Andy?"

"Jesus Christ! You sure play hardball. Don't you ever give up easily?"

"Is that why I'm here, Andy? If that's the case, I think we are wasting—"

"Hold your horses, little brother! Let me finish what I have to say." Andy put the coin in his trouser pocket and sat down on the bed. He crossed his legs, grabbed the TV remote, and reduced the TV's volume.

"So what is it then?" William became agitated.

"The BOD wants to reinstate you. They will increase your salary and double your bonus. They think you are a fine young man who did a good job for the company." Andy looked around, got up, and switched off the air conditioner. "It's cold!"

Andy sat down again on the bed. "As I was saying, William, the BOD has talked to some top brass in the government, and some of your argument seems to be reasonable—but it doesn't mean that the policy on the environment can be changed to your requirements. Far from it. Nothing works immediately, Will. It takes time. At least you have started the first step, and the ball is rolling uphill. Be pragmatic, Will," Andy pleaded.

Finally, William nodded. He knew that changing the developing country's mentality about the environment was a monumental task. Even advanced countries couldn't deal with the environment effectively.

"Good! I knew I could count on you, Will." Andy rushed toward William and shook his hand. "So we are back in business! All for one and one for all!" Andy suddenly took hold of William's head and rubbed the top of it with his knuckles.

"Ow!" William screamed, but the pain was minimal.

"Another thing, Will." Andy released William from his grip. "The government, through one of its ministries, has decided to create the Environment Action Committee, better known as the EAC. You can recommend two of your friends to sit on this committee. And please be fast about it." Andy opened the door, smiled, and left.

William closed the door and nodded to himself. Andy's proposal was fair. He was back in business. William took off his clothes and rushed to the bathroom. There was cause for celebration, and he would celebrate with Susan.

Chapter 57

Michael liked Raymond's attitude and productivity. Once, in the middle of the night, Michael's pregnant wife craved and demanded durians, which could only be obtained forty-five miles out of town. Raymond volunteered to help and drove all the way to get the custard-looking fruit back to Michael in less than two hours.

Michael also liked to have Raymond as his companion whenever he drove around to monitor his business throughout the Malaysian Peninsula. He even took Raymond to Singapore and, to Raymond's delight, involved them in an orgy with prostitutes working there.

So Michael has weaknesses, Raymond thought as he cuddled the girl in his arms.

Michael took Raymond to one of the subsidiary company's board meetings. It was the first time Raymond had sat with top-level executives. He sat next to Michael and was only a spectator.

Michael was banging on the table and shouting. Everybody was quiet. Michael took out a file and threw it onto the table. Raymond played with his fingers, pretending not to notice. Some of the members of management were not happy with Raymond's presence, for they knew he was only an office boy.

"Five hundred and fifty houses! Only seventy-seven taken up! Are these houses made of straw? Is that why people don't buy them?" Michael sat on his chair and whirled around. That was what he always did when he was angry at a board meeting.

"Mr. Chuan, remember, we told you the location is a bit isolated and out of the way."

Michael suddenly swung forward and stared with burning eyes at his marketing manager. "Are you blaming me?" Michael barked at the top of his voice.

"No, sir," the manager timidly answered.

Michael looked around, but nobody dared to say anything else. Michael cooled down and took a deep breath. "I have waived down-payment deposits and legal fees. We have offered a three-hundred-dollar cash bonus to the first two hundred and fifty buyers, but still, no one is interested."

Raymond raised his head when he heard of the special promotion. He slowly put up his hand. Raymond became nervous, as many eyes looked at him as if piercing his heart. Michael saw him.

"Yes, my friend? What is it you want to say?"

"I am not a member of this board, and I guess this is just some sort of suggestion. Raymond noticed that the glow in the eyes of those present was getting stronger. Their facial expressions were unfriendly.

"Continue," Michael said.

"I have a lot of friends back in the East who would be more than willing to buy these houses. I saw the design, and it is good."

Michael's younger brother, Andrew, who was his second-in-command, rose. "You think it's that easy, Raymond? Like this is some sort of Monopoly game?"

Michael asked his brother to sit down. He looked at everybody else, and they all stared away from Raymond and looked down. Michael faced Raymond. "Why don't you try to help out? Who knows? You might work some sort of miracle."

"I'll try, sir. But I can't promise anything."

"Okay, Ray, I'll get the company to pay for your expenses, including airplane tickets, lodging, and transportation, but please get me results." Michael decided to gamble on Raymond, and Raymond gladly agreed.

Raymond packed his finest clothing and flew with a first-class ticket to Jesselton with a different image. This time, his thinning hair was properly trimmed and kept, and he wore branded polo shirts and trousers and Bailey shoes.

He stayed at Pan Pacific Hotel and waited patiently for William while he dined on the finest food. Raymond had asked William to bring along some friends. While Raymond was enjoying his dinner, William arrived with six of them—five businessmen and one teacher.

"Hello, boys! Please don't hesitate to join," Raymond said.

Everyone was happy and partied together with Raymond, except William. He was not interested in the food. He watched Raymond and saw a changed man.

"I'm one of the partners for a public listed company, Will! We deal in a lot of stuff!" he boasted to William.

"So what is it, Ray? Why did you call us here?"

William observed his friends toasting and enjoying the splendors of Raymond's lifestyle. Raymond sipped some red wine. "I've come all the way here to offer you free houses!" Everybody kept still, and suddenly, all of them burst into laughter.

"I'm not joking. You can have free houses. It's all in West Malaysia, in the town of Bentong, Pahang, at the crossroads of the future East-West Highway."

Raymond sipped some more red wine as he noticed their laughter subside. He cleaned his lips with the white napkin on his lap.

"Free houses, eh?" William asked sarcastically.

"Yeah! Free houses!" Raymond answered.

"Can I have, let's say, two units?"

"Sure, Will! Just fly over, and you'll get two units."

"No! Make it four units!"

"Okay! Four units!"

"Wait a minute, Ray. Maybe I'll take twelve units!"

Raymond threw the napkin onto the table. "Make up your mind! How many do you want? Is that the last count?" No one present could believe his ears. The teacher, Mr. Judge, approached Raymond and patted him on the back.

"I would like eight units," Mr. Judge whispered in Raymond's ear.

Raymond stood up, called the waiter for the bill, and took a final sip of the remaining wine. "I'm real tired now, and I want to sleep. If you are interested, call up the Star Angle Travel Agency. Here is the phone number. They will arrange for you all to fly to KL, and from there, you all will sign the sales and purchase agreement."

***

William and his friends all flew to Kuala Lumpur, and Raymond took them to a tall building where he supposedly worked as a partner. Some of them had never been to Kuala Lumpur, and they marveled at the awesome sight.

They all sat and waited outside the company's legal department, and after twenty minutes, they were all called in. Each of them received a pile of documents to sign. They looked at each other.

"Don't you smell something fishy going on, Will?" Mr. Judge asked William with curiosity and hesitation as he looked through the papers, unable to grasp the contents' true meaning.

William flipped through quickly. He scanned carefully certain passages of the documents. "It looks all right. It is just a standard document. Okay, boys! Free houses! Let's sign!" William told his friends, and they all eagerly scribbled their signatures on the legal papers.

Mr. Judge suddenly stopped and whispered to William. "We haven't seen the houses!"

William pointed toward the paper. "The house is free, Judge! As a teacher, you will not get this opportunity again in your lifetime. If anything goes wrong, we don't lose a single cent!"

So Raymond made an arrangement that William and nine of his friends would get twelve houses each. Within a period of no more than five days, Raymond had sold off 120 units.

Raymond brought William and his friends to a nightclub. William requested permission to leave. "Ray, I have a more urgent and pressing matter to settle. Please continue enjoying with the rest of them. I've got to make a move now."

After William left, Raymond assigned girls to each of William's friends. Mr. Judge was the happiest of them all.

The next morning, Michael heard about Raymond's success. He summoned Raymond to his office, and when Raymond arrived with a hangover still blurring his mind, Michael hugged Raymond tightly. Raymond sat down and slowly produced all the receipts for the money he had spent on transportation, lodging, and entertainment for their clients.

"Well done, my friend!"

"I am doing this all for you, Mike!"

Raymond spent one week resting. With some substantial leftover cash, he traveled to Phuket, Thailand, and enjoyed himself there. He wanted to forget everything for a moment: his miserable home, job, wife, and kids. The beach was beautiful, and the girls were fantastic.

When Raymond returned to work, he received the best news of his life. Michael had promoted him to be the general manager of Rapid Rise Construction, one of Michael's subsidiary companies. Michael gave him a generous salary, a fully furnished four-room bungalow near the worksite, and a four-wheel-drive vehicle.

"Is there anything lacking, Ray?" Michael asked as he leaned back in his big chair.

Raymond thought for a while. "What about entertainment allowances?" Raymond said with confidence.

"Done!" Michael said.

As Raymond walked away from Michael's office, he noticed that Andrew was following him. Raymond quickened his steps, but Andrew was still behind him, catching up. As Raymond raced toward the elevator, Andrew caught his left shoulder and pulled him to a stop.

Slowly, Raymond faced Andrew. Soon two tough-looking shorthaired guys arrived and stood by Andrew's side with their arms crossed. Whoever they were, they weren't friendly. Andrew walked slowly around Raymond. Raymond looked at the floor, pretending not to notice.

"You came from nowhere, and now you are the big boss, eh?"

"I didn't ask for the job, Andrew. It was offered to me."

"You want me to tell Michael what you just said?"

Raymond stood still and shook his head. Andrew kept circling him like a hawk ready to pounce on its prey. "Who are you? Where do you come from? Why are you having problems in East Malaysia?" Andrew asked. These disturbing questions made Raymond jittery.

Did he do a background investigation on me? Raymond thought to himself.

"One thing is for sure: I don't trust you!" Andrew gripped Raymond's collar and pulled him closer to him.

"Oh, come on, Andrew. I've done a good job for your brother, haven't I? Be reasonable." Raymond seemed to be begging him.

"I don't trust you!" Andrew shouted.

"I trust him! I trust him more than you!" Michael screamed. He was standing with his hands on his hips several yards away. Suddenly, the two tough-looking men became timid like wet rats, and they quickly left. Andrew looked at his brother, released his grip on Raymond, and walked away slowly.

Michael walked toward Raymond. He suddenly burst into laughter as he saw the pale face of Raymond. He grabbed Raymond by the neck and pulled him close to the elevator.

"Come! Let's have some brunch together!"

Michael's laughter turned to a smile. The elevator opened up, and they jumped inside. Michael kept staring at Raymond. Raymond took out a cigarette. The lift took them down to where Michael parked his car. As they were walking toward the vehicle, Michael suddenly stopped. He faced Raymond and tapped his shoulder.

"Andrew is always like that, Ray. He is a cautious person. He is a quiet type but tends to be aggressive sometimes. But he is a nice man. You will learn to like him soon."

Michael gave full authority to Raymond to handle the job at the construction site. It was a glorious day for Raymond. He could now exercise his own judgment. There was another property development project going on in Bentong: six rows of shop houses surrounded by six hundred units of low-cost homes.

It took Raymond twenty minutes to locate his new house. Raymond stepped into his fully furnished new home and inhaled the fresh morning air. He put down his bags, walked toward the kitchen, and opened the refrigerator. It was fully stocked with food. He closed it and walked toward the veranda. From there, he could see the construction activities going on downhill.

At the construction site, the foreman greeted Raymond as if they had anticipated his appointment. The letter from Michael describing his new job was still in his pocket. The foreman led him to the site's office, which was made of a forty-foot cargo container. Raymond stepped in, and the room was cold because of two powerful air conditioners.

"Good morning, sir! We were expecting you. My name is Nathan. I am the chief engineer at this site."

Raymond shook his hand and saw they had prepared a small space for his work. "Don't I have my own office?" Raymond asked.

"We can make arrangements for you to have your own room. But we need another container for that. Here we all work in cramped areas. A proper office is only available in KL and Port Dickson," Nathan told Raymond.

"So get me a container. I need my own room to work."

"I'll get it done straightaway. I hope you are better than Mr. Yong. He was the general manager here before you took over. I heard he was transferred to KL and assigned to the cold room."

Raymond looked puzzled. "What's a cold room?" he asked.

Nathan stopped his work and looked up. "Oh, it's just a term invented by Michael. It is a purgatory office."

"Why?" Raymond asked.

"Because you came in, sir." Nathan stared at Raymond and then slowly turned away from him and continued his work. Raymond smiled.

In a matter of days, Raymond got his own forty-foot container with a two-horsepower York air conditioner. He also ordered an expensive chestnut table and a big executive chair. He decorated his new office and charged it to the company.

The financial controller for the project protested, but Nathan told him that Raymond was the boss's pet and that they should not annoy him. Raymond was happy with himself.

What an achievement! I can level myself with that birdbrain William!

Raymond studied his new job thoroughly. He made it a point to understand the work. He had never been in the construction business, so he bought and studied a construction manual.

He showed interest in the day-to-day routine activities and problems. He formed strong bonds with the workers at the site, and they all learned to love him. Most of all, he enjoyed developing a rapport with the material suppliers.

Raymond always took the suppliers out to a nearby nightclub. Instead of the suppliers paying for the entertainment, as was customary, Raymond volunteered eagerly to pay the bills. Like the workers, the suppliers too loved Raymond.

Chapter 58

WILLIAM HAD TRAVELED A lot for the past few months since the present government had won the election and the mandate to rule for another term. He went to all the important towns and some developed villages. He met with more people than ever before, and Moses was grumbling about the extra load of work.

William stayed up all night as he studied field reports, paperwork from Ramlan and Ramon, statistics he'd obtained from various government and private organizations, and verbal feedback from the business communities. He made critical assessments of the newspapers he read, especially the financial news.

William slept for only a few hours each night. Moses watched with concern as William seemed to turn into a hermit. One day as William sorted out the reports and wrote in his diary, he suddenly stopped, as he felt he couldn't think anymore. Moses arrived and gave him coffee. "Thanks, Mossy!"

Moses grinned and walked out of the room.

William read a newspaper headline. The Asian economy was going to roar ahead for another decade. He read another one: "Thumbs Up for the Malaysian and Southeast Asian Economy."

This time, William was not going to Kuala Lumpur to meet up with Andy. Andy wanted a break from city life and wanted to stay out of the busy streets for one week. He wanted to continue working in a pristine environment in East Malaysia. William proposed three locations, but Andy had one in mind.

Labuan was a tiny island about one hundred miles from Jesselton and only thirty-six miles from the Kingdom of Brunei. In the nineteenth century, the sultan of Brunei had ceded the island to the British as a token of gratitude because the British had helped to stop piracy in that region. The British had named a small town on the island Victoria after a powerful British monarch at the height of the British Empire.

The British had intended to transform the sleepy island into another Singapore, but due to the poor location, they'd abandoned the idea. It continued to be a quiet, peaceful town, and the only way the island could survive economically was for the British to declare her a free port within British Borneo. The island had also been the scene of heavy fighting during World War II and the only part of Borneo to witness a battle between the Allied forces and the Japanese Imperial Army.

Now the island was one of the most serene and peaceful places in the world, only interrupted by occasional petty problems and, rarely, serious crime. In 1994, the government had given the island international offshore financial center status, which many islands in the Caribbean had, and thus, tourism played a new role. The island was beautified with the intent of transforming it into a garden paradise. It was also a place where the government did not tax on alcohol and cigarettes, and many tourists were delighted with the cheap entertainment outlet.

William brought Andy out to the sea, where a professional diver guided them to see two sunken ships. The watery tomb was now home to various species of marine life, especially century-old grouper fish, which flocked together, seeking refuge and food there. Lobsters were in abundance. After all, Labuan was located in the South China Sea, which was home to endemic tropical marine life not seen anywhere else.

On the boat, the diver told William and Andy that what they were seeing might not last another fifty years, so this was the best time to see it. He explained that overfishing and fish bombing would destroy the ecological balance unless the government put a stop to these activities. William looked at Andy. Andy looked away.

Andy and William stayed at the Waterfront Hotel. They rested and swam in the pool. The relaxing mood made Andy refuse to be interrupted by any phone calls and to hear any reports from William. Both of them wore sunglasses.

"I think I will bring my wife the next time I come here, Will. She will love this place."

"I can't help it, Andy—I have to talk about the reports now."

Andy took off his glasses and frowned. "Please, Will, don't spoil the day. I'm more eager to do our job than you, but right now, give me a break, will you?" Andy continued to enjoy the blazing sunlight frying his body. "Okay, Will. We will discuss it tonight. Agreed?"

William smiled and nodded.

There were no seats left at the hotel's coffeehouse. William's eyes continued to scout but couldn't find one. They decided to walk to a nearby food stall. Both of them wore batik shirts to suit the humid environment. At the food court, there were plenty of empty tables. Not many people were around. They sat down at a corner table, and both ordered fried rice.

"Look, Andy, I'm noticing some disturbing signs regarding what is about to happen in the future."

Andy seemed uninterested. He was focusing on his dinner.

"Are you listening?"

Andy raised his head. "Go ahead! I'm listening." His mouth was filled with food.

"Recently, I've spent a lot of time talking with the businessmen. All say the same thing. Business is expanding, and they are acquiring more working assets, borrowing more money from the banks, and employing more people."

Andy nodded while enjoying his food. "So? That should be a good sign then."

"That's just the beginning of the story, Andy. All of them have positive expansion. Some are having millions of dollars monthly turnover in their books. But all of them are experiencing the same problem: not enough cash flow to turn their business."

Andy looked puzzled. "I don't quite get you, Will," he said.

"They are highly geared, Andy. Their businesses are nothing but credits and debts. For example, a factory expanded his business, but he supplied his customers on credit terms. He, in turn, will owe the transportation company, who will owe the tire and spare-part shops. Don't you get me, Andy? The economic growth is based on borrowed time and money! And time will catch up to them! That's scary, Andy. Aren't you scared?"

"What is on your mind, Will?" Andy began to take slight interest in the conversation as he sipped his coffee.

William took out his small notebook. He skimmed what he had written and looked back at Andy. "Our country's growth rate since 1987 is incredible. It is eight percent every year."

"That's to achieve our vision for 2020, Will!"

"It is a bubble ready to explode, Andy. The current account deficit is widening yearly. We are going to hit the wall, Andy! When I was in Singapore, I overheard people who claimed to be speculators crying out, 'I smell blood!' Doesn't it scare you, Andy?"

"So what action do you propose for the government?" Andy put his hands on the table. He seemed annoyed at what William was saying. He picked up his coffee cup and sipped again.

"Propose that they reduce the growth rate and increase the tariff on imports."

Andy jumped out of his seat. "Are you out of your mind?" he yelled. Andy noticed that everybody was looking at him. He sat and whispered to William, "Do you realize what you are proposing? It could spell increased unemployment and declining business. Do you realize what it could do to the government politically?"

"I know it is a bitter medicine to swallow, Andy. But remember what I said today. Our economy is in big trouble."

Andy remained silent and then said, "Give me your report, and tomorrow morning, we will go through it carefully. Then I'll see what

I can do with it once I'm back in KL, facing the big boys. You're giving me a lot of problems to solve, Will."

"At least we are giving them warning. Andy."

Andy persuaded William to close the subject for the night and asked him to take him around to enjoy the nightlife. They had a good time together, and they went back to their hotel room at three o'clock in the morning.

"See you, Will!" Andy was drunk.

"Good night, Andy." As William was about to enter his room, a lady passed by. William couldn't help noticing her beauty. His eyes followed her. She smiled at William. William raised his hand slowly to say hi. She went straight into Andy's room. William smiled.

Chapter 59

RAYMOND APPROACHED THE BIG office of a successful hardware supplier named Mr. Lim. Over two generations, Mr. Lim's company had expanded from a small grocery store to a huge trading house for construction materials. Mr. Lim enjoyed dealing with Raymond, as he asked for no bribes, unlike the others before him. Raymond observed that Mr. Lim's office had the typical Chinese setup. Mr. Lim invited him in when he saw Raymond outside his office.

"Please sit down, Ray," Mr. Lim said.

Raymond sat. "I would like you to supply me with fifty metric tons of high-quality timber."

Mr. Lim started wondering. "Why do you need so much timber?"

"It's for the formwork to shape the concrete."

"With high-quality timber?" Mr. Lim thought for a while. Then he smiled and laughed. "But I don't have that much. Whatever I have I will supply you. You are the boss. To be delivered on-site?"

"No, I'll get the materials from your warehouse. Can you issue the invoice right now so I can get Michael to release the money to you as soon as possible?"

Immediately, Mr. Lim instructed his secretary to prepare it. "Is there anything else, Mr. Raymond?"

"That's all, Mr. Lim. And thank you for your cooperation." Raymond requested permission to leave.

For the next several hours, he went around the town to solicit more timber. Mr. Lim's supply was not enough. He needed more. Some tried to give him under-the-table money, but Raymond refused.

He only asked for invoices. After going around, he went back to the construction site and continued his routine work.

Early the next morning, Raymond went to Kuala Lumpur to catch up with Michael before he left for Australia. Raymond brought the invoices and the wage list for the workers at the site.

"What is it, Ray? I've only got a few minutes for you. I hope you understand." Michael hugged Raymond.

"It will only take a few minutes of your time, Mike." Raymond noticed Andrew looking at him. "We've got to settle this before you go, Mike." Raymond showed Michael the papers he'd brought from Port Dickson. Michael briefly looked at them. He looked at Raymond and smiled. "Okay, settle them!"

"Can you release the money today?"

"Jennifer, can you prepare these for payment?" Michael looked at Raymond. "Just ask whatever is required from her, Ray."

Raymond rose from his seat and saluted Michael. "Have a pleasant journey, Mike!"

"Thank you, Ray. Take care of my company. I will have a nice surprise for you when I get back."

Raymond walked away from Michael toward Jennifer and immediately worked out the details with her. Jennifer gave a cash check of $250,000 to be released to Raymond. He rushed out of the office. He was shivering with excitement. Suddenly, Andrew stopped him.

"I'll get you one of these days, Ray," he said.

Raymond suddenly felt cold. However, he mustered enough courage to push Andrew's hand away from his shoulder. He walked quickly and didn't turn around to see Andrew.

Back at Port Dickson, Raymond negotiated with Philip, the pimp who had helped him months ago. Raymond held his discussion at the Port View Hotel coffeehouse, and he made sure nobody else knew where he was.

"Okay, Philip, I have fifty metric tons of fine timber ready to be carried away from five different locations. Can you get people to buy it?"

"How much?"

"Half of the market price?"

"What? Anytime! When can we start?"

"Tonight. Mobilize transportation, but don't use trucks from Port Dickson. Get ones far from this place. Once the transaction is done, you deposit the money to this account." Raymond wrote the account number on his cigarette box and gave it to Philip. "Thirty percent of the transaction will go to you as your commission."

"Is this legal, Ray?"

"Trust me! Everything will be okay."

"Thank you, Raymond."

Philip made arrangements with his cousin, who had the means to transport the bulky commodity. By midnight, they'd whisked away the timber without raising any suspicions. The next morning, Philip sold off the timber easily in Johore Bahru to a Singapore businessman. The deal was too good to ignore.

Philip did as he was instructed, and Raymond fattened his account with another deal. Philip was more than happy to get his commission. Raymond went to the site and paid token sums as wages to the laborers and staff.

"I talked to Michael, and he told me that you will get the balance of your pay as soon as he comes back from Australia." Raymond walked toward his office. Suddenly, he turned around and stopped. "Yes, Nathan? What seems to be the problem?"

"Mr. Raymond, it is unprecedented for our wages not to be paid on time. Can you go back to the headquarters and resolve this problem?"

Raymond lit his cigarette and scratched the sand with his right shoe. "Don't you understand? Michael is overseas, and he will be back in a month. I talked to him yesterday morning."

Nathan approached Raymond. "It will demoralize the employees, sir!"

Raymond remained silent with his mind working to get himself out of this dilemma. "Never mind! I'll talk to the workers, and I will go back to KL and solve this matter."

Raymond dined with the workers in a nearby seafood restaurant, and with his convincing persuasion, he managed to assure them that everything would be settled smoothly and urgently. The workers accepted his word and continued working with enthusiasm.

One week passed. Andrew had heard rumors that a scandal had been going on at Port Dickson. He sent one of his bodyguards to check out the rumors and pinpoint the culprit. He had someone in mind, but he needed a little more evidence.

In a few days' time, Andrew had enough information to drag Michael back to Kuala Lumpur. Andrew summoned Nathan, and both worked out with Jennifer all the papers and documents Raymond had handled. Andrew and Nathan continued to work all night, and finally they finished the job. Andrew grinned.

Raymond felt uneasy when he heard he was to report for duty in Kuala Lumpur this time and to leave his work immediately. He didn't know that Michael was already back in town. Raymond hadn't planned for this. He'd planned to quit and leave the place a few days before Michael returned from Australia. Raymond suspected somebody had discovered his activities and informed Michael about them. However, it was too late to escape now. He had to face Michael.

When Raymond arrived at the corporate headquarters, all the staff members were silently staring at him. Some shook their heads; others smiled. When he reached the main office leading to Michael's room, Andrew was standing there, staring at him with a cunning smile. Raymond ignored him and walked toward Michael's office.

"Good morning, Mike! I didn't expect you to be back so soon." Raymond sat in front of Michael. "It is good to see you back," Raymond continued.

"Well, Raymond, those house buyers are supposed to pay up. Why haven't they?"

"They still can't get bank loans, Mike! They are working on it."

"I don't care how they raise their money! They can get it from a bank loan, or they can borrow from their rich uncles, but they must pay up!" Raymond had never seen Michael lose his temper this way. "Another very big problem is that you have committed a serious crime."

"What crime, Mike?" Raymond said, feigning ignorance.

"Breach of trust! Don't pretend, Ray! That will be seven years behind bars!"

Michael took out some documents and threw them in front of Raymond. Raymond slowly looked at the papers. He then looked up at Michael. Michael looked serious. Raymond took a deep breath and said, "Give me time, and I will return the money to you. If you report me, you will not see your money."

Michael was not convinced, but he had no choice. Michael thought for a while. "By this afternoon at one o'clock, I want my money!" Michael shouted. "After that, you're fired!"

Michael and Andrew waited for Raymond to return. It was already two o'clock, and there was still no sign of Raymond. Andrew looked at Michael and smiled at him. "I told you, Brother! He cannot be trusted! You can see by his face."

"Okay, Andrew! Please don't torture me again. I've made a mistake."

Michael's admission satisfied Andrew.

An account clerk rushed in. "I have a friend who knows Raymond. She told me you can find Raymond at the Grand Continental Hotel! He is there right now."

Michael and Andrew immediately rushed out of the office and headed straight to the hotel. Michael instructed Andrew and the bodyguard to wait in the lobby while he confronted Raymond in the coffeehouse. Michael took off his coat and passed it to Andrew. He saw Raymond sitting with an indecent-looking man. Without asking, Michael sat next to Raymond.

"I want my money back, or you go to prison! I'm going to lodge a police report, Ray!"

"Mike, if you drag me to prison, I will bring you down with me!"

Michael bit his lip and stared at Raymond and Philip. "You are threatening me, Ray?"

"Yes! I am threatening you! Remember? You always go to the Legend Hotel, and you ask me to book your room and wait in the lobby. I taped you making love with an influential government secretary's wife, Mike! The wife of the man who gave you multi-million dollars government projects! And the other one was a bank manageress whose husband is a rich tycoon, who generously gave charity to your church. You want to play a rough game, eh, Mike?"

Raymond's revelation startled Michael. He became disoriented.

"This tape can demolish your relationship with your loving wife and also the Christian movement who treated you like a prophet," Raymond said.

"You sure are one ungrateful bastard! How could you do this after what I have done for you?"

Raymond looked at Philip. Philip sneered and said, "Well, Mike, that's how we survive in this world."

Michael stood up. "One of these days, you will meet your match, Ray. God is merciful!" Michael spoke slowly, filled with emotion.

"You know something, Mike? There is no such thing as God! He is only the imagination of desperate people like you!"

Michael walked out in a hurry. Raymond could see Michael and Andrew arguing in the lobby, but finally, they all left the hotel together. Raymond felt relieved, but he was also worried that Michael would ignore his threat and lodge a police report against him. He was playing a poker game with Michael, and it seemed Raymond had won this round.

"Are you okay?" Philip asked.

"Do you think I can be okay with this stupid problem?"

"You looked confident just now. Now your face is so white!"

Raymond kept silent. Then he walked away toward the washroom. Inside, he washed his face and looked in the mirror. He continued to wash his face several times, until his collar was all wet.

I now have three hundred thousand dollars! I'm better off than William! I'll show this to him. No, wait! I'll make more money, and then I can pat his head. I'll ask him, "Who is better now—me or you?"

Raymond moved out of his rented room in the city slum and took up residence at the Palace and Marble apartment complex in a luxurious three-room apartment on top of a hill overlooking the oldest part of the city. It was a high-class residential area but densely populated because of the condominiums mushrooming all over the hill.

He rented the apartment for $3,000 a month. It was semi-furnished and was located on the sixth floor. The complex had a swimming pool, a gym, laundry, and a twenty-four-hour security service. Raymond had elevated himself now, and he felt proud of his achievement.

Every night, he would ask Philip to send hookers from different countries and continents to fulfill his lust. Raymond enjoyed his new lifestyle, uninterrupted by the thought of impending future problems once his money ran out.

Chapter 60

"RAY, WHEN DID YOU arrive?" William came out of his office and greeted Raymond.

"Where is the asshole son of a bitch?" Raymond looked around, noticing that Moses was not in the office.

"He went for a holiday. He will be back tomorrow—if he can catch the flight home."

"I hope his plane crashes!"

"Don't be like that, Ray. He is a nice guy if you know him personally."

William took Raymond for a ride around town, and they talked about the good old times. Raymond suggested William call for a reunion with their other classmates, but after a while, he gave up the attempt, as they were all too busy and preoccupied with the coming Christmas and New Year's.

"You came at the wrong time, Ray!"

"Didn't realize time passes so quickly, Will. It's almost New Year's again."

"Why don't we drop by this shop here, Ray? It looks pretty quiet."

Raymond agreed. William parked the car, and both of them stretched their arms because of the tiring trip in the car. They took a spot right below the fan. Both ordered lemonade, which was the best drink during the hottest part of the day.

"I don't work for Michael anymore, Will. When he decided to take back your houses, I considered that he had broken his promises. I would rather resign than watch my friends get double-crossed. He promised free houses, and then he suddenly considered the houses as sold."

"What do you do now?"

"I'm dealing with used cars from Singapore. Singaporeans must dispose of their vehicles after five years; that's their country's law. They can't sell the cars in Singapore, because the tax will be too high. So we help them sell their cars in Malaysia. But we must build a unique rapport with the Malaysian customs officers, if you know what I mean."

William nodded. He understood what Raymond was involved with. Raymond continued bragging about his love life and the different girls he had slept with. William smiled and enjoyed hearing Raymond, but he was unsure he believed him.

"Why do you need so many girls, Ray?"

"Variety is the spice of life!"

"Prostitutes?"

"Are you degrading me? I don't have sex with rented flesh. Mine is the real thing. Office girls, single and married secretaries, receptionists, waitresses—you name it! I don't buy sexual services, Will. They are attracted to me. I tell them no money and no strings attached. They agree, and it is between two consenting people. So what about you, Will? Still going out with Theresa?"

William shook his head.

Raymond noticed that William did not want to discuss the subject. "Well, okay, time for me to go back to KL. Can you take me to the airport?"

"That soon, Ray? What about your wife and children?"

"I'll meet them next time. I don't think I have the time now."

"No time?" William asked in amazement.

"Got a lot of work to do back in the city, Will. How I love the city!" Raymond said as he stood up and paid for the drinks. William obligingly took him to the airport and waited with Raymond.

Did he come all the way from KL just to drop by and say hello to me? William thought. The motive seemed illogical. *It doesn't make sense!*

He shook his head and diverted his attention to a more important matter. William had proposed an important plan to Susan, which she'd eagerly accepted. Both were now anticipating a grand day they could remember forever—a day that they hoped would begin a new chapter in their lives.

Chapter 61

CHRISTMAS CAROLERS WERE SINGING hymns mildly outside. The boy looked out and saw young children his age singing a tune about an evergreen at his neighbor's house. After receiving some gifts, the children began to disperse. The snowfall was getting heavier every moment.

A Christmas hymn still played on the radio inside their home. It was soothing to hear it while looking at the towering Christmas tree. The boy watched the empty tree. There were no lights or presents.

"Come here, Son! Help Mama with the pie! I made it just for the two of us."

After they enjoyed the pie, both of them sat by the window, watching the weather turn into a blizzard. The boy gazed at the mounting snow close by. He then played with his old toys.

"Mama, who is Father? Why isn't he with us? Why does Godfrey get to spend time with his father?"

Catherine looked at her son and hugged him tightly. "Your father left us before you were born. You're too young to know. Actually, he and I were never married. He promised to marry me, but I'm still waiting for that."

He watched his mother cry. "Is there a place where there is no snow?" the boy said, changing the subject.

"Well, child, not unless you want to stay in the tropics, which are among the hottest and most humid parts of the earth, and there is no snow there. And those places are always infected with diseases. I prefer the snow."

"It's boring, Mother! With the snow, I can't play outside!"

"You will learn to live with it, Son. Believe me."

"I want to travel to the tropics when I grow up."

"You have to be a soldier then."

The Christmas hymn gained strength. The melody was enchanting. He closed his eyes tightly to forget everything but the music that he could only hear once a year. *When I grow up, I want to be a soldier. I want to go to the tropics,* he thought again.

"Al! Al, are you okay?" Maria gently shook Aaron's shoulder.

Aaron's memory faded, and the lady standing in front of him was no longer his mother but Maria, who now stayed with him. Aaron looked at his surroundings. Maria had prepared their dinner; the Christmas tree was well decorated and full of lights and presents. Maria walked to the kitchen and came out with more food and drinks.

Aaron stood up and walked toward the tree. He looked at it carefully and slowly squatted down and stared at the presents. He tried to refocus on his vivid memory. *It's a long time since I left jolly good England,* Aaron thought to himself. *I've forgotten how the snow felt and where Mama's grave lies.*

"Dinner is ready, Al!" Maria had prepared the table while waiting for Aaron. Aaron looked somber. Maria didn't want Christmas to be spoiled, but she had to understand the many problems Aaron faced. They both sat down, and Aaron grabbed Maria's hand and held it tightly.

"Maria, for the past several years, I have been spending my Christmas alone. Can you believe that? All alone! No tree! No dinner! Just myself and the beer." Maria put her other hand on top of Aaron's, which was still holding her other hand. There were tears in his eyes, and Maria felt Aaron's emotion.

"I don't know whether to be happy or sad. But it's happy, I guess!" Aaron said.

"Try to enjoy our Christmas, Al! We'll enjoy tonight and be sad together tomorrow."

Aaron chuckled at what Maria had said. There were smiles on both of their faces.

"Our dinner is getting cold," Maria added.

Just as they were about to start, Aaron and Maria heard a soft Christmas song outside his apartment. They sat still and tried to listen. The singing continued. Aaron stood up and walked to the door. He put his ear to the door. The voices were coming from right behind. Aaron immediately opened the door.

"Surprise! And merry Christmas!" Susan screamed.

Aaron was speechless. He was overjoyed. Instinctively, he hugged her tightly and didn't let go for at least half a minute.

"Daddy, this is William. He is the one who suggested we come visit you. He insisted on paying for my trip, and since I missed you so much, I made it a point to come see you."

Aaron vigorously shook William's hand. "Merry Christmas, Will!"

"Merry Christmas, Mr. Johnson!"

"Susan has been talking all the time about you. Indeed she has! Have we met?"

"Many times, sir! When I was a teenager."

"Ah yes. You took care of Susan once, didn't you?"

William smiled in hearing that.

"I am sorry I couldn't remember, Will. Indeed I am getting old."

"It's all right, sir. I understand."

Maria approached Aaron and held his arm. "Oh, I forgot!" he said. "Remember Maria, Susan?"

Susan walked toward her and hugged her. "How could I forget Auntie Maria? She was so nice to me."

Aaron walked toward the table and waved for them to follow. "Come in, ladies and gentleman! Sit down, and enjoy our dinner."

As they were about to sit down, there was another knock on the door. They all looked at each other. Again, Aaron walked to the door and slowly opened it, and again, Aaron got a happy surprise. It was Cecelia and her two kids. The girl shouted, "Granddad!" Aaron hugged his favorite and only grandchildren. Aaron instructed the kids to go to the dinner table. The kids nodded and ran to the table, where Susan and Maria also greeted and hugged them.

Aaron turned toward Cecelia and hugged her. She said, "My father heard you were staying here, and he told me. I decided to wait for Christmas to surprise you."

Aaron smiled. *What a happy coincidence,* he thought to himself. "Come in, Cecelia!"

"Can I talk to you privately?" she said. Aaron looked at the children and turned back toward her. He nodded, followed Cecelia outside the apartment, and closed the door slowly.

"I'm going back to my old job, Dad."

"Oh no! Cecelia, please don't."

"I have to! There is nothing I've done right. My childhood failed, my life as a teenager was a mess, and my marriage fell to pieces. The only thing I seem to excel at is what I have been doing—my old job!"

"Cecelia, please give more thought to this. What about your children? You must consider them!"

"I've thought about that too. That's why I decided that you are the best person to look after them. You didn't fail to raise your children, Daddy. I know you are thinking that now, but it's Elaine who destroyed their lives! Please take good care of them. I'll be visiting them twice a week. Don't worry!"

Cecelia kissed his cheek and left. It was a happy and sad Christmas for Aaron.

Chapter 62

AN ORGY WAS GOING on at Raymond's apartment. Philip had brought two male friends and eleven prostitutes to enjoy the closing of the year. It was a wonderful moment for Raymond. He looked out from his balcony with a bottle of red wine in his left hand. He looked at his watch.

"Ten! Nine! Eight!" They began the countdown. "Four! Three! Two! One! Happy new year, everyone!" The topless girls screamed at the top of their voices as they hugged and kissed the outnumbered males. Raymond held two girls in his arms, and a third was squatting down and opening his trousers. The morning was memorable for Raymond.

Raymond woke up from his sleep. Naked bodies littered his room, and he stared at the one whom he had not tried out yet. He looked at her sleeping near the bathroom door. *Shit! I have only managed to try four girls. What a waste!* he thought to himself while looking sternly at the youngest of the hookers.

He got out of his bed and walked toward the living room. He lit a cigarette. It was almost broken in two, but it was the last one he could find in his home. After he lit it, he slowly moved to retrieve his bankbook from one of the drawers. He looked at it and sighed.

"Well, it's depleted. But it will last for another three months, I hope," he murmured softly to himself. Raymond watched the horizon and saw the beam of light coming out of the darkness, getting brighter with the passage of time.

Raymond helped himself to a can of beer. He had never seen the sun come out of the mountain and end the dawn. On this first of January, he was determined to watch her come out. He sat down and sipped his beer slowly.

"What are you doing waking up so early, Ray?"

Raymond lost his concentration. He turned around and saw Philip. "Hi, Phil! Happy new year!"

"What are you doing?"

"Just trying to watch the sun breaking the dawn."

When Raymond turned back, he saw that the sun had already come up. "Dread! I missed it again! You disturbed my concentration, Philip. Now I have to wait for another year."

Philip shook his head in disbelief. "Only small children play that game," he told Raymond. "Ray, do you know the guy with me? The big fat one?"

"I didn't manage to know any of them, including the hookers!"

"He is a very rich man, Ray. I think he is a multimillionaire."

Raymond stood up and walked toward Philip. "You don't actually know him?"

Philip nodded. "I just knew him yesterday. He asked me to get a model for him. He was willing to pay a handsome price for it. I got him one, and he paid three thousand dollars!"

"Bloody fool! Why am I paying for him to enjoy here? Why doesn't he fork over the money?"

Philip persuaded Raymond to calm down. Raymond was still babbling. "Please, Ray! Just listen to me."

Raymond stopped babbling. "Okay. I'm listening." He crossed his arms.

"I am the one who invited him to this party. Last night, he really enjoyed it. And he'd like to be friends with you. He said he's never enjoyed such a spectacular New Year's."

"So what benefits do I get?"

"Why don't you go out with him for breakfast? Discuss with him. Talk to him."

"I hope there is something to gain, Phil. I don't like to waste money on useless people."

Raymond had breakfast with the man. He was fat and slightly taller than Raymond, and he was an extremely rich man. His name was Ma Foo Yee, and soon Raymond addressed him as Mr. Ma, which the man liked.

Raymond came to know that Mr. Ma was once in a triad in Hong Kong and sold illegal drugs to mainland customers in China. He had built strong contacts with the authorities, which explained why he had not been caught. But as his business had grown, so had the risk. Finally, the authorities had told him that he had overextended himself, and the exposure of his business was imminent.

Mr. Ma had decided to stop his activities immediately, and he'd immigrated to England and stayed in London's notorious Chinatown. He'd decided to make his business legal and started a fish-processing plant in one of Thailand's coastal towns. He imported the processed fish to England and sold it to oriental customers in Europe.

"You deal with fish?" Raymond asked.

"Yes! Lots of fish!" Mr. Ma answered, still eating. He was putting so much food into his mouth that Raymond could hardly understand what he was saying.

Suddenly, Mr. Ma stopped and struggled to put his hand inside his pocket. He took out a photograph and gave it to Raymond. Raymond took it and studied it.

"I'm looking for this fish. I used to get some in Thailand. Now I can't find it."

"It seems common." Raymond looked carefully at the picture.

"Common? I did some research on it. I went to several fishery departments in Thailand and also England. I referred to encyclopedias of fish. Nobody seems to know what type of fish it is."

"Why are you looking for this type?"

"There is a big market among the Chinese community in Europe for this kind of fish. They say it is an aphrodisiac. That's what the Chinese believe."

Raymond concentrated on the picture. "No wonder the rare fish population is depleted. The Asians seem to have no limit to their cravings and superstitions!"

"Why bother? Make more money, and that is the most important thing," Mr. Ma answered.

Raymond smiled. "That, my friend, is the best statement, and I totally agree with you."

Mr. Ma felt flattered. He wiped his mouth and burped loudly without excusing himself. "Mr. Raymond, if you can get this fish, I will gladly pay you thirty-five British pounds per kilo for it."

Raymond's sense of hearing sharpened. "I'm listening."

Mr. Ma sipped his orange juice. "I said I'll pay you thirty-five pounds per kilo."

"I know where to get this fish, Mr. Ma."

"You do? You really do? From where?"

"That's my secret, Mr. Ma."

The fat man wiggled, trying to straighten his cumbersome body. His face moved closer to Raymond's. "I'm really serious about this business. If you can find those catches, I will gladly deposit some money now."

Raymond laughed. "No need for a deposit, Mr. Ma! Once I get it, then you pay me."

Raymond had seen the fish before. He remembered that it was sold cheaply on the east coast of Borneo, and some of the factories there bought it to process it into fish balls. Raymond secretly made a trip to Sandakan. He met some of his contacts among the fishermen and fishmongers. He was cautious not to encounter those he had cheated years ago.

Raymond showed them the photograph. They recognized the fish immediately but told Raymond that nowadays, it was almost impossible to find. Raymond was disappointed. However, he continued his search in the important towns all along the east coast of Malaysian Borneo.

Finally, he met a man who assured him that he could obtain such fish easily in the Indonesian Borneo town of Nunukan, close to the southeastern Malaysian border.

Scum infested this place, including pirates, smugglers, pimps, and notorious con men. Business transactions included the smuggling of desperate Indonesian females looking for work in Malaysia, who found out later they were forced into the immoral flesh trade. Illegal logs, which were supposed to be banned for export, were barter traded and ended up in the many factories in Malaysia. Goods subjected to high tariffs in other ports of Indonesia were charged zero duty in Nunukan.

Raymond couldn't believe he'd ended up in this sickening place. The city streets were dirty and dusty, and it was humid. There were many people, tribes, and funny occupations. Raymond looked out from his two-star hotel's lobby. The hotel air conditioners had all gone out and were about to be serviced for the fifth time in less than eight hours.

"Mr. Raymond, my name is Abdul, and I believe you are looking for this." The man unwrapped an object and showed it to Raymond. Raymond was delighted. His trip was not in vain after all. It was the fish he was looking for.

"If you can get many of this fish, I will gladly pay you ten Malaysian dollars per kilo."

"That is a very good offer! I will try my best, Master Raymond."

Raymond waited for three weeks on the island; his money was depleting quickly because of the hotel lodging and his unstoppable desire to sleep with girls. Furthermore, he was offering a high price for such fish, while everybody else was buying at less than one Malaysian dollar per kilo.

Finally, Raymond packed the goods and sent off five hundred kilos to London by air through the Malaysian airport at the border town of Tawau. From there, it would take one day for transit activities at the Kuala Lumpur International Airport before the goods could be shipped directly to London. Raymond could not wait there because of the many enemies he had created long ago. He had to go back to Nunukan.

Raymond had almost no money left. He was beginning to get worried. It had been three weeks already since he had exported the fish. *What if it is the wrong fish? What if it is similar in shape and color but still a different fish? What if Mr. Ma insists it is the wrong fish even if it is the right fish? What if Mr. Ma tries to cheat me?*

The thoughts bothered Raymond. He still owed some money to Abdul, and if there was no news, he would be stuck in this destitute place, and Abdul would haunt him forever.

Four weeks and two days passed, and still, there was no news. Raymond had the telephone number of Mr. Ma, but the telecommunication system was still primitive. He could not make any calls outside Nunukan. He had a cell phone, but he could not call out. He could only receive calls. Raymond was getting impatient. So was Abdul, who paid him a visit at the hotel every day.

Raymond's cell phone suddenly rang. He picked it up and listened.

"Hello, Ray! How are you doing? Sorry for the slight delay. Can you give me your account number, please?"

It was like a voice from heaven to Raymond. He was relieved to hear Mr. Ma talking to him. "I sold off those fish in only three days, Ray! Sensational, isn't it?"

Raymond gave Mr. Ma his account number. Raymond immediately went back to Tawau and saw his account grow another eighty-four thousand Malaysian dollars after converting from English pounds.

He went back to Nunukan and paid off Abdul. "Now is the beginning of my prosperity!" Raymond said in a loud voice. He went outside the hotel and walked around the town. He dressed simply so that criminal elements trying to prey on people who looked successful would not target him.

"Hey, you bastard!" someone yelled, and Raymond turned around. "You must be a son of a bitch!"

Raymond smiled. They hugged each other. "It has been a long time. We never hear from you, Devin! What happened?"

Devin smiled back at Raymond. "Your dear brother lives like a king here! Everything is cheap! Everybody is poor! So where is a better place than here?" Devin replied.

"What is your business here?"

"I smuggle rice from Indonesia into Malaysia. What are you doing, Ray?"

Raymond took out the photograph and showed it to Devin. "I sell fish, Devin. Just like the good old days. Only this time, it is much better!"

Raymond celebrated with his long-lost brother at a small seafood stall near the harbor. He proposed a toast to him, and they drank beer. Devin informed Raymond that after he'd left Jesselton, he had gone straight to Singapore and stayed there for a while. He'd gotten an Indonesian girlfriend, who'd brought him to her hometown on Bantam Island, which was close to Singapore. Devin told Raymond that he liked Bantam and intended to stay there permanently. He'd ventured into the business of seaweed production. It had failed because the location was not suitable due to heavy pollution from Singapore's busy harbors and industrial waste.

"After that, a friend brought me here to Indonesian Borneo and told me seaweed grows very well here." Devin was partially drunk as he kept up with his life story. "But here, people do not make money through the straight ways. You understand me, Ray? Everybody is a crook here!" Devin stood up. "Everybody is a bloody crook here!" Devin shouted at the top of his voice.

"That's enough, Devin! Everybody is looking at us!"

Devin laughed as he continued drinking his beer. "Don't worry. They don't understand English. You know, Ray, I find it more profitable to smuggle rice. And I'm happy with my job."

"Good for you! You must have a lot of connections here."

"I have a friend who works at the governor's office. He is in charge of all his letters and communications. But he is only a clerk."

Raymond became interested. "Devin, you mean to tell me he has access to all the governor's documents?" When Devin nodded, Raymond chuckled. "How strong is the governor?"

Devin had had enough of his drinking, and he closed his eyes tightly. Raymond waited patiently for him to respond. "In Indonesia, the governors are like warlords and very autonomous within their own provinces. The only people they fear are the Indonesian president and his children. But the president never disturbs them as long as they are loyal to him. So they control the army, the police, the regional bureaucrats, the land, and licensing!"

Chapter 63

TWO MONTHS HAD PASSED since the first successful shipment. Now the catches were miserable. Abdul managed to get less than one hundred kilos of fish. Raymond couldn't believe his luck was turning against him. He summoned Abdul to his temporary office in his hotel room.

"I am also very eager to catch the fish, Tuan Raymond. But I've looked everywhere. I have even traveled as far as the Maluku Islands. Even if you offer me a very high price, the problem is, the fish are nowhere to be found."

Raymond held his head. A migraine started to torture him after he received this news. "You have searched everywhere?" Raymond looked up, hoping for a new suggestion from Abdul. Abdul nodded and bowed his head. Raymond thought the weather or season must have contributed to the decline. "When will they appear in huge numbers?"

"This fish do not have a season, Tuan Raymond. But they just seem to disappear."

That night in his hotel room, Raymond discussed a scheme with Devin. He was beginning to see a bleak future in his fish business and had to do something to keep it alive. He explained to Devin in great detail what he had in mind.

Devin laughed. "You are one smart jackass, Ray!"

"Can you work it out?" Raymond asked his brother.

"Leave it to me. By tomorrow, I will get what you want. But you must pay my friend one thousand US dollars up front, or he will not do it for you."

Raymond smiled. Devin stroked his hair. Half of it had turned white.

Raymond requested Mr. Ma meet him in Kuala Lumpur. Three days later, Mr. Ma arrived from London with two of his bodyguards and a frail-looking adviser who was his accountant. Raymond waited patiently for him to arrive at the Kuala Lumpur Shangri-La Hotel.

"What is it, Ray? Where are my fish?" Mr. Ma sat with Raymond and instructed his adviser to sit near him. The bodyguards sat at a different table, but their cautious eyes were always looking at Raymond.

"The fish have a season, Mr. Ma. We anticipate it will be August before they will appear again."

"So what have we to talk about? It is a long journey from England, you know." Mr. Ma requested a menu from the waitress. He whispered something to her, and she smiled. "See you tonight, okay?" he said.

The waitress nodded. "What do you want to have for your lunch, sir?" she asked.

"Oh yes. Give me pizza, fried noodles, and a hamburger."

"Be right back, Mr. Ma," the waitress replied politely.

Raymond observed Mr. Ma carefully. He noticed he would do anything for ladies. He was a compulsive womanizer. He watched Mr. Ma as Mr. Ma stared at the waitress. He also stole a peek at a lady dining close by with her husband.

"Mr. Ma, would you be so kind as to study these documents? My brother, Devin, got a timber concession—about a hundred thousand acres of virgin jungle in Indonesian Borneo." Raymond handed him the papers.

Mr. Ma glanced at them quickly. "What do you want me to do?"

"There is a rich timber tycoon from South Korea who is willing to purchase the concession. He is still waiting for an answer, and he is waiting in Manila, Philippines."

"Then why do you need me? Why don't you just sell it to him?"

"We can't do that, Mr. Ma. He knows his way very well in Borneo. He could go directly to meet the governor, and then we'll get nothing out of this deal. But if we purchase the concession first, there is no way he can double-cross us. The permit has a period, Mr. Ma. It will expire in December next year. We must act quickly."

"How much is the Korean willing to pay per acre?"

"Three hundred US dollars."

"How much capital do we need to buy the land?"

"About one hundred US dollars per acre."

Mr. Ma took a closer look at the documents and consulted with his adviser. The adviser took the papers and walked away. One of the bodyguards followed him. The food arrived, and Mr. Ma looked delighted. He slapped the waitress's backside, and she winkled at him.

"Let's have lunch, my dear friend!" Mr. Ma said to Raymond. Raymond shook his head and declined the offer. Raymond was watching the adviser as he disappeared into the lobby and into the business center.

Half an hour later, the adviser came back. He handed the documents to Mr. Ma and whispered in his ear. Mr. Ma looked serious. Then, suddenly, he laughed loudly. Raymond had been getting a bit nervous, but he felt relieved when the fat man laughed. Mr. Ma grabbed Raymond's hand. "Mr. Chew here did a thorough check of the documents just to make sure. They are indeed authentic. You've got yourself a deal, Ray! I'll wire the money tomorrow, but I will start with a deposit. That will be five hundred thousand US dollars."

"You will not regret this, Mr. Ma!"

"Better not make me regret it, or you will regret it," Mr. Ma said, laughing, as he looked Raymond in the eyes. Raymond looked down. Mr. Ma stood up, walked near him, and held Raymond's shoulder. "Work this thing out, and both of us will be rich. Understand?" he said, and Raymond nodded. "Now I have to go. You settle the bill!"

Raymond was jubilant. Immediately, he invited Devin to Kuala Lumpur, and they celebrated as they waited for the wired money to arrive. They both stayed at the Federal Hotel. The next morning, they sat in the lobby and discussed business.

"We just can't simply spend the money, Devin."

"Who cares? He will not be looking for us in Borneo."

"Neither can I ever return to KL! I don't like the idea of not coming back to KL."

The discussion was intense. It took all morning for them to realize they had not had their breakfast. They went for lunch at the hotel's coffeehouse and continued their discussion. It was a difficult windfall for Raymond—he had too much and didn't know what to do with it.

"Why don't we invest the money for a quick return? As soon as we make more than a hundred percent gain, we return the principal sum," Devin suggested.

Raymond shook his head. "Where can we invest and get a hundred percent return?" Raymond continued pondering.

"We can invest in the currency market," Devin said.

"Devin, currency trading is very risky business."

"But it has high returns! I have a close friend in Singapore called Jebir. He made a killing and became an instant millionaire when he bet against the Mexican peso. Now he is one of the best gurus in currency speculation."

The idea convinced Raymond, and he and Devin set off for Singapore to meet with Jebir. Devin took Raymond to a high-rise office in Singapore. The sixth, seventh, and eighth floors all belonged to Jebir. Raymond learned that Jebir was involved not only in currency trading but also in the stock market, properties, and shipping.

"How much money do you want to invest?" Jebir asked.

"We have about five hundred thousand US dollars." Raymond felt proud telling him.

"Only five hundred thousand? However, because of your brother, I'm willing to help you invest wisely."

Devin looked at Raymond and smiled.

"I and all of my family members are about to bet two hundred million Singapore dollars that the Malaysian dollar will rise."

Raymond looked puzzled. "Are you sure, Jeb?"

"Are you trying to insult my wisdom?" Jebir said, and Raymond quickly shook his head. "Good! I'm betting for the Malaysian dollar to rise because their currency is too undervalued. Malaysian politics are stable, economic fundamentals are sound, and the stock market is booming. Follow me, my friend! I will prove to you that I'm putting all my money on the Malaysian dollar, and if I am daring enough, what is a miserable five hundred thousand US dollars?"

"That sounds reassuring, Jeb. What do you think, Devin?" Raymond said.

"I say we go for it! Once we strike it rich, we give Ma his money back."

Indeed, Jebir did prove to them that he'd bet a large amount of money on the Malaysian dollar. As soon as Raymond received the money from Mr. Ma, he went straight to Singapore and deposited it with Jebir.

Chapter 64

I T WAS 1997. A financial crisis hit Asia like the meteor that hit Earth billions of years ago. It started with Thailand, and the Thai baht became devalued. Then nations all over Southeast Asia felt the contagious effect. Soon the Indonesian rupiah plummeted, followed by the Malaysian currency. Stock markets all over Southeast Asia, except in Singapore, crashed with no remedy insight.

The Malaysian government, using their central bank, tried to support their currency by selling off their dollar reserves, but the odds were overwhelmingly against them. Finally, the government abandoned the attempt to save the Malaysian dollar, and it spiraled out of control and lost 60 percent of its value against the US dollar.

Raymond watched helplessly as the world collapsed around him. He kept monitoring the developments online. One day he couldn't stomach it anymore and went to look for Devin.

"This is all your fault, Devin! You idiot! You and your friend Jeb!"

"Don't blame me! You made the decision!"

"I want you to contact Jeb and ask him to save whatever is left."

"I can't!"

"What do you mean you can't?"

"His entire office closed yesterday. He has closed shop."

"Jesus Christ! We are going to be sucked into the black hole, Devin!"

Raymond and Devin quickly packed their belongings. Devin left the hotel and helped Raymond out at his apartment, and soon they were ready to leave for Nunukan.

"It's lucky I did not use up all the money," Raymond said. He thought he was smart. Suddenly, there was a loud knock on Raymond's door. Both Raymond and Devin were startled. Raymond walked toward the door.

"Who is it?" Raymond shouted.

"We are here to inspect the conduit system in this apartment," a voice replied.

"I didn't send for anybody," Raymond responded.

"The landlord sent for us," the voice replied.

Raymond opened the door slightly. Suddenly, the door was pushed open from outside, and Raymond fell down. Raymond looked up. Devin stood still.

"Well, well. Going somewhere, you two?" Mr. Ma instructed his bodyguard to tie Raymond and Devin to chairs, and the tough gangster roughly gripped their faces.

"You know, Ray, one day in KL, I was walking around. I considered myself lucky when I had a chat with your good friend Michael. Oh, he said a lot of good things about you. He had a lot of faith in you. After that, I decided to check your movements—from Nunukan to KL to Singapore. I found out what you did with my money. If that was the business deal, Ray, I could have done it myself."

Raymond struggled. "This is Malaysia, Mr. Ma! You cannot kill a Malaysian citizen."

Mr. Ma laughed as he waved a tooth extractor in his hand. "Who is talking about killing you? I never kill people in my life, no matter how bad they are. However, when I was young, I had an ambition to be a dentist."

Devin peed in his pants upon seeing the pliers in Mr. Ma's hand. Raymond wiggled desperately to loosen himself.

"Now I can fulfill my ambition without certificate and anesthetic," Mr. Ma said. "This is going to be fun! Or would you like the sharpened bicycle spoke dipped into ten-day-old human excrement? I can poke that on your legs, and you can watch them fall off!"

Mr. Ma smiled as he approached Raymond. Devin struggled harder and was murmuring through his gagged mouth. Raymond turned his face left and right vigorously. "Please, Mr. Ma! Let's be reasonable! I'll pay you back all your money!"

"How? By trading your dirty, smelly asshole?"

"We will use our sister Susan as collateral. You can use or abuse her as you like!"

"Why do I need your sister? I can get thousands of girls if I want them."

"She is a virgin! No men have touched her. Enjoy her young body as you please. Once we get the money, you can release her. We don't want anything to happen to her, so she is good collateral."

Mr. Ma thought for a while. He slowly put the pliers away. Devin relaxed and loosened himself. "Don't play tricks on me. I will find you," Mr. Ma said.

"We won't, Mr. Ma," Raymond answered.

The bodyguards released them. They quickly untied themselves. Mr. Ma and his men began to walk away. Raymond rubbed his painful jaw to relieve it.

"I will give you one week to bring your sister to me. And I will give you three weeks to retrieve my money. Is that understood?" Mr. Ma said. Both Raymond and Devin nodded.

After they left, Devin looked at his wet pants. "Okay, Ray, we can now report the matter to the police!"

"Are you nuts? He will buy his way out of the law and find us and kill us! What we can do is buy time. We send Susan to him first, and we figure it out along the way."

Chapter 65

ANDY INFORMED WILLIAM THAT he was required to fly immediately to Kuala Lumpur. He advised him to check in at the PJ Hilton Hotel. William groaned whenever Andy gave a short-notice instruction to him. William was in the midst of negotiating with the state government to discount repayment for the loans they gave to local students. William decided that Ramlan should handle this case for him.

William arrived in Kuala Lumpur late at night. He had never stayed at this hotel, and it took some time for him to find it. As soon as William checked in, the room telephone rang. William picked up the receiver. It was Andy.

"Will, your appointment to meet the BOD will be at eight o'clock tomorrow."

"What? I thought you said the appointment would be at nine."

"Don't worry. The most they can do is fire you."

"Did I do anything wrong?"

"No, I meant there is nothing to worry about. Just be yourself."

"Okay then. Eight o'clock." William put down the receiver. William had a hunch that the board of directors wanted to know more about the financial crisis affecting Asia, which William had predicted almost a year ago. However, he wondered what questions they wanted to ask. Besides, he had never met the BOD. That was supposed to be Andy's job.

William had his breakfast at the coffeehouse at six in the morning. He read the morning paper and went through some of the documents that he anticipated would be the topic of discussion. William never liked surprises, and this one was intolerable to him. It was getting on his nerves already.

His cell phone rang. "Hello, Susan! Guest what? I'm in KL already. Once I've finished—" William heard Susan crying. "What's the matter, Susan? Are you all right?" Susan tried to catch her breath. William waited anxiously.

"They kidnapped me, Will! Please help me!"

"Who kidnapped you? Where are you?"

"Help me, Will!" Susan pleaded.

William immediately stood up and left the table and his briefcase. Andy appeared and greeted William. William pointed repeatedly to his seat. Andy made a gesture to indicate that he didn't know what William was talking about.

"Andy, my table is there! Wait for me and look after my briefcase, and I will be right back!"

Andy was shocked as he saw William run out of the hotel. He slowly walked toward William's table, sat down, and waited.

"Okay, Susan, calm down. Try to explain slowly."

"My brothers kidnapped me!" Susan stammered.

"Who kidnapped you?" William waited for an answer.

"Raymond and Devin!"

William headed to the taxi stand and waved. "Where are you now, Susan?" William jumped inside and asked the taxi to move.

"Where to, sir?" the taxi driver asked.

"Anywhere! Just drive!" William screamed. "Where are you now, Susan?" William asked again, impatient and worried.

"I don't know, Will! They blindfolded me when they took me here. I've to go now, Will! They are back!"

Susan hung up. William was at a loss. He was in the process of meeting the board of directors, which had been the most important thing happening to him, and now another urgent problem had cropped up. William instructed the driver to take him to the center of the city.

Which hotel? Which part of the street? How am I going to find her? I don't have any leads at all! These thoughts were clogging William's mind. He paid $100 to the taxi driver and asked him to wait for him.

William walked around like a madman. He didn't care that people looked at him. Suddenly, his cell phone rang, and he answered quickly. "Andy! Andy, I have a big problem, and I will not be able to be with you. Sorry!" William sat on a fire hydrant close by. Then the phone rang again. He listened. It was Susan.

"Where are you, Susan?" William asked with anxiety.

"I don't know, Will! Everything is removed from this room."

"What about a towel? Do you see an address or a name on the towels?" William waited for an answer.

"No! The towels don't say anything!"

William's mind was working quickly. "Can you escape outside?" he asked.

"Devin is just outside the room!" Susan responded.

"Please look outside the hotel window. There must be a landmark."

Susan remained silent. Then she said, "I can see a McDonald's on the opposite street, and there is a Hong Kong and Shanghai Bank and a Malayan Banking building just beside this hotel." Suddenly, Susan hung up.

"Susan! Susan!"

William wasted no time and began his difficult search immediately. He went to the nearest McDonald's and asked around. Nobody seemed to know anything. He went to the next McDonald's. Again, nobody knew.

"Please! This is important! This is a matter of life and death! Can you tell me where there is a McDonald's restaurant opposite two banks?" William showed the employees the names written on a piece of paper. Nobody knew where the place was. William walked away, almost giving up hope.

"Excuse me! That's the place I used to work, near Malayan Banking, opposite McDonald's," a customer said. It was a stroke of luck. He explained to William the location. William thanked the man and rushed out.

Arriving at the bank, he looked at the McDonald's on the opposite road. He saw a hotel nearby. William crossed the road and walked into the hotel. Suddenly, he saw Raymond talking to a few people. He hid beside a pillar. He moved quickly to the reception counter and took a hotel business card.

William went outside the hotel and made a call to the hotel operator. "Raymond Johnson, please," he said.

The operator placed him on hold for a moment. When she returned, she said, "Oh, I'm sorry, sir; the line has just been barred."

"There is an urgent message from his father. His mother is extremely sick, and she needs to get in touch with him."

The operator paused for a few seconds. "Why don't you see him yourself and tell him, sir? His room number is seven zero nine."

William walked inside the hotel and saw Raymond still talking. William slipped into the elevator unnoticed. William was pouring out cold sweat. He had never encountered a problem like this in his life. When the lift reached the seventh floor, William slowly walked out.

There was an empty water jug outside one of the rooms, and William took it. When he reached the room, he stood away from the peephole and knocked on the door strongly. The door opened, and suddenly, William pushed it with all his might.

Devin was thrown back and lost his balance. William rushed in and banged his head with the jug. Devin collapsed to the floor. Susan rushed to William. They hugged each other, and quickly, William pulled her away from the room. As they rushed to the elevator, William decided not to use it, for fear of encountering Raymond.

They took the stairs instead. They didn't enter the lobby but went through the hotel kitchen. William told Susan not to stop running, and they quickly disappeared. William took Susan straight to the airport, and they waited for the next flight to Jesselton. They didn't bring anything except whatever they had with them.

Raymond was furious. He slapped Devin, who had just recovered from the blackout. He slapped him again. Devin tried to control his speech. He still was disoriented from the strong impact on the front of his head.

"Where are they, Devin? Where are they?"

"I don't know, Ray!"

"Who came and rescued her? Who? Answer me!"

"I think it was—"

"Don't think, you shit-ass! We don't have the time!"

"It looked like your friend William!"

Raymond pushed away Devin and stood up. There was fury in his facial expression, and his eyes were glowing. Raymond shouted. Suddenly, fear crept into Raymond's mind as he thought of Mr. Ma.

Raymond combed the whole city looking for Susan and William. He asked Philip and his gang to help out with the search. They couldn't find him. Time was running out for Raymond. Soon Mr. Ma would be looking for him instead. Raymond discussed with Devin the possibilities of Susan's whereabouts.

They decided there could be only one place: East Malaysia. Devin did not like the idea of going back there, but Raymond insisted they must find Susan. They took an early morning flight to Jesselton.

Raymond and Devin searched everywhere. They went to William's office, but he was not there, nor was he at his apartment. He asked the workers around William's father's home and plantation, but there was no sign of William and Susan. Raymond had no choice but to fly to Sandakan and look for her at his father's home. If Susan was there, that would be the end of Raymond's scheme.

"Hello, Dad! It is so good to see you. Boy, do I miss you!"

"How do you do, Son? Do you happen to be by yourself coming here?"

"Yes. Yes, I'm by myself coming to see my good old father!"

"How thoughtful of you, Ray!"

Raymond walked into Aaron's apartment. "Daddy!" Raymond's kids screamed.

Raymond extended his arms and held his children tightly. "How are you, little guys?" He kissed his children but quickly released them. He had more important things on his mind. Maria came out of the kitchen. She quickly held Aaron in her arms. Aaron hesitated to respond and remained still. Raymond hadn't expected Maria to be around, and he became uneasy.

Maria smiled at him. "Good to see you, Raymond!" she said. Raymond remained silent. He just gave a little nod and turned toward his children.

"Grandpa always brings us to see the orangutans!" one of the kids said proudly.

"Grandpa is bringing us to Turtle Island this Sunday! Right, Grandpa?" said the other.

Aaron smiled. "You're very right, children!"

Raymond stood up and turned toward his father. Both of them walked toward the balcony. "Did you happen to see Susan and William recently, Dad?"

"You aren't going to ask about Cecelia?" Aaron said, shocked.

"No. I just want to know where Susan and William are right now."

"Susan is studying in KL, Ray. I don't know where William is. Why are you suddenly showing an interest in her?" his father asked.

"I love her, Dad, and I care very much for her." Raymond quickly left without saying good-bye. Aaron was speechless. Raymond's kids quickly rushed to Aaron, and he hugged them tightly.

Raymond flew back to Jesselton, feeling relieved that she was not with Aaron. But now there was another riddle for Raymond to solve. Where was his missing sister, and where was William? Raymond hurried to meet Devin at the Palace Hotel, and they started a long session of brainstorming.

"If only we had access to flights' passenger lists." Devin sighed.

Raymond was thinking hard. Devin's statement awakened him. He stood up and held Devin by his shoulders. "You just spoke the magic words!"

Devin was puzzled. "Did I?"

Raymond got the telephone directory and searched. He found what he was looking for and made a call.

"Hello! Salim? Remember me? Raymond! It has been a long time since we met. So, my old classmate, I need a favor from you." Raymond talked for fifteen minutes and then replaced the receiver. "Got it, Devin. I've got their destination."

Chapter 66

"How long are we going to stay here, Will?" Susan lay on his chest as they pondered.

"Be patient, Susan. Your safety is the most important."

They'd spent hours in the hotel room in a city alien to both of them. They were not bored, as they enjoyed each other's companionship. Aaron had strictly advised them not to leave the hotel room. They were scared.

"I'm sorry you have to miss your classes, Susan."

"I'm sorry I interrupted your work, Will."

William's eyes were watching TV, but his mind was somewhere else. He could not see the logic of the whole situation. Susan's brothers, who were supposed to protect her, were the ones committing this crime. William knew that if he took the matter to the police, they would classify it as family affairs. The police would not treat it as a crime. They would call the family members and ask them to settle things among themselves. Besides, there was a possibility that Raymond might use money to buy his way out of trouble.

"It's all in the family, Will. Devin hurt Theresa."

William looked at Susan. "You knew this?"

Susan nodded. "Daddy told me."

William was shocked. "Your daddy knew?"

Again, Susan nodded. "Sure he knows."

William raised his body a little and adjusted Susan's head on his chest. "Raymond told me he, Linda, Theresa, and Devin were the only ones who knew."

Susan's eyes looked brighter. "They didn't know Maria knew. Maria saw what happened and rushed to get help. But by that time, it was too late. Theresa was raped by a worker passing by. Daddy lodged a police report against the man. He was charged. But Daddy didn't report Devin."

Suddenly, they heard the door being unlocked. They both jumped out of the bed, shocked to see three men standing in front of them: Raymond, Devin, and Mr. Ma.

"Well, look what we have here!" Raymond exclaimed.

William and Susan held each other tightly. William saw that Raymond's and Devin's faces were filled with anger. Mr. Ma was smiling. William pushed Susan behind him. Both were scared, but William tried to act calm.

"I won't give Susan to you, Ray! Not to anybody!"

"You are right, Ray. I have never seen such a beautiful girl." Mr. Ma looked at Susan with excitement.

William pushed Susan farther backward. Mr. Ma tried to touch her, but William pushed away his hand. Mr. Ma did not mind forgoing his money. Susan was worth it. Mr. Ma laughed, believing he would get his prize. He turned toward Raymond, and his laughter stopped. His happiness turned to worry. "What is that gun for, Ray? That isn't necessary!" Mr. Ma said.

Raymond pointed the pistol at William. William cleared his throat but pretended to be composed. Susan threw away William's hand and moved forward to cover William. William tried to push her back, but she refused.

"He is the source of my problems, Mr. Ma. He turned my life upside down!"

Mr. Ma walked toward Raymond and tried to take the gun away from him. Raymond pushed him and turned the gun on Mr. Ma, who suddenly moved away toward Devin. Mr. Ma put up his hands. He regretted telling his bodyguards to wait in the lobby.

"Please be reasonable, Raymond. There is no need for this. If you kill him, you are committing murder," Mr. Ma said.

"He double-crossed us! And he hit my head with a jar!" Devin walked toward William.

William and Susan stepped back and found themselves cornered against the wall. Mr. Ma, the big, tough guy, now looked frightened. He tried to slip away, but Raymond again pointed the gun at him. Mr. Ma stopped.

"I might be a big-time gangster, but I never get involved in murder!" Mr. Ma cried.

"I think we have no choice, Mr. Ma, but to shoot William," Raymond said.

"Hey, I don't want anything to do with your action, Ray!" Mr. Ma said.

Susan was crying loudly.

"Nobody can hear you in this small hotel, Susan! Believe me. It is owned by Mr. Ma's friend. What a coincidence!" Raymond laughed. Mr. Ma stood still. William closed his eyes tightly.

"Hold it right there!" Suddenly, Aaron burst in, ran in front of William and Susan, and shielded them. "If you want to kill him, you'll have to kill me first, and I wouldn't do that if I were you. The police are everywhere below!"

Raymond asked his father to move away.

Aaron stayed put. "Please, Raymond. Come to your senses!"

Raymond hesitated.

"Just kill all of them!" Devin shouted. Devin rushed to Raymond and took his gun. Devin pointed the gun at them.

"No, Devin! No!" Raymond shouted as Susan cried more loudly. "You can't kill our father!" Raymond yelled.

Devin ignored him and squeezed the trigger. Raymond rushed in front of Aaron, and the gun blasted. Raymond fell to the ground.

"No!" Aaron shouted. Susan screamed. William and Mr. Ma were stunned.

"Everybody, hands up! Metro Manila Police!"

Mr. Ma immediately raised his hands. Devin just stared. He dropped the gun. Aaron was holding Raymond, who was bleeding profusely from the left side of his chest. Susan was still crying, and she joined her father in holding Raymond. William stood still, too scared to say or think anything. Two young Chinese men rushed in.

"Mr. Ma, we have been monitoring your movements for a long time," one of them said. "We are Hong Kong police detectives, and you are wanted for money laundering and smuggling drugs inside your fish." They handcuffed Mr. Ma and took him away. The Manila police officers arrested Devin. His face looked lifeless.

"I don't regret anything, Daddy," Raymond stammered. Blood continued to ooze out of his chest. "What I did was always right!" His dying eyes looked up at William. "I'll beat you one way or another. See which one of us reaches heaven first!" Raymond smiled.

William slowly bent down and cradled Raymond's head in his hands. Susan held Raymond's hand. Aaron knelt next to William, weeping. Raymond succumbed to his injury and died. Aaron and Susan sobbed as they held the lifeless body of Raymond.

Chapter 67

AARON, LINDA, SUSAN, MARIA, William, Cecelia, and her two kids watched Raymond's casket being lowered into the grave. William and Aaron paid for his funeral. It was a modest one. The ladies and the children were all weeping. Aaron and William kept their thoughts to themselves. Raymond was buried at the Manila North Cemetery. Aaron registered him as a Catholic. The church bell rang in the distance, as if to mourn Raymond's departure.

Aaron slowly walked away. He wept again, thinking of Raymond and Devin. Devin had been charged with manslaughter. Aaron had tried to help, but the prosecution wouldn't let him go. Aaron took out a cigarette and smoked.

He couldn't help noticing that the cemetery was filled with squatters. They called themselves the caretakers. The slum there was different from the ones littered all over Southeast Asia's big cities. The inhabitants were clean, and they practiced mutualism. They helped family members of the deceased and the Metro Manila authorities to clean up the place, provided they were allowed to stay.

A sudden cool breeze passed Aaron, as if the dead were trying to tell him something. He thought about the cemetery on top of the hill in Sandakan. As Aaron was smoking, he saw a peculiar picture on a simple tomb. He walked toward it and looked at the portrait carefully. He turned cold. He put his fist to his mouth. Beside the picture, the name displayed was Fiona.

He called over a caretaker close by to see the grave, which had been overwhelmed by weeds. The man looked at the tomb carefully and nodded. He faced Aaron.

"Her name was Fiona. Nobody knows her surname, and nobody knows where she came from. We heard rumors that she had a Chinese boyfriend. The man's wife came to know of his affair with Fiona, and she immediately dumped him and went back to Taiwan. His business collapsed, and Fiona left him. We also heard that her boyfriend committed suicide after his business failed. She hung around Mabini Street with American tourists. She became addicted to drugs. She contracted diseases, and one of them was AIDS. Her friends from the street helped to pay for her funeral."

Slowly, the caretaker left Aaron to himself. Aaron dropped down. He was sure he knew who Fiona was. He looked up at the sky and prayed to God. He prayed that the grave he saw didn't belong to Elaine. He prayed Devin would be freed, and he prayed that all of these horrible things were just bad dreams. Aaron stood up and walked slowly away. He turned to look at Fiona's resting place one more time.

"Who is it, Daddy?" Susan asked while all the others were standing close to her.

"Nobody you know, Susan." Aaron put on a brave face and smiled.

Maria rushed to hold Aaron up. Aaron wept. After that, he took a deep breath. He hugged Linda, Susan, and the children. He then approached Cecelia and hugged her too. Finally, he faced William and forced himself to smile. He pulled William toward him and hugged him too. They then all walked together, holding hands.

Only Aaron turned back around to see the lonely tomb one more time. Then he turned to the left and observed the fresh grave of his son. There was nothing they could do now.

"Rest in peace, both of you, and may God bless your souls."

COMING SOON!

VICEROYS
OF
GOD

DON PETER